The Rose Stone

by

L. A. Kelley

The Rose Stone

Cover Art by *Jennifer Greeff*

The Wild Rose Press, Inc.
PO Box 708
Adams Basin, NY 14410-0708
Visit us at www.thewildrosepress.com

Publishing History
First Edition, 2022
Trade Paperback ISBN 978-1-5092-4167-5
Digital ISBN 978-1-5092-4166-8

Published in the United States of America

I took a stumbling step back and froze at the snap of a twig underfoot. "It's a hallucination," I whispered. "It can't hurt me."

Without warning, the heavy body pounded across the forest floor, rapidly closing the gap between us. Through the brush, I glimpsed a scaly hide. "Screw it. I'm out of here."

I did an about-face and shambled in the opposite direction, cursing my legs. Why didn't I remember to bring the cane into the dream world? The lurker in the trees followed, thumping steps drawing closer. I could almost feel hot breath on the back of my neck. Blind panic urged me faster, but I was slowed by a stumbling gait and thick foliage that snatched at my clothing.

Thud!

A heavy body landed right behind me, shaking the ground. Claws clamped my waist, dragging me to a halt and lifting me in the air. The self-defense class Melanie talked me into one summer rushed back. I struck out blindly with my fists and connected with something squishy. I grabbed it and yanked hard. There was a tearing sound and an inhuman bellow. The claws opened. I tumbled to the ground and got the first good look at my attacker. A scream froze in my throat as I came face to face with a walking horror.

In point of fact, face wasn't the right word.

Chapter One

I clenched my fist until the hand tremor subsided and then shot an uneasy glance at Melanie. Her attention remained fixed on the laptop, and I relaxed, certain she hadn't noticed a thing. As the seconds ticked by and she continued to study the screen, my spirits lifted. The test results couldn't be hopeless. Anxiety had tied a big honking knot in my stomach for nothing. Sure, that's it. My best friend hadn't let me down. Only good news awaited. I settled back in the chair.

Another minute passed, and my heart thumped. Bad news?

I gnawed on my lower lip. Worse than bad? Damn her poker-face.

A crimson-colored haze filtered into my peripheral vision, and I suppressed a surge of panic. The eerie distortion had come and gone the last few days and I chose to ignore it. Just as I chose to ignore other symptoms until they made it impossible for me to work. I blinked hard and muffled a sigh of relief when the haze disappeared.

Despite the nagging headaches and the dull cramp in my limbs, or maybe because of them, my senses heightened. I had recently discovered anxiety made a person acutely aware of their surroundings, and every random input hammered at me: the faint astringent smell of Melanie's office in the medical center, the slight *tick* of the blinds as they swayed in response to air currents flowing from the vent, the muffled voices from the parking lot outside the ground-floor window.

The silence lengthened, and my nerves drew taut as a bowstring. I shot a fusillade of thoughts in Melanie's direction to will her obedience. *Don't say it. Whatever you do, don't say, "I'm sorry."*

Melanie looked up from the monitor. Her previously stoic expression twisted in despair. "Jess, I'm so sorry."

My mouth went dry. This wasn't supposed to happen. I had it planned. The results would be optimistic. I had scads of options for treatment.

Melanie leaned forward and took my trembling hand. "The brain tumor is more pervasive than we believed." Her voice was barely above a whisper.

I struggled to draw a breath, the air suddenly heavy and oppressive. Despite nothing but clear skies out the window, it felt like a storm building.

"I know it's a lot to take in, but…" Melanie trailed off. Her gaze flicked to the report again.

"But what?" I said with a bitter laugh. "It's worse than a death sentence? Do I become a zombie?"

"No, but your condition deteriorated faster than expected. A lot faster. I've consulted specialists. They've never known a case like this. It—it caught us off-guard." Melanie's voice broke, and she swallowed hard.

"How long?"

"Jess—"

"How long?" I demanded.

Melanie licked her lips. "If the tumor continues to grow at the same rate, you'll be incapacitated in a month—maybe less."

"Incapacitated," I whispered, the shock not quite sinking in. "Such a cold, clinical word for a vegetable. Why don't they call it something nicer like kale? I'll become a nice big bunch of kale. That's not so bad."

"You hate kale," said Melanie with a faint smile. It drained from her face, and she squeezed my hand. "Jess, you'll have to make different living arrangements soon, but I can help. I'm so sorry I dumped this on you at once, but time isn't on our side."

I yanked my hand away from her and rose to my feet, gripping the back of the chair to steady my shaky legs. "I have to get out of here."

"Jess—"

"Melanie, I love you like a sister. Maybe more, since I never had a sister to compare. You've been my best friend since we were kids, but I can't do this right now."

Melanie jumped up from her seat. "Where are you going?"

"A bar."

"You don't drink."

"I'll learn."

"Jess…"

I sighed. "Please, I need some alone time." Away from the antiseptic odor of a medical center, far from kindly people walking the halls in hospital scrubs, and patients leaving with nothing worse than a bandage covering a flu shot.

"You shouldn't drive," Melanie said. "You shouldn't have driven here. You promised you wouldn't because of the tremors."

"It's the last time, and I swear, this is an actual for-real promise. I don't want a poor schlub ending up in the ER with tire tracks across his face because of me."

"I'll drop by after work, and we'll talk then," said Melanie. "I sent a new prescription to the pharmacy that should help ease the tremors. Have you had any hallucinations? If so, the symptoms are worsening, and you must check into a hospital at once."

"I haven't seen a thing." I conveniently ignored the crimson haze. If I were fated to die today, no way would it be face down in a plate of hospital food. "I'll go straight to the pharmacy and then home. It's only around the corner from my place."

"Okay. Use the cane, too. It'll help."

"Sure." But not slow the course of an agonizing death. Nothing could do that. I grabbed my purse. "If you're wrong about this and I turn into a zombie instead, I'll eat your brains first with plenty of spicy salsa because you hate spicy food."

Melanie pulled me into a hug. "Deal." Her voice cracked.

I blinked hard, forcing back tears, and dashed out to the parking lot. Dash wasn't entirely accurate. The tumor's location caused pain and headaches along with muscle weakness in my legs and an intermittent tremble in my hands. I walked like a sailor who had enjoyed too much shore leave, only I didn't enjoy anything.

I leaned against my car, gulping deep breaths of air, and a lump rose in my throat. My old crappy car, the one I planned to replace since my career took an upswing. Now I wouldn't get the chance. I rubbed my eyes, determined not to blubber in public, and got into the driver's seat. I gripped the steering wheel so hard my knuckles turned white. My hand shook, and I sat on it. It felt like a creepy vibrating sex toy. My ex-boyfriend Elliot would have approved, but ex-boyfriend Elliot was, thankfully, gone from what remained of my life. I didn't have to listen to his opinions anymore.

"Not now," I moaned, and mercifully, the spasm ended.

The air was stuffy in the car, and I lowered the window. A man and woman walked toward me across the parking lot. He held her hand and said something. She laughed. At the sight of their happy faces, blistering rage bubbled inside me, and I shot them a death glare. How dare they laugh when I'd never laugh again? The woman turned toward me and caught my eye. My expression must have unsettled her because she swiftly looked away.

"Terrific," I muttered. "Start the car before the cops show to confront the crazy woman in the parking lot."

I drove with extra care and, as promised, went directly to the pharmacy. The drive-thru had five cars in line so I parked and shambled inside, taking careful steps to the counter, stopping often while pretending to examine displays to hide my unsteady gait.

The pharmacist handed over the pill container. "This is a new medication. The drug is potent, and I haven't filled the prescription before. The directions are clearly marked, but it can have serious reactions if you take too much. Be sure to call the doctor immediately if you experience adverse side effects. Do you have any questions?"

I forced a smile. "Nope, thanks." Side effects were no big deal when knocking on death's door.

I parked the car in my space behind the condo and

gave the steering wheel a last pat. "You'll go in my will as a donation to the local PBS station; the cranky starter is their problem now." I took the stairs to my third-floor loft at a sluggish pace, gripping the banister tightly to steady myself. Propped against the wall in my apartment was the hated cane, just where I'd "forgotten" it. Melanie had brought it to me a few days ago. It was metal with a padded T-shaped top instead of a crook. While her concern was heartwarming, the cane was a constant reminder that my old independent life had crashed and burned.

Sunlight streamed through the tall windows and the skylights overhead. Despite my gloom, a smile twitched my lips. I loved this place from the instant I'd laid eyes on it. I lucked out, too, since the inheritance from my parents covered the purchase price. The brick walls and concrete floors hinted at the loft's former industrial use, perfect for an artist. Half the wide-open area was dedicated to living space and the rest to my studio, infusing the air with the scent of turpentine and oil paints. Best air fresheners ever.

My career began in graphic arts, and I found extra work on the side as a book illustrator and cover designer, eventually starting my own business. It suited me better since I was able to work at home and take a drive to the country whenever the need for fresh air beckoned. At times, it felt as if there wasn't a drop of oxygen left in the city. My special love was fantasy stories. Fairytales grabbed me at an early age and never let go. As the business grew, I became picky about assignments. Forget covers with boring, angsty heroines with heaving bodices, gazing in adoration at an overbuilt swordsman. Besides, they were thrown together from stock photographs on the computer. Instead, give me a picture book to illustrate with flying pigs, and I was in heaven.

I turned an affectionate gaze to the easel, the floor spattered with paint that escaped the drop cloth. I never bothered to clean underneath. The colorful smears filled me with pride. It meant steady money coming in and I was a genuine artist. My old blotchy smock hung on a hook by the deep sink. Shelves with art supplies covered the walls. Usually, a few unfinished canvases sat next to them, but recently, my career was on a roll. I connected with local picture book writers in need of artists. My work had garnered great reviews, a few awards, and more contracts. Business took off. I exhibited my own pieces locally. The last few original paintings sold for high prices at an art show, so the walls were bare. Thus, a new plan formed. No more book covers. I'd work on my paintings on the side and sell prints from my website. One day, I'd write and illustrate my own fairytale. I'd been itching to do that since I was a kid.

Then my life caved in.

First came headaches and then intermittent tremors. Eventually, it became difficult to stand at the easel. I convinced myself it was overwork and muscle strain. I was a pro at denial, the reason my boyfriend lasted as long as he did. I kept hoping Elliot would morph into Mr. Right. He had the perfect qualifications— handsome, charming, and steadily employed—but men don't grow into the role. Either they are from the beginning, or they aren't. He wasn't, but it took me too long to admit it.

Melanie noticed the change in me first. She's been

my best friend since the day we met in elementary school. Melanie Carpenter and Jessica Stone were two peas in a pod, except one pea veered to medicine and the other to art. Dr. Carpenter was darn good at her job, though. As hard as I tried, I wasn't able to hide the change in my gait from her, and she insisted on a complete examination and blood work. Those tests became more tests which became more tests, and then the awful word "tumor" reared its ugly head. Today in her office came the worst-case diagnosis I had previously refused to consider.

Without warning, the streams of bright sunlight through the windows shifted from amber to rose, deepening the color in the brick walls. My heart thrummed in wild panic. The eerie effect had been faint and at the edge of my vision until today. Now, it was more vivid and had a slight shimmer. I blinked hard. The wall returned to normal, and I ran a shaky hand across my brow.

My eyes burned and I rubbed away tears. How long before I was unable to hold a paintbrush ever again? The tumor would steal my physical strength first until my body became unresponsive to the slightest desire but leave my mind screaming to get out. But the only exit was a lingering death.

Maybe not.

Warnings from the pharmacist drifted back to me. "A potent drug. Adverse reactions." Wasn't that simply a nice way of saying an overdose was terminal? A desperate idea took shape. I had a choice between a slow, painful death by inches or a quick am-scray into peaceful nothingness.

I grabbed the bottle and stumbled into the

bathroom. As if my body suspected my intent, the tremor returned. I opened the pill bottle and spilled some on the floor but managed to get most into my mouth. Grimacing at the sour taste, I filled the water glass and downed them in one gulp. I limped to the couch and leaned back in the cushions with a sigh, waiting for the end.

I didn't have to wait long.

My stomach gurgled and made a loud *blorp*. I shot to my feet and weaved to the toilet just in time for the undigested pills to have a burial at sea. I rinsed my mouth and then flushed. "This isn't fair," I moaned. "I can't even die right." Worse yet, I'd have to fess up to Melanie to get a refill. On the other hand, I could say a hand tremor made me spill the pills, and they accidently landed in the toilet. I peered at my pale face in the mirror and gave a wry chuckle. "Lucky for me, the tumor makes a great alibi."

The chuckle exploded into a laugh. For some strange reason, the unexpected purge produced a sudden burst of energy. The pent-up tension since Melanie broke the awful news vanished in an instant. I felt good right now. Nope, I felt great, full of life. I was able to move, feel, and scarf down a tub of cookie dough ice cream. Today was certainly not the day to die. Creative juices flooded my veins and solidified into an uncontrollable urge to paint something, anything. It grabbed hold of me and refused to let go.

I set up the last clean canvas on the easel. I bought it during a clearance sale at an art supply store years ago because it was cheap and then stashed it in a corner. It was larger than my preferred size and I never found the right inspiration. I ran my fingers across the surface with a smile. I loved this part, imagining the possibilities. I didn't even need a firm idea, only the hunger to create. A blank canvas was a mystery waiting for me to solve. What would be there when I finished? If I hated the result, there was always the option to paint over it and start again. Thinking of the freedom offered by the hidden possibilities brought a smile to my face.

The first decision was whether to use oils or watercolors. This definitely cried out for oils. Normally, I started with a pencil outline to get a sense of the structure and arrangement of the composition, but not today. I donned my smock and picked up the palette and my favorite palette knife. A few pills may have gotten into my bloodstream after all because my hand was rock steady as I mixed the paints. Alizarin red there, a touch of cobalt blue here, then a dab of yellow ochre. I used the palette knife instead of a brush to blend the colors on the canvas. Without conscious thought, they became a shape, and I stepped back to examine the result.

A rose.

Not an actual rose, but an idealized flower symbolizing the strength and courage to face adversity. Even the formidable thorns had meaning. Whoever wore this symbol never ran from a fight.

Who wears the rose?

I put down the palette and switched to a pencil, hurriedly sketching the figure of man around the rose. Broad shoulders carried the weight of heavy responsibility. My warrior had high cheekbones, deep brown eyes, and a noble bearing, but there was kindness in him, too. He wasn't classically handsome and would never make the cover of a romance novel. I grinned. But he had dimples, definitely dimples.

The symbolic rose was centered on his chest, as if worn as an emblem. That felt right, but I needed more details, his incomplete features bugged me. I was stuck at a creative dead end and couldn't continue until every aspect of his face was clear in my mind, but my mind was blank. With rising frustration, I grasped the palette knife and studied the unfinished man. For some unknown reason, he captured my attention like nothing else I'd ever done, and it was impossible to walk away. I'd experienced waves of inspiration many times before, but this one was different.

The sunlight from the window shifted. Color surrounded me, vibrant pink hues deepening to brilliant crimson, spilling across the painting, brightening the rose. Not so much a haze, but a glowing aura, blocking out everything but the rose, setting the petals ablaze with color. "Perfect," I whispered. Drawn by the extraordinary effect, I clasped the palette knife tight to my chest and with my other hand touched the canvas.

Spinning, whirling, falling into the depths of the crimson light, I lost feeling in my body but wasn't afraid. If this was death, it was kinda fun. My eyes closed.

"Oof!"

I hit with a thump, whooshing the air from my lungs, then sucked in a breath and groaned. I was no expert but assumed death didn't come with a hard landing. I must have passed out and hit the floor and cursed my stupidity. If I were bleeding, I'd have to clean the mess before Melanie arrived or I'd never hear the end of it. I rubbed a hand across the floor, hoping for the touch of concrete and not a pool of something warm and sticky. Instead, my fingers entwined in a soft, springy mass.

"What the…" My floor had no carpet, and this felt like grass. My artistic air freshener had disappeared, too. Lush floral notes replaced the omnipresent smell of paint and turpentine in the loft.

I opened my eyes. My jaw dropped. "Not possible," I whispered.

The loft had vanished. I lay face up in a glade, surrounded by thick piney woods, one hand clutching the palette knife. Faint pink tinted the foliage, but it vanished as I scrambled to sit. Overhead, a sky with ominous gray clouds was barely visible between the heavy overhanging branches.

A stiff breeze, rife with earthy forest scent, batted my cheek. My heart skipped a beat at soft chittering overhead. Leaves rustled as furry creatures scurried across tree limbs as if my sudden appearance startled them.

I staggered to my feet, gulping in a lungful of clean, fresh air, and gawked at the unfamiliar surroundings. This was deep woods and not the local park with manicured walkways. The weather report predicted clear blue skies today, but the gathering clouds overhead hinted at a coming storm. Brush and trees ringed the small clearing. Big trees. Not the local pines, but massive conifers with flat needles that looked as if they had stood for hundreds of years. I'd never seen such trees near my home. I'd never seen such trees ever. Nothing was familiar. I touched a trunk. The dream tree was eerily solid.

My mouth dried. "How can this be real? Where am I?"

Did hallucinations have clear scents and sounds? Shoot, why didn't I ask Melanie more questions or grill the pharmacist about the side effects from those stupid pills?

Because you were afraid of the answers. How do you feel now about using denial as a treatment for a terminal illness?

I rubbed the back of my neck. "Kinda dumb, actually."

I took a step and grimaced as a painful muscle spasm shot through my leg. I flexed my fingers and winced. They hurt, too. That much hadn't changed. I still had the palette knife, so dropped it in the smock's pocket. Convinced I had completely lost my mind, I placed a finger on my neck and didn't know whether to be happy or rattled at the steady pulse.

"Okay. I choose to believe I'm alive, but something is very wrong with this scenario. Maybe it's not a normal hallucination. I-I must have fainted and gotten a hard knock on the head. This might be a coma." Panic flared inside me. "Calm down. Try to wake up." I took a deep breath and shouted, "I'm awake now." The vision of the primeval woods remained stubbornly in place.

A rumbling growl reverberated through the trees, and my heart raced. "All righty. Attracting attention might not be the brightest idea until I figure out what's going on."

The little animals overhead chittered again, but this time their conversation had a frenzied aspect. My arrival gave them jitters, but that sound caused wild-eyed terror. Branches shook as they dove for cover, knocking bits of leaves and twigs to the forest floor. In an instant, stillness reigned. Even the stiff breeze had dropped.

Cold sweat trickled down my spine. "Okay, Jess. I really mean it this time. Wake up now."

Dried vegetation on the forest floor crunched under the weight of a large, heavy something lumbering through the woods. No more than fifty feet away came rustling brush and a low, rumbling snarl. Branches ripped apart as the ominous sound forged a beeline in my direction. Then the noise stopped, but the eerie stillness of the forest offered no comfort. The silence lengthened as if that something was waiting, listening.

Breath caught in my throat. I took a stumbling step back and froze at the snap of a twig underfoot. "It's a hallucination," I whispered. "It can't hurt me."

Without warning, the heavy body pounded across the forest floor, rapidly closing the gap between us. Through the brush, I glimpsed a scaly hide. "Screw it. I'm out of here."

I did an about-face and shambled in the opposite direction, cursing my legs. Why didn't I remember to bring the cane into the dream world? The lurker in the trees followed, thumping steps drawing closer. I could almost feel hot breath on the back of my neck. Blind panic urged me faster, but I was slowed by a stumbling gait and thick foliage that snatched at my clothing.

Thud! A heavy body landed right behind me, shaking the ground. Claws clamped my waist, dragging me to a halt and lifting me in the air. The self-defense class Melanie talked me into one summer rushed back. I struck out blindly with my fists and connected with something squishy. I grabbed it and yanked hard. There was a tearing sound and an inhuman bellow. The claws opened. I tumbled to the ground and got the first good look at my attacker. A scream froze in my throat as I came face to face with a walking horror.

In point of fact, face wasn't the right word.

This was no dream, it had to be a nightmare. A creature loomed over me with a gaping maw that emitted a strident buzz. Instead of eyes, waving stalks fluttered from indentations around the top of its head. It had a scaly metallic hide and a pouch slung over its back. One of the stalks bent at a sharp angle, vibrating more than the others and dripping a black oily substance. My stomach heaved. That must have been the squishy thing I grabbed.

A scratchy metallic *click-click-click* issued from the creature, and then a droning monotone filled my head. *Where is the one who holds the spark?* The creature's mouth hadn't moved.

To my horror, it bent over me, and tendrils fluttered across my body. "No spark," it rasped. This time, I was sure it spoke.

The inner voice rose to a screech. *The spark is here. The power called.*

I smacked the nasty tendrils aside and scurried backward. "Get those stinking things off me. What spark? Who is that?"

She hears? There was a slight pause and more clicking. *Bring her.*

The creature's hand shot out. I dodged to the side, cursing my clumsiness but wasn't quick enough. It grabbed my right forearm like an iron clamp. The sleeve had been pushed back and its touch was hard and cold, more metal than living tissue. Jerking me to my feet, the claws scratched my arm. The sting of blood droplets brought another surge of terror. That hurt. Nightmares could terrify and wake me in a cold sweat with a thumping heartbeat, but never had they caused actual physical pain.

Burning torment ripped across my shoulders as the monster lifted me in the air. "Put me down," I yelled, squirming in its grip.

The ungainly talons didn't grasp well, and I began to wriggle free. The creature unslung the sack across its shoulder with the obvious intent to drop me inside. I kicked at the chest, hitting a hard, ungiving surface akin to pounding a wall. The wall couldn't care less.

The blunt edge of the palette knife was hardly a weapon, but in desperation I snatched it from my pocket and swung at the waving tentacles. With unnatural strength backed by a flood of adrenaline, I stabbed the one fluttering weakly. The force of the blow snapped the palette knife in two. The stalk sheared off and fell twitching to the ground, bleeding black ooze and spitting a trail of sparks. The remains of the flimsy blade stuck in its head, leaving me holding the wooden handle with part of the jagged metal shaft protruding.

The creature's roar shook the leaves on the trees. It didn't let go but flicked opened the sack and dropped me inside. The top cinched shut, and it swung me, I presumed, across its back. I landed with a hard thump, jarring my teeth. The cramped confinement was terrifying enough, but when it began to run, every footfall slammed me up and down.

The thought of meeting this thing's master chilled my blood to ice water, and I fought a wave of mind-numbing hysteria, searching for escape. I jabbed with the broken palette knife blade and nearly cried out when a pinprick of light appeared. I forced in the tip and rocked it back and forth. Despite the wild ride, the hole increased. In a frenzy, I tore at the sides until the opening was big enough for a foot. A few more seconds and I'd wiggle through. Once I hit the ground, adrenaline coupled with blind fear might help boost me up a tree. The monster's body was large and bulky and the hands strong but clumsy. Not the best build for climbing. Neither were mine, but if I had any chance, a break for freedom had to come now.

"For the Rose!"

At the sound of the man's voice, the creature snarled and skidded to a stop. Hoofbeats neared, followed by a bird-like screech from overhead. The bag swung violently back and forth. I slashed in desperation at the hole and with a *rrrrip* the opening widened enough to free both my feet.

I heard a *twang*, and the monster stumbled, howling with rage, and released the sack. The sudden drop caught me by surprise. I hit the ground hard, and the palette knife slipped from my hand and fell through the hole. I managed to stand, no easy feat.

The ground shook with movement, more hoofbeats and heavy thumping. The monster's bellows interspersed with the wild bird screeches. I froze in panic, fearful of being trampled in the melee and not knowing which way to dodge. A hand gave me a hard shove to the side. I stumbled against a bush but stayed on my feet. Then came a final deafening scream, and a heavy body hit the ground.

Someone grabbed the sack, and a blade sliced through the tough material over my head as if it were tissue paper. As the bag slipped past my shoulders, instinct and those self-defense lessons took over. Heart pounding, I struck out blindly with a hard right jab.

Chapter Two

A man with a sword in hand stumbled back rubbing his cheek and let out a curse.

"Keep your hands to yourself, buddy," I said, fists balled in a defensive stance.

"Buddy?" he sputtered.

The monster and its severed head lay on the ground, an arrow sticking from its chest. The man lowered the hand from his face, and I gaped at him. The stranger bore a startling resemblance to the rough sketch in my painting, except he had an old scar on his cheek. A bow and quiver of arrows was slung over his back. He wielded the sword with expertise and wore a tabard embellished with a rose over a leather jerkin, but not any rose. My rose—identical to the stylized figure I painted not more than an hour ago.

From behind the man came snorts of laughter. Two teenagers in similar clothing, swords held high, rode into the clearing and dismounted from...? They certainly weren't horses. The large animals had lop-ears and features reminiscent of a cross between a goat and a llama. By my rescuer stood a third one. The goat-llama peered at me, eyes shining with intelligence and a hint of amusement, as if it also enjoyed a good joke. Roses woven into the saddlecloth matched those on the humans' tabards. Roses were even etched into the sword blades.

The girl sheathed her sword and bit her lip. She regarded her companion with barely restrained hilarity. "Bram, did I hear a curse escape the captain?"

The young man was a year or two older and his lips twitched in a half-hidden grin. "Surely not, Abril. You know he forbids cursing among the Rose Guard as it displays a lack of self-control. Our captain never breaks his own rules."

The captain scowled at them. "The breach, Sergeant?"

"It held long enough for two more to enter," said Bram, and his expression darkened. "After the squad killed them, Abril and I came in search of you."

"Racer spotted the third in the woods," said the captain. "It took her."

Abril gawked at me. "They never take captives."

"Three carvers," said the captain, rubbing the scar on his cheek. "This is troubling news." Despite the fact they apparently killed a trio of monsters, none of them looked like celebrating. "Wind surge?" he said.

"The lyrs sense nothing yet," said Abril. "Perhaps the breach sealed quickly enough."

"Even so, stay alert. Pity, we had no time to wait for our drummer. Danya would know for certain." The captain nodded at the corpse, his expression grim. "Never have so many carvers passed the boundary. We must return to the garrison at once and send word to Stone Keep."

"Excuse me," I shouted, struggling with the sack entwining my legs. "What's going on? What is that thing, who are you, where am I—"

"Peace, my lady," said the captain gently. "We mean no harm. My name is Griffin, captain in the Rose

Guard. Bram and Abril are under my command. Allow me to free you." He removed a dagger from his boot, the blade embossed with the same stylized rose. I froze, eyeing it with alarm.

He made no threatening moves, but offered the dagger to me, hilt first. "Or free yourself, if you'd rather."

I gave him a wary look and took the dagger. The blade was razor sharp and with one swipe, the sack fell away. I stepped out and nearly stumbled at a muscle twinge. "Are you injured?" he said with alarm.

"No. I'm fine. It's nothing." The smock sleeve covered the scratches. I mentally cursed the weakness in my legs and clutched the dagger in a two-fisted grip. I had no expertise in knife-fighting but having a pointy thing in my hands triggered a surge of confidence.

"Keep the blade, my lady, if it offers comfort," Griffin said.

Nothing in his manner sent alarm bells screaming, unlike the monster on the ground, which even in death brought shivers. I glanced at the dagger and then the way the captain held his sword with easy confidence. Dream or not, I had a funny feeling that, if necessary, Griffin could disarm me in his sleep. With one hand tied behind his back. I returned his weapon, and he slid it back into his boot.

The body of the creature called a carver emitted a nauseating reek. The tendrils had been severed and the same oily black substance dribbled from the wounds. Judging by the corresponding goo on the captain's sword blade, he was responsible. The severed head also had long parallel rake-marks that didn't resemble cuts from a sword. My heart skipped a beat. They had torn open the skin to reveal the shiny gleam of a metallic skull.

Abril scrutinized me with a puzzled look. "I've never seen the like of your dress. Are you an artisan?"

"I'm an artist. I paint."

"What are you doing here?" said Bram. "Are you new to the garrison? We had no word of arrivals, and the people know to stay well clear of the boundary and avoid the heights during an alert."

I couldn't tear my gaze from the carver, a nightmarish mixture of machine and flesh and shuddered. "What was that thing?"

Griffin raised an eyebrow. "You don't recognize a carver?"

Bram murmured an aside, "She must be in shock if the scourge of the Commonwealth is unknown."

Scourge? Commonwealth? I stared at them. They stared back. These people looked genuine. So did the entire landscape. I saw it, smelled it, touched it. With a sudden impulse, I jabbed the captain sharply in the chest with my finger. "Ow," I said, shaking away the sting, more confused than ever. "Solid as a rock. This can't be a dream, but it's a heck of a hallucination."

"I assure you, madam," he said dryly. "I am quite real."

I snorted. "Great, a hallucination with an attitude. Enough with the madam, though. You may as well call me Jess until I wake up. Oh, and thanks for the rescue, Captain Griffin, even though I'm hallucinating everything."

"As you wish, Lady Jess." He smiled at me, and I had an unexpected flutter of pleasure at his dimples. I had been right to add them. They softened his chiseled

22

appearance. The captain snatched a clump of leaves and wiped the remainder of the black goo from his blade. After ramming it in the scabbard, he went to the corpse and with the toe of his boot nudged the stump of the palette knife protruding from the carver's head. "Yours?"

"Uh-huh, but I don't want it back."

Abril bent over and picked up the handle lying on the ground. "An unusual choice of weapon," she said, peering at it with curiosity. "What is it?"

"A palette knife to spread paint." I shrugged. "A girl's gotta use what she's best at."

Abril chuckled and gave it back to me. "A wise attitude. I have often said similar to my father." The captain shot her a look, and although Abril's demeanor became solemn once more, a twinkle lingered in her eyes.

"Why was the carver after you?" asked Bram. "Carvers kill. They never take prisoners."

I dropped the handle of the palette knife into my pocket and shivered. "They eat people?"

Bram gaped at me. "When they hunger, otherwise, they destroy any living thing in their way. Their purpose is to spread terror."

"What are they?" I demanded. "It has a metal skull, but it's covered with hide. Is it a machine or alive?"

"Both," said Griffin. "Where are you from?" His eyes widened. "Have you come from outside the boundary?"

"Boundary?"

Thunder rumbled overhead. The captain's mount pawed the ground and shook his head while the others tugged at their reins. "Questions will wait," he said, regarding the sky with a frown. "The lyrs are uneasy. We must leave and make for the safety of the garrison. Lady Jess, we have no spare lyr, so you and I must ride together. Have you ridden before?"

I gave his animal a wary look. "I can ride a horse. This is kinda like a horse."

"Horse?"

"Never mind." I approached the captain's lyr and cautiously patted his neck. He turned his head, gave a curious sniff, and then butted me gently. I chuckled and scratched under his chin. "You're a good boy, aren't you?" The lyr leaned into my hand and made a soft trilling sound between a nicker and a bleat.

"Cirrus approves of you, and a war mount does not give affection easily," Griffin said with obvious surprise.

He cupped his hands, boosted me into the saddle, and then swung in behind me. The saddle was wide with a strange T-shaped pommel that reminded me of my cane. It was a snug fit for two and I scooted tight against the captain so we both had enough room. Even with his leather outfit, Griffin's warmth seeped into me. I was glad he couldn't see my face as I was sure a flush rose to my heated cheeks. It had been a while since I had a man this close.

"Are you comfortable?" he asked.

I cleared my throat. "Quite." In fact, this was more than comfortable. Having his arms around me to hold the reins was downright agreeable. Bram and Abril mounted, and we followed them through the woods.

Griffin urged his mount to a trot. He tightened his grip around my waist, and my heart beat faster in response. He didn't have traditional good looks, and with the faded scar on his cheek, displayed none of the carefully crafted perfection of book cover models. He was young, early thirties, but carried himself with the unruffled confidence of a professional warrior who'd seen more than his share of battles. Honestly, for conjuring a hallucination, I'd done a spectacular job. Kudos to me.

As we rode, I wrestled with the vague notion of familiarity, too, as if Griffin and I had met in the past. Surely, I would have remembered. Had I passed him on the street and then culled his face from my subconscious?

We reached a glade. It would have been a lovely place for a picnic except for the corpses. Three men and another woman in the same rose uniform sat on lyrs. Two monsters, bristling with arrows, were minus their heads. A dozen yards away was a glistening shimmer barely visible through the foliage as if someone hung a semi-transparent curtain between the trees. Only a blurred outline of the forest could be seen on the other side. I started to ask what it was and then caught another whiff of that nasty acrid stink from the dead carvers and pressed my lips together to keep from gagging.

"The breach?" said Griffin sharply.

"Collapsed," said one of the men. He motioned in the direction of the shimmering curtain. "The boundary is secure."

"A small bit of good fortune," said Griffin. He pursed his lips and whistled. A shrieking blur dropped from the sky and a bird with the semblance of a hawk flew straight at my head. Startled, I leaned back into Griffin and flinched, expecting the worse. At seemingly the last moment before a collision, the bird pulled up a pair of vicious-looking talons and landed gracefully on the oversize pommel.

With flapping wings and a chorus of shrieks, more followed, landing lightly on the pommels of the other soldiers. The only one without a feathered passenger was Abril. My heart pounded, but whether in shock or disbelief I wasn't sure. This situation was quickly becoming overwhelming. Everything in this hallucination was so real, the carvers, the woods, now these birds and the captain's arms around my waist. Though that part was still nice.

"No fear, my lady," said the captain. He reached out and stroked the bird's head. "Racer is my warbird. You must have seen them at the garrison."

"I-I'm not from around here."

"Racer fights with me. No eyesight is keener than a warbird. He is able to spot a carver from afar, send me the location, and then distract the creature until I strike the killing blow. After the carver was killed, Racer flew off to watch for signs of the wind surge. Racer, say hello."

"Wind surge?" I asked.

The warbird cocked his head and peered at me with stunning intensity. A hawk's eyes were yellow, but his were crystal blue, the color of the sky. They drew me in, and as with the lyrs, held intelligence in their depths.

Words flowed into my head. *Jess of the Rose Stone.*

I inhaled a sharp breath. "He knows my name."

The soldiers stared at me, and Abril blurted, "She heard Racer."

"Captain," said Bram. "I have never known a

warbird to communicate with someone not sworn to the guard."

The bird on Bram's pommel shifted its weight from side to side. *She is of the Rose Stone, but not of the Commonwealth.* I stared at it, the other bird's voice spoke clearly to me also.

"What do you mean, Sojourn?" asked Bram.

Sojourn swiveled his head to peer at Racer who began to chant, *Rose Stone, Rose Stone, Rose Stone.* The other birds joined in, their hushed twitters filling my head.

"Where are you from?" demanded Griffin of me. "How did you get here?"

Before I could say, "No clue," a dank wind buffeted my face. Thunder boomed; powerful reverberations rolled through me.

The surge is building, said Racer. *Flight will be difficult.*

"Lead the warbird legion to the garrison and alert them of our arrival," said Griffin. Racer let out a cry, and, as one, the warbirds launched into the air. "Hurry," Griffin shouted to the others. "The wind surge is rising fast." The lyrs bounded away.

The hand tremors had subsided again, and I clasped the T-shaped pommel, knees clenched tight to the lyr. The animal's movement was more graceful than a horse, but the rough terrain still made for a jolting ride. I hadn't been in the saddle for a while, and it took several teeth-rattling seconds to find a comfortable rhythm.

The sky grew darker by the minute, roiling angry clouds formed a churning mass overhead and blocked the sun. Fear welled in the pit of my stomach. I had never seen a storm develop so quickly.

We broke through the woods and arrived at the edge of a steep incline strewn with rocks jarred loose from the cliffs above. I shifted in my seat and warily looked over the rim. We'd have to dismount and find shelter. No horse would ever be crazy enough to attempt such a descent.

Apparently, lyrs had less in common with horses than I surmised. With a graceful bound, Cirrus hurtled over the side and the rest of them followed. The lyrs zigzagged from one pile of shifting detritus to another, occasionally jumping over larger boulders that blocked the way. With each leap, Cirrus picked up speed. He didn't even seem to look where he was going and simply plummeted headfirst downhill. I gritted my teeth at the ache in my knees. The scratch on my forearm from the carver throbbed, too.

I yelped at a hard jolt. "This is insane. Why can't I wake up?"

My words drowned in a roll of thunder. "Did you say something, Lady Jess?" shouted Griffin.

"Yes. No. Never mind." I tried blinking to clear my vision, but the hallucination remained stubbornly intact. I rode a bunny-eared goat-llama in a frantic race down a cliff, held tight by a man dressed for a Renaissance fair.

The logical explanation must be a reaction from those stupid pills. But how? They weren't in my stomach long enough to dissolve, so I couldn't have gotten a full dose. So much for the inadequate warning label about possible side-effects. I made a mental note to have a stern word with the pharmacist.

The lyrs landed at the bottom of the crag and raced away. The sky was murky gray, and the clouds whirled, as if stirred by an invisible hand. Not even a speck of sunshine peeked through them. Turbulent wind whipped billows of dirt off the ground, and the world was bathed in dreary half-light. With a *splat*, a raindrop landed on my cheek, but I didn't dare let go of the pommel long enough to brush it away.

The troop rode at a thundering gallop, and my heart pounded against my ribs as the wind became an icy blast. The path veered sharply around an outcropping and then widened as we entered a valley. In the distance was an impressive stone wall, the same gray color as the surrounding cliffs.

Abril rode beside us. She shifted in the saddle and shot an uneasy look behind. Her eyes widened. "Wind surge!" she shouted.

I turned my head to peer around Griffin and immediately wished I hadn't. A tower of black clouds built over the top of the ridge we had descended. Lightning bolts streaked through the interior leaving tracks of internal flames. I watched in horror as earth sucked from the ground beneath the clouds reached thirty feet into the air and became a swelling wave. Chunks of debris from the forest floor swirled inside the boiling mass. For an instant, the wave teetered on the brink of the cliff. Then it toppled, barreling over the side. Straight as an arrow shot from a bow, it headed right for us.

Air pushed ahead of the wave hammered our backs. Flecks of saliva dripped from the lyrs' mouths, but they didn't slow their manic race to the garrison. We thundered past farmhouses, windows and doors shuttered, the grain in the fields bent low by the force of the advancing wind.

Turrets ringed the garrison's walls. Men and women in uniform stood guard on a walkway between them. They called out, beckoning us to hurry. Our road led straight to a massive gate, but it was shut tight.

Blurs circled one of the turrets. The warbirds' raucous cries added to the frantic urgency. One of them broke away and dove in front of us.

Faster! cried Racer.

My sweaty hands clung to the pommel as the lyrs galloped to a sure collision with the gate. At the last moment, it swung open with a grinding creak. The lyrs' hooves clattered over gray cobblestone and into the keep. The gate slammed shut behind us, and Griffin reined to a halt. The troop turned around, the lyrs' flanks heaving. The roar on the other side of the wall was deafening, becoming louder and louder, like the approach of a runaway train. I sat paralyzed in the saddle, gaze fixed to the gate.

The wave hit with an earth-shattering boom. The ground shuddered, and Cirrus took a skittish sidestep. The giant hinges groaned. The wave plowed into the gate and rose higher and higher, until visible above the wall, reaching to the sky. Suspended inside were whole trees ripped from the ground. I was unable to breathe or move a muscle, waiting for the wave to crest and bury me beneath tons of debris. I pressed back into Griffin's arms and opened my mouth to scream. His hold on me tightened, and the scream died on my lips.

All eyes turned to the sky, including those of the lyrs. The tip of the unnatural wave of destruction wobbled toward the garrison. Then, with what appeared to be infinite slowness, it curled backward and disappeared behind the wall. From the other side came a tremendous crash and then blessed silence.

The tension drained away, and my body sagged in the saddle. "I-I thought we were done for."

"A wind surge has never defeated the wall of High Point Garrison," said Abril proudly.

I took several deep breaths, and my stampeding heartbeat slowed to a respectable trot. "I-is it gone. Are we safe?"

"Yes," said Griffin. "You really have no knowledge of a wind surge?"

I chuckled weakly. "Trust me, I'm pretty sure I would have remembered. Where did it come from?"

"As to where and how, we do not know, but they always occur after a breach," said Griffin. "They're increasing in strength as more carvers force entry. If a drummer seals a breach quickly, the surge is stopped, otherwise, we run to safety." His words had a savage tint. This man obviously didn't approve of running from anything.

Drummer? Wind surge? Breach? I had nothing but questions. What kind of crazy world had my mind created?

The giant gate opened again. Outside were mounds of dirt, rocks, and the remains of shattered plant life, the piles now illuminated by the amber glow of fading daylight. I could barely see beyond the rubble to the ridge, but the sky above was mercifully clear. The ominous clouds had vanished as quickly as they formed. The inhabitants of the garrison must have often dealt with the wind surge's aftereffects because they were well-prepared. People arrived in carts drawn by teams of lyrs. They had shovels, ropes, axes, and other implements and hurried outside to clear the entrance.

A woman in uniform edged through the crowd and hailed Griffin. "That was close, Captain. The warbirds alerted us, but we feared you wouldn't make it back in time. Is it true three carvers passed the breach?"

"Yes, I'm afraid so."

She drew a breath as if to steady herself and then shot me an undisguised look of curiosity. "The warbirds said you brought a visitor. They had many questions."

Although my nerves were still shaky, the notion of being the center of conversation among the warbirds was unexpectedly funny, and I pressed my lips together to keep from snickering.

"Fortune and the speed of the lyrs were in our favor today," said Griffin. "Have the other patrols and drummers returned?"

"Yes, sir, hours ago. Single carvers attempted two other breaches, but the drummers thwarted them. They sealed the boundary before any made it through."

"Send the guard to check the surrounding farms and make sure the inhabitants are safe. I will be at headquarters and see to our guest. Has Danya returned?"

"She's still at the farm attending the birth." She stiffened. "You fear the wind surge caught her on the road?"

"No. Danya warned breaches were imminent today. She would have noted the rise of the wind surge and sheltered in place. Send a message that I need her at once."

Griffin nudged the lyr to a walk. My heartbeat had returned to normal, but a nasty case of the jitters refused to die. Perhaps Griffin sensed that, because while his hold around me eased, he didn't completely let go and I was grateful.

As we left the gate behind us, I looked around. This wasn't simply a military base, but a settlement. Narrow lanes spread out from cobblestone streets lined with shops and homes, windows and doors shuttered tight. On the top of the wall, a man in uniform struck a gong with a hammer. The sound reverberated, bouncing from alley to alley. The all-clear signal? Doors and shutters opened with a clatter, and faces peeked out, awash with relief. I expected the military presence, obviously Griffin and the others were soldiers, but this small vibrant community had surprising diversity. Like Griffin's squad, the inhabitants had varied skin tones, reflecting a blending of cultures. Not the typical, white-washed fairytale, but exactly how I would have drawn them.

People huddled in doorways, chatting in excited voices. When they spotted our troop, they waved and shouted, but at the sight of me, they gaped in curiosity and whispered behind their hands. Possibly the gossipy warbirds had filled them in on the unexpected guest, too.

The main street led to a building in the center of the garrison, constructed of the same stone as the walls. The windows were open, shutters pulled back, and welcoming lights shone within. People gathered in a courtyard at the bottom of steps to the entrance. They must have been waiting for us because once Griffin, Abril, and Bram dismounted, they hurried to take the reins.

Griffin patted Cirrus' nose. "Many thanks, my friend. You earned your rest."

The lyr nuzzled his hand and turned his head to

look at me. If he had an eyebrow, I got the distinct impression he would have raised it. "Absolutely," I said, throwing myself over his neck in a hug. "You're way better than a horse." I meant every word. Cirrus bobbed his head as if in complete agreement, and I laughed.

The adrenaline rush had passed, and I leaned back in the saddle, light-headed and inhaling deep lungsful of crisp air. Every muscle ached. It had been hours since I ate or drank anything and weeks since this much physical activity, even if it were imaginary. I took in the sky, the stone walls, the people surrounding me. An uneasy prickle of doubt crept in. If this wasn't a dream or a hallucination, where the heck was I and how did I get here? I gave my head a mental shake to dislodge the crazy notion. This place was definitely not real.

Griffin held out his arms. "Lady Jess, allow me to help you down."

I leaned into him and with a grimace, eased my leg over the saddle. He lowered me gently to the ground, but my weak legs teetered once they bore my full weight. I would have fallen, but Griffin caught me by the waist and held me close. "You're injured," he said in alarm.

"No. I have a medical condition that affects my legs—why am I explaining this to a dream?" I snapped, irrationally angry at an embrace that felt much too real.

His eyes twinkled. "Since you haven't yet wakened, why not rest until you do? This dream has questions he wishes to ask."

"Fine," I grumbled, squirming from his grip. "But I'm okay now and don't need help."

"As you wish."

A man hurried from the keep informing Griffin dinner waited in the main hall. The captain nodded and ordered him to bring Danya as soon as she arrived.

"Who's Danya?" I asked. "You mentioned the name earlier."

"The garrison's chief drummer."

Drummer again. Oh well, maybe there was dinner music.

I limped down the corridor, Griffin at my side, Abril, and Bram behind us. Griffin stayed within arms' reach but didn't move to assist me. I sensed his eyes studying me discreetly. "So," I said, "I'll ask the first question. What is this place?"

"High Point Garrison, the most northern of the forts," said Griffin. "We keep watch on the boundary."

"Boundary of what? Where exactly am I?"

"You are in the Commonwealth of the Rose."

"Yes, but what is it?" I asked with growing exasperation.

"I don't understand." From the way he knitted his brows in confusion, he plainly didn't. "It is our place, our world."

"On Earth?"

He stared at me. "Where else would we be?"

I sighed. "Never mind. You're in charge here?"

"I am." His voice held a hint of pride.

"So, the symbol on the uniforms represents the Commonwealth."

"The Rose Guard, protectors of the Commonwealth. You don't remember?"

"I remember everything in my life, where I was born, where I live, my favorite coffee shop—"

"Coffee?"

35

"Don't interrupt," I said a trifle testily. "I remember where I buy my paints, the cost of canvas. How many times do I have to explain that you and your people are hallucinations or a dream or something else I haven't figured out?" I blew out my cheeks in frustration. "Sheesh, I get cranky when I'm hungry."

Griffin gestured ahead with a twinkle in his eye. "Then it's fortunate dinner awaits us."

We came to an open door. I sniffed the air, and a smile spread across my face. Inside was a dining hall where servants set steaming dishes on a long table. The room had a wooden floor polished to a high gloss. Windows with ornate, stained-glass depictions of a rose let in the last of the fading light. A fireplace on one side offered cheery warmth to cut the chill. Instead of logs in the fire, a woman tossed a dark brown brick-shaped object into the hearth. Another woman lit sconces on the walls filled with large candles of the same color. They gave off a pleasant herbal scent.

"I apologize for the roughness of the surroundings," said Griffin. "This is a frontier outpost, but we have the basic amenities." He added lightly, "Perhaps, if it's not to your taste, you can dream of another."

I grinned. "For a hallucination, you're very funny—and tolerant."

Abril snorted a laugh, and the captain shot her a disapproving look. "Am I?" he said dryly. "I'm not regarded among my guards for either good humor or patience."

"Well, that must be a result of my imagination then. I approve of what I've done, so I'll keep you this way." I scrutinized him from head to toe. "The roguish

36

good looks work for me, too. Even the scar."

"Roguish good looks?" said Bram with an innocent expression. "I can't say as I've ever noticed that in our captain."

"Oh, yes, and the dimples are a nice touch, too," I said. "Nope, I won't change a thing."

Abril appeared on the verge of another laugh until the captain sent her a scathing look. She turned her head away and bit her lip, eyes gleaming. He inclined his head toward me. "My thanks, Lady Jess. I shall endeavor not to disappoint."

I plopped in a chair with a weary sigh and reveled in the heat from the fireplace as it eased the ache in my bones. A servant placed a bowl of stew in front of me. It had chunks of meat, vegetables, and little dumplings.

"Eat, Lady Jess, and then we will talk more," said the captain.

I didn't have the strength to argue, and besides, I was starving. I gave a spoonful of stew an experimental nibble and then dug in with gusto. It was delicious. A little voice in my head insisted it wasn't logical. Food didn't have a taste in a dream, but I was hungry and told the inner warning to shut up and mind its own business.

Griffin poured brown, steamy liquid into an earthenware mug and handed it to me. I took a sip. The ingredients were unfamiliar, but the taste refreshing, and I drained the cup. I suspected a mild stimulant, too, because the earlier chill vanished, and pleasant warmth coursed through me. I tugged on the neckline of my shirt. Since I started eating, the temperature in the room had risen dramatically, although the flames in the hearth weren't large.

As my hunger disappeared, my spirits lifted. "If all hallucinations are as delicious as this, I'll recommend them to my friends," I said cheerfully, finishing the last dumpling.

None of the others had spoken during the meal, but now Bram regarded me intently. "Why are you convinced we are hallucinations? I assure you, Lady Jess, I feel quite real."

"As do I," said Abril. "How did you come to the heights? There are no settlements nearby. You don't live at the garrison, and I've never seen such clothing. The ridge is a treacherous climb without a lyr."

"That's a great question, and I'd like the answer myself. I was at home and took new medication." I coughed. "A teensy too much. I went to my easel and started to paint." I squirmed in my seat and felt my cheeks warm. "It was strange though. The man I sketched resembled you."

Griffin's brow furrowed. "How can that be? We have never met. I'm certain I would have remembered, but…" He paused as if unsure and eyed me sharply. "There is something familiar about you."

A pleasant sensation pinged through me. *Down girl.* "As I said, you're a hallucination. I painted a rose first and then added you afterward."

Abril and Bram exchanged startled glances with the captain, and he narrowed his eyes at me. "What kind of rose?"

"It's identical to the one on your uniform, more stylized than real. Funny that, my usual work is very different. Anyway, I was working on this figure study. Then I suddenly felt lightheaded and thought it might be a reaction to the medication. The world went crimson-colored and hazy. I had a sensation of falling and hit hard. I opened my eyes and lay in the middle of the woods. Everything had a faint glow at first and then cleared. The next thing I knew that carver thing got wind of me, and I ran for my life through the woods. By the way, Captain, thanks again for the rescue," I said with a smile.

His eyes sparkled. "I hardly think it is necessary to thank a dream, Lady Jess."

I chuckled. "Nevertheless, I'm grateful, and everyone can drop the 'lady' bit and call me Jess. Since you're figments of my imagination, there's no reason we can't be on a first name basis."

"Then I would be honored for you to call me Griffin. Why did the carver take you captive?"

"I have no clue. It only said a few words and didn't make much sense."

Griffin blinked. "Carvers never speak to us."

"Well, it wasn't really the carver. I heard this nasty voice in my head, but the carver heard it, too. It gave him orders."

Griffin's demeanor changed in an instant. He leaned toward me, a wary light in his eyes. "What did it say?"

"Something about a spark. It was surprised I heard and ordered the carver to bring me to it."

Griffin grabbed my arm and demanded harshly. "What spark? Where is it?"

I shook off his grip. "How should I know? I have no idea what it was talking about."

"Forgive me, Jess," said Griffin. "But you are in great danger if the darkling hunts you."

"What's a darkling?"

His jaw tightened. "The carvers' master. Many years ago, it unleashed havoc on this world and nearly destroyed us. The darkling remains hidden on the other side of the breaches."

"Through the boundary?" I asked.

"No, it's different," he said. "The boundary is a protective wall encircling the Commonwealth. The breaches attempt to pierce the wall, but they originate from someplace else, the darkling's lair. We don't know where it is. The darkling communicates with the carvers through silent talk. Drummers such as Danya can tell when a breach forms and give warning, but you are the first I know of to hear the darkling's commands."

"Start from the beginning," I said. "You know my story, so tell me about this place." I tugged a finger again at the neck of my shirt collar. "Man, it's hot in here. Can you open a window?"

A noisy screech came from outside and then a brisk *tap-tap-tap* on the glass. Griffin rose from his seat and lifted the sash. Racer sat on the ledge and poked his head inside. His electric blue eyes peered directly into mine.

"Trouble?" Griffin asked.

No. The legion wishes to see.

Racer flapped his wings and flew into the room. He landed on the table in front of me, avoiding the dishes with no difficulty. I gaped as a dozen of his friends swooped in behind him and alit around us. Startled, Bram and Abril pushed back their chairs and got to their feet, leaving me surrounded by warbirds studying me with large blue eyes.

I gripped the armrest. "Um, hi?"

Rose Stone.

I shifted in the seat. "Right, sort of. You're Racer. I met you on the ridge. Thanks for your help, too."

Victory against the enemy is always sweet.

Rose Stone! The echo of a dozen thoughts from the other warbirds reverberated round the room. *Rose Stone, Rose Stone, Rose Stone.*

Griffin leaned toward me, the intensity in his expression unnerving. "Why do Racer and the other warbirds call you the Rose Stone?"

"Well, I'm not *the* Rose Stone. I'm *a* Rose Stone. My full name is Jessica Rose Stone."

The three humans gawked at me as the warbirds continued to chant, *Rose Stone, Rose Stone, Rose Stone.*

"Hush," I said, and their chittering in my head instantly quieted. I fanned my face. It felt as if the temperature had risen another ten degrees in the past minute. "What's the big deal? It's only a name."

"It's not simply a name," said Griffin.

"Jess, can you hear me?" said a voice from above.

I hopped from the chair and stared in wonderment at the ceiling. "Melanie, is that you?"

"Jess," yelled Melanie. Her voice was louder now. "Open your eyes."

A rosy haze crept into my peripheral vision. "I'm awake. Where are you?"

"Right here. Open your eyes."

"Who are you talking to?" demanded Griffin.

"It's my friend, Melanie. Can't you hear her?" I ran a hand across my brow. My skin was scorching to the touch. "Why is it so hot in here?"

"Jess, you're flushed with fever," said Griffin. My legs trembled, and I swayed on my feet. Griffin grabbed me and his hand brushed against the scratch made by the carver.

Pain shot up my arm, and I flinched from his touch. "Ow, that hurts."

Griffin rolled up the smock's sleeve and gasped. "A carver wound."

My whole body was on fire now. "I'm fine," I mumbled. "Just a scratch, no need to fuss. So hot…" It was hard to think. My lips didn't connect to my brain anymore.

Muscular arms lifted me off my feet. Griffin held me close, his face creased with worry. "Jess, why didn't you tell me the carver injured you? Their claws have deadly poison."

"Don't be silly, dreams can't hurt…" The hazy glow closed in, blurring my vision. The scent of a rose filled the room. I inhaled deeply, and the essence enveloped me, cooling my blood. In the background, Griffin shouted orders. The table disappeared, so did the walls. My field of view constricted, closing like a narrowing tunnel, until the only things that remained were Griffin's eyes peering deep into mine.

"Cool hallucination," I murmured. "I'll sure miss you."

"Jess, come back."

Was that Melanie or the captain? "Griffin," I called. "Where are you?" He faded from view and through my mind roared Racer's triumphant cry.

Rose Stone!

Chapter Three

My eyelids fluttered open.

"Hey, it's about time. Welcome back," said Melanie.

I blinked. "What are you doing here?"

"Don't you remember? I told you I'd drop by after work. What happened? I couldn't wake you and was worried. A few more seconds and I'd have called an ambulance."

I sat up and looked around. For a moment, it seemed as if a touch of pink tinted the walls, but the color vanished so quickly I couldn't be sure. High Point Garrison was gone. Instead, I lay on the couch in my loft, still wearing the smock. I ran a hand through my hair damp with sweat. "I, uh, fell asleep."

"I was going to use my spare key, but the door was open. You shouldn't leave it unlocked."

"Oh, I guess I forgot."

"It must have been a heck of a dream. I called, but got no answer, so I came in and found you on the couch. Who's Griffin?"

I gaped at her. "What?"

"Griffin. You were calling his name, rather insistently. I assume Griffin was a man, or was it a half-lion, half-eagle kind of thing?"

I chuckled. "He was most definitely a man."

Melanie grinned. "Oh, one of *those* dreams."

"It might have been, if I wasn't so rudely interrupted."

"Are you sure you're okay?" said Melanie. "You still seem a little out of it."

I put a hand to my cheek. It was cool to the touch. "The fever's gone," I muttered.

"What fever? Are you sick?" She grabbed my wrist to take my pulse.

I yanked it away and made a face at her. "I'm fine, Mother. There was no fever. I felt a little warm, but I'm back to normal now."

Melanie eyed me askance. "As your doctor, I'm the better judge of that. Sit still and I'll get you a glass of water." She went to the kitchen sink. "Are you hungry? I can make something."

"No, thanks, I had a bowl of stew…um, opened a can of stew." I scratched my head. I should have been starving. I was too nervous to eat that morning and only had a cup of tea for breakfast but felt comfortably full.

Melanie returned with the water. I took a sip and the muzzy disoriented feeling of being in two places at once drifted away.

"How about a cool washcloth for your head?"

"Geez, don't fuss so much."

"I'm a doctor and your busybody friend. It's what I do." She went into the bathroom and stormed out a moment later with a scowl on her face and a clenched fist. She opened her palm and shoved it under my nose. On it were a few white tablets. "I found these on the floor along with the empty bottle. What did you do?"

"Um…"

"Jess, did you take them all at once? My God, we have to get you to a hospital—"

44

"No need. I swallowed a teensy more than advised, but they didn't stay down long enough to do any harm."

Melanie's eyes filled with sorrow. "Jess…"

I stood up and threw my arms around her. "I'm sorry I frightened you, but I'm okay now. I promise I won't do anything stupid for the rest of the day."

"I wish I believed you. Jess, please don't give up hope. I made a few calls today." Her voice quickened with excitement. "There's a doctor at the university who developed a new procedure for tumor extraction."

I stared in disbelief. "I thought the tumor was inoperable."

"Conventional surgery is out of the question, but this new technique is experimental and involves a medication to shrink the tumor so an operation is feasible. He's conducting medical trials, and according to the research I've seen, has had very good results. His name is Dr. Owen Turner. I checked around and he has an excellent reputation. I crossed my fingers and emailed your files to him after you left today, and he called me this afternoon. He didn't promise anything but is eager to discuss your case. Jess, I have good vibes about this. I made an appointment for you to see him tomorrow. I'll tag along and pick you up at nine sharp. What do you say?"

"Don't you have patients who need you?"

"You need me more, and I've already arranged coverage."

I swallowed the lump in my throat. "I say you're the best friend ever and I'll be ready. Thanks, Mel." I jabbed her playfully in the arm. "Stop hovering now. I swear, I'm okay. You'll be happy to know I'm filled with the sudden urge to paint."

Melanie brightened. "That's great. You haven't picked up a brush in a while and you're wearing your smock. You must have been busy already."

"Let's say, I was inspired."

She went to the easel. "The rose is so pretty, but not your usual style."

"I'm experimenting."

"I like it." She squinted at the canvas. "I see you roughed in a man. Is he holding the flower?"

"Not exactly. It'll be on his tabard."

"His what?"

"It's a tunic. Knights wore them, except Griffin isn't a knight, no armor. He's a guardsman."

Melanie chuckled. "You named him. That's adorable."

"Yes, well," I stammered. "It seemed to fit. I decided to do a fairytale, different from anything I've done before. I'm still working out the details."

"You always loved a good fantasy, even as a kid. Nice dimples, by the way." She cocked her head. "Something about him is vaguely familiar. Is Griffin a model from one of the book covers you've done?"

"No. I don't think so, but you're right." I hid a smile. "I have a feeling I've seen him before, too. Recently, actually."

"Well, I'll leave you to it, and don't forget to lock the door this time."

"Yes, Mother." I locked the door behind her and leaned against the wall, staring at the familiar surroundings of the loft, and experiencing a strange disconnect. A moment ago, I was in another world and now I was home. I still felt Griffin's touch and heard the concern—no, the fear in his voice when I collapsed.

Did I die there only to come back here to die from a tumor?

"Ridiculous," I said with a shake of the head. I'd either experienced a seriously vivid dream or a bizarre hallucinogenic aftereffect from the medication I managed to keep down. A tinge of guilt washed over me. I should have told Melanie how real the fantasy world seemed, but she'd probably insist I head to the hospital, and I was fine now. The last thing I wanted today was more medical tests.

"The Rose Stone." I snorted a laugh. "Oh, brother."

Confessing to Melanie would only upset her, and I enjoyed the adventure even though it was imaginary. Ex-boyfriend Elliot had our dates planned to the minutiae. Spontaneity was a crime. His notion of a feat of daring was to try a new restaurant before the reviews were in.

I rubbed the back of my neck. What happened to the girl I used to be? My free-spirited nature had dissipated over the years, replaced by dull, solid stability and the need to make a living. It had been a while since I felt so wild and unchained—as if life held infinite possibilities, and I only had to be brave enough to reach for them.

I closed my eyes, recalling the taste of dust in my mouth from the desperate ride to safety in the garrison and shivered at the memory of the boom as that horrific wave slammed into the gate. Now, that was certainly an adventure. I smiled. Griffin's arms around me had kindled more of a flame than Elliot ever did.

Another burst of creative fire prodded me to the easel, and I reached automatically for my old trusty palette knife. It was gone. My heart raced. I shoved aside art supplies in a frantic search, but the knife wasn't on the tray, the worktable, or the drop cloth. I stared at the pocket of my smock.

"No." My mouth went dry, and I swallowed hard. "Not possible." I slipped my hand inside and touched a wooden handle. With thumb and forefinger, I pulled out what remained of the palette knife. The metal shaft was broken, and the jagged tip held a dried black substance with an oily sheen.

"P-paint." My voice shook. "It has to be paint." I held it to my nose and smelled a faint acrid scent, the blood of the carver. I dropped the handle on the drop cloth and kicked it away, eyeing it like a venomous snake poised to strike. "Calm down. There must be a rational explanation. I-I must have broken the palette knife and forgot. I stuck it in my pocket when the hallucination began." Of course, that didn't explain the missing blade. I rolled up my sleeve. On the skin where the carver grabbed me were traces of faint pink lines.

I gawked at my arm, willing the marks to go away, but they remained stubbornly in place. "I-I scratched myself without realizing it." I ran my fingers across them and felt slight warmth, the kind from a healing wound. I snatched back my hand. My legs shook, but not from physical weakness this time, and I leaned against the worktable for support.

I peered at the rough sketch of Griffin. "Are you real?" I got no answer. Blood rushed to my head. There was only one logical explanation. I had to be unconscious in a hospital bed. My broken brain had me in its grip and refused to let go. Soon my breathing would stop, and death would claim me. My shoulders sagged. I was so tired of the fight. What was the point of continuing?

Relax. Give in. Let go.

A surge of anger shook me right to my bones. I wasn't unconscious, and those people in the Commonwealth didn't roll over and die when things got tough. Griffin wouldn't. He charged the carver without thought to his own safety. He'd have fought a dozen to the very end and stood fast at the wall to face the wind surge without a blink. Maybe my stupid, rotten brain was trying to tell me something. Death only came when a person was no longer able or willing to fight.

Well, not today. The hovering clouds of gloom scattered. I grabbed a paintbrush and waved it in defiance. "Real or not, I'm not dead yet, and I've got work to do." Was it a rush of adrenaline or hope that the appointment with Dr. Turner tomorrow wouldn't be in vain? Either way, the shaking in my hand subsided. Back and forth, brush to palette to canvas. More color here, less there, switching brushes and mixing paints. I worked in a fury, unable to rein in the explosive burst of creative adrenaline.

When the light finally faded, I stopped to study the canvas. Griffin was complete. The tiny, detailed brushwork had surprisingly delicate precision. I had never worked this fast on other projects. I barely remembered painting the tiny stitches onto the rose emblem on his tabard, lightly dabbing with a brush whose bristles were slightly thicker than an eyelash.

His outfit wasn't clean and tidy but spotted with blood from the carver and dirt from the wild ride to the garrison, the faded scar high on his cheek. I saw Griffin with perfect clarity, better than a photograph. His deep brown eyes captured my gaze and asked, *Well, my lady.*

Am I to your liking?

I flashed a broad grin. "You certainly are. As a matter of fact, you're the best portrait I've ever done, if I do say so myself."

He was more real than a fairytale hero. Even when authors and publishers raved about my book covers, the fantasy men always looked fake to me. I pulled their images from stock photos. They displayed no unique personality, nothing but identical chiseled good looks. They probably went to the same gym and drank the same protein shakes. That was the way publishers liked to see them, but this portrait was different, no phony imperfections to make him appear tough. He *was* tough—a born leader—but his voice and touch hinted at a softer side hidden from his troops.

I blew out my cheeks in disgust. "Girl, you have a fertile imagination." I touched the emblem centered on his chest, pleased with the result. Funny to have a flower symbolize a fighting force. A warbird was more fitting, but it seemed the name Rose Stone struck a chord with everyone. Evidently, it held great significance.

Rose Stone...I frowned. The phrase rang in my head and not because it was part of my name. I swear I'd heard it once in a different context, but where? A dim memory from the past flickered but disappeared into the distant recesses of my mind before I latched on. I wracked my rotten brain for a hint to no avail. What a pity I woke before learning the full backstory from Griffin. Only tantalizing snippets remained; the carvers were bad, the mysterious darkling that controlled them was worse. What was the Rose Stone and how did I fit into the picture?

Of course, I could always write my own story. I perked up and ran through a dozen different plotlines culled from a love of fairytales, but nothing seemed right. This painting had one special story, no other fit, but I didn't have the details yet.

My burst of energy drained away and left me swaying with fatigue. I hung up the smock and cleaned the brushes and palette in the sink, rolling my stiff, cramped shoulders. I was hungry all of a sudden, too. That satisfying fullness from the imaginary stew was gone, so I rifled through the refrigerator and threw together a quick dinner. It was nowhere near as good as those dumplings. The tremor in my hand returned, but the pain was less intense. Putting my health out of my mind and concentrating on something else for a while had done me good.

I took two pain pills Melanie prescribed and staggered into a hot shower. Today had definitely been a weird jumble of mixed emotions. It started out horrible, a wallow of hopeless despair. A few hours ago, I almost surrendered, but now my spirits soared. I was inspired to paint again. Instead of seeing tomorrow as one step closer to death, a dollop of cautious hope took root regarding this new doctor and his experimental procedure.

I crawled into bed and pulled the comforter to my chin. *Comfort and hope, that's what I need.* My eyes closed as my muscles relaxed. The medication took effect and the last of the pain faded away. The sounds of the city outside my window hushed and then vanished.

As I drifted off to sleep the image of Griffin appeared, but unlike the confident portrait on the canvas, this one was worried.

Muted voices murmured from far away.

"Can you heal her?" said Griffin.

"I have done what I can," said a woman. "The poison had time to work its curse and now runs through her veins, but she is strong. However, she must wake soon, or she never will."

"Don't surrender, Jess," Griffin whispered. Warm breath caressed my ear as if he stood right next to my bedside. "The battle continues." I felt a touch on my hand.

"I won't," I murmured. "I want to see you again."

"She answered," Griffin said in excitement. "Did you hear her?"

"No, but she seems to have formed a connection to you."

"What's happening?" cried Griffin. "Her body is fading."

"I do not know. The drum will lead her to our path, but she must have the courage to follow."

Tap, tap, tap. The rhythmic thrumming had a hypnotic beat.

"Jess," said Griffin, his voice becoming inaudible. "Come to me. Follow the path."

****

Tap, tap, tap.

My eyes opened to the soft patter of rain hitting the skylight. For a few disorienting seconds, I stared at water droplets trickling down the glass pane. Then reality flooded in. I was home in bed, not in the garrison's hall. I reached for my cellphone to check the display. I'd overslept. Melanie would be here any minute.

I sat up and rubbed my temples, jolted by the intensity of the dream. I swear I had heard Griffin call, felt his breath on my cheek, and the touch of his hand. There was a woman with him, too, but not Abril. She said I had to find the courage to follow the path.

I stretched and yawned. "Follow the path?" I mumbled. "What path?" Odd how the story continued in my dreams. It was getting pretty good, too, but my stupid brain needed to add some finer points to nudge the plot along.

My arm itched. I gave an absentminded scratch and then peered at my skin, eyes widening in astonishment. The faint pink lines had vanished. Had they been there when I got into bed last night? I couldn't remember.

I threw on clothes and hurried to the easel. The smock rested on the hook where I left it and the broken palette knife in the same spot on the drop cloth. I prodded it with my toe. I hadn't imagined that, at least. My lips twitched in an unconscious smile at the finished portrait of Griffin, and I touched the canvas, tracing the lines of his face. He had called for me in my dream. He wanted to see me again. That was nice. I got a warm, fuzzy feeling and then shook my head in 'disbelief. "A painting wants to see me again?" I chuckled. "Girl, you have completely lost it."

There was a knock at the door, and Melanie arrived bearing coffee and muffins. As I ate, she studied me with her "doctor eyes."

"Quit staring," I said. "You give me the creeps."

"You look a little better this morning. How are you feeling?"

"I'm okay, and, no, I didn't take more pills than prescribed. I won't do that again—not without giving advance warning."

Melanie made a face. "Gee, thanks. You're too kind."

Her gaze wandered to the easel, and she walked over to take a closer look. "Hey, you got a lot done to this guy since yesterday."

"I had a sudden burst of inspiration."

"He's cute. A shame he isn't real."

"Yeah, a shame." I stifled a grin.

"He's kind of a mess, too. Why did you paint him so dusty?"

"Captain Griffin was on patrol and killed a monster called a carver."

"Oh, he's a captain now. Never heard of a carver. What is it?"

"A tentacle-headed freak with humongous claws. Part machine, I think. They're not from around here," I added lightly.

Melanie leaned in and studied the canvas. "You're sure he's not a model? I swear he looks familiar or maybe I heard the name before. Griffin rings a bell."

"Trust me, Griffin would never model. He isn't a man obsessed with his looks." I cleared my throat. "I had another dream about him." Melanie snickered, and I shot her a look of disapproval. "No, it wasn't one of *those* dreams. Get your mind out of the gutter. He was searching for me."

"And you wanted him to find you."

My heart gave a tug. "I suppose I did."

"Pity. Is he single?" Her eyes held a wicked gleam. "You can have fun times with him even if he's imaginary."

"Wow, for a doctor you have a filthy mind, and I

think he's single."

"You think?"

"I didn't notice a wedding ring and forgot to ask. I'll be sure to bring it up the next time I see him." I peered at the painting and couldn't help but smile. "I'm going to call it *The Rose Stone*. Griffin is captain of the Rose Stone guards."

"What's a Rose Stone?"

"Haven't a clue."

"It sounds like one of the fairytales you're so fond of. The Rose Stone," she murmured. "Funny, that sounds familiar, too, and not because it's part of your name...well, we'd better go. We don't want to be late for the appointment with Dr. Turner." She motioned to my legs. "Do you need help with the stairs?"

"I'm slow but can manage. Get the car, and I'll meet you out front."

"Okay. Don't forget the cane."

Melanie left. I went to the closet and grabbed my jacket and then inspected the painting one last time. My heartbeat raced as a rose-tinted aura danced around the edge of the canvas. I closed my eyes. "Go away," I hissed between clenched teeth. When I opened them again, the aura had disappeared, and I breathed a sigh of relief. Griffin's portrait now seemed to hold a questioning look as if he wondered where I was going. "Don't worry," I said lightly, patting the canvas. "It's just a doctor's appointment. I'll be back soon." I grabbed the cane on my way out the door.

The hospital complex sat on the outskirts of the university, an imposing collection of buildings dating from the original stone edifice of the nineteenth century to more modern structures of gleaming steel and glass.

Melanie parked in the lot of the research center, and we took the elevator to the top floor.

"Nice place," I said. "I hope my insurance covers this."

"Don't worry about that. Owen told me since this is a trial procedure, once you're accepted, costs are waived."

"Owen? You're on a first-name basis." I nudged her. "He must be cute."

"He asked me to call him that when we spoke on the phone," she said in a huff. "And I suppose the picture on the center's website isn't totally tragic."

"Ah, you checked him out. That's adorable."

She glared at me. "Behave."

Dr. Owen Turner's office window overlooked the broad expanse of green separating the research facility from the university's main campus. He was younger than I expected, in his early thirties, and greeted both of us with warm, welcoming handshakes. He wasn't classically handsome but exuded nerdy charm. He also didn't wear a wedding ring. I shot a glance at his desk. No pictures of a spouse or kids either. Melanie had nerdy charm, too, and a love life even less successful than mine. Two kind-hearted nerds might make one awesome pair.

Dr. Turner showed us to seats at a table with an open laptop. "I was going through Jess' medical records again. As you know, the tumor is in a tricky location, even more inaccessible than other patients who've been through the procedure. I won't lie, tumors such as this are nasty. They act as if they have a mind of their own and don't give up easily. Jess, have you had any hallucinations?"

I shifted in my chair. "I-I'm not sure. I had a detailed dream with different noises, smells, and tastes. It felt very real."

Melanie's brow instantly creased with worry. "You don't experience complex sensory input in a dream. That sounds more like a hallucination to me."

Dr. Turner leaned forward. "She's right. Tell me what you saw and felt."

"I drifted into another world that seemed completely real. Most of the plants and animals were the same, but others were different. Soldiers were on patrol, and one of them rescued me from a monster. They were as surprised to see me as I was to see them, as if I unexpectedly popped into the middle of their lives. We rode to an outpost, and wind attacked us." I kept my attraction to Griffin to myself. That was too awkward to share.

Melanie raised an eyebrow. "The wind attacked you?"

"Yeah, it followed us down the mountain, and we barely made it to the garrison in time. We rode on these animals, and I felt the bounce in the saddle and smelled the woods around me. Griffin was the man in charge, a captain of the guard. We had dinner, and the food was excellent. I remember how it tasted, and when I woke on the couch, I wasn't hungry." I forced a smile. "Last night, I even thought I had scratches on my right arm where the monster grabbed me. Silly, huh?"

"Scratches?" said Melanie. "Let me see." Before I uttered a protest, she snatched my arm and yanked up the sleeve. "I don't see anything."

I jerked my wrist back. "Of course not. It was dark, and I was tired. I told you I didn't notice them this morning, so it must have been a mixture of a wild imagination and vivid dreaming."

"That's not a dream," said Dr. Turner, gently. "Dreams don't have such detail and plots are disjointed. They can be repetitive, like sufferers from PTSD who relive the same harrowing event but don't last long and suddenly jump from one scenario to the next without logical flow. Even people who have repeated nightmares have other dreams, too." He drummed his fingers on the table and peered at the monitor with a frown.

I gripped the armrest. "I'm sicker than you thought."

Dr. Turner patted my hand. "It means the disease has progressed faster than we believed. I need to run a new MRI and start you on medication to prevent hallucinations."

The idea of losing contact with my imaginary world was strangely disquieting. "They didn't bother me," I blurted.

"You can't function in real life if you can't tell the difference between fantasy and reality," Melanie said. "Do you want to wander around the city in a daze talking to yourself?"

"No, I suppose not." I turned to Dr. Turner. "Is there any way to tell when you enter a hallucination?"

"Not often. That's the difficulty. Stimulus tweaks the senses, perhaps a color or a scent and the mind latches on. The brain's electrical impulses give it life, so no matter how strange the mental image, the person reacts as if everything is normal."

"So, if I ate a bowl of stew in a hallucination, I'd believe it was an actual bowl of stew."

"That's right. They can be extremely detailed, impossible to tell apart from reality. I once treated a patient who believed he was in Paris. He 'saw' Paris around him and even heard me speak French. He assumed I'd taken him there for treatment. You can talk to a person in a hallucination and generally they hear you but may not accept what you tell them is the truth. That's why medication at the onset is important to curb the symptoms and prevent the patient from acting irrationally and causing unintentional harm to themselves or others."

I looked from Dr. Turner to Melanie, their expressions displaying nothing but compassion. They'd never believe the Commonwealth of the Rose was real, even if I showed them the broken palette knife. They'd say I imagined it, but I must have. It had been a hallucination and ending it was for the best. Why fight it?

The reason hit me with a bang. Because in my heart I wanted to go back and hear the rest of the story of the Rose Stone, and a larger part of me wanted to see Griffin one last time to say goodbye, even though the desire to say goodbye to a hallucination was totally nuts.

I sat up straight. "Okay. Prescribe any treatment necessary. What's next?"

"I'll explain the procedure so you can make an informed choice," said Dr. Turner. He went into a detailed account, including the chance of multiple side effects from the experimental medication, but only the gist of it mattered to me. If this new treatment worked, the tumor would shrink enough to make an operation to remove it possible.

Melanie listened in rapt attention, every so often posing a technical question, but I sat in silence. Why worry about potential side effects and the odds of success verses failure? I heard what I needed to hear. Dr. Turner had thrown me a fragile lifeline. I had every intention of clinging to it.

"The decision is yours, Jess," said Dr. Turner. "I won't lie. This is a high-risk procedure. We've had impressive successes, but also failures, and we continue to tweak the medication to find the most effective dosage. Very powerful chemicals will be pumped into your body, and too much can be as dangerous to your health as the tumor. I can't guarantee this treatment won't hasten your death."

"But patients have been cured?"

"Yes. We began trials six months ago, and ten people with tumors previously considered inoperable had them shrink enough for surgery, and we successfully removed them. Five others died during treatment. Two of them were in surgery at the time, and their conditions rapidly deteriorated. Three were in recovery. For those patients, the stress of the treatment and operation proved too much."

I sat up straight. "Ten healthy people walking around is better than a guaranteed death sentence. Let's get started."

Melanie hugged me. "I'll be with you every step of the way."

"This is a medical procedure," said Dr. Turner with a twinkle in his eye. "So naturally it involves a ton of paperwork to fill out. I'm sorry about that. I hope it will be the worst part for you. I'll make arrangements for a new MRI today and compare it with the one Melanie did. After that, we'll have a better idea how big the tumor has gotten."

Dr. Turner escorted me to a clerk, and I filled out the paperwork. The forms didn't flash warning lights, but each sheet stressed the fact the undersigned volunteered for an experimental procedure with possible unknown side effects. I knew how to read between the medical lines. There were no guarantees.

Melanie had gone off with Dr. Turner. I signed the last dotted line with a flourish and even drew a little rose beneath that lifted my spirits. Melanie returned with two cups of coffee and gave one to me. "The MRI tech is standing by. Owen said whenever you're ready."

"You and Owen seem mighty cozy. Are his intentions honorable? I hope not. Life is more fun that way."

"Stop playing matchmaker."

"You like him. I can tell by the way you glare at me." I turned to the clerk and asked, "Is Dr. Turner married?"

"I don't believe so," she said with smile.

"There you go, Mel. All clear."

"Stop butting in," Melanie hissed.

"I bet he wouldn't have asked you to call him Owen if you had warts."

"Shut up and follow me."

We went directly to the MRI lab, and I smirked at Dr. Turner, cup in hand. "You bought coffee for him, too," I whispered. "Sheesh, you work fast."

Melanie shot me a look that clearly conveyed "zip it," and I went to a changing room. I tossed the empty coffee cup and slipped on scrubs, shapeless drawstring pants with a pullover shirt. A few minutes later, I sat on the MRI table, my hands cold and clammy. I rubbed them on my thighs and tried a few deep breathing exercises in a fruitless attempt to calm myself. I'd been through the same procedure not long before but being shoved into an open-ended tin can hadn't gotten any easier.

I warily regarded the MRI machine. How come I never noticed it resembled a gaping mouth eager to swallow me whole? My heart thumped a frantic beat. Why was this so scary? An MRI was basically a harmless picture, and the table wasn't uncomfortable. I patted the sheet, confident I could nap here easily. Maybe it was the slight claustrophobia that overcame me along with the necessity of remaining absolutely motionless inside a long narrow tube.

"Just smile and say cheese," I muttered to myself.

The technician looked up from the control panel. "Did you say something?"

I flushed. "Nope. Not a thing."

Dr. Turner came over and regarded me kindly. "Feeling uneasy?" he said.

"I'm a bit anxious." I coughed. "Possibly, more than a bit."

"No problem. I'll be right back."

He returned with three pills and a glass of water. "One is a new medication that's had excellent results easing tremors, the other is for muscle pain, and the third a relaxant." I downed them and then lay flat on the table. Soon, pleasant lethargy seeped into my arms and legs. This wasn't awful. My hands stopped moving and my legs felt normal, no pain at all.

"Ready?" said the tech.

"Fire away."

"Now, it's important to remain absolutely still," she said. "I'll be in the monitoring room watching with Dr. Turner and Dr. Carpenter. You'll hear my voice through the speakers and be able to talk to me."

"I remember the procedure."

"Good. Don't worry. Everything will be fine."

I tensed momentarily as the table slid into the tube, but then relaxed. "Nice meds," I murmured. "My compliments to the doc."

The tube was quiet except for a faint hum. The pleasant lethargy now seeped from my arms and legs and filtered into my head. My mind drifted, and the image of Griffin's portrait appeared. Why was he so fascinating? The urge to paint began again, but more than that was the need to complete what I started and add more details around Griffin. He should be mounted on Cirrus.

A prickle of unease inched along my spine. Something wasn't right with Griffin's expression. I had painted a confident warrior, but now his facial muscles tensed and worry lines blanketed his eyes. I yawned. I would have to fix that when I got home.

"Jess," said the technician through the speakers. "If you hear me, give a thumbs up." I complied.

"She's back," said a faraway voice. "Jess, talk to me."

I yawned again, my thoughts muzzy. The technician sounded like Griffin. Something must be off with the speakers. "I can hear you fine."

"Good," said the technician. "Now, relax. When the scan begins, you'll hear banging noises. They're rather loud, I'm afraid, but don't worry. You won't feel a thing. Some people find it comforting to think of them as drums."

"Okie doke."

Bang...bang...bang...bang.

Bang, bang, bang.

Thump-tap-thump, thump-tap-thump.

The clamor of the MRI changed from a strident bang to a rhythmic thump. It grew louder and more incessant and had a compelling rhythm I didn't notice last time. The beat was hypnotic, soothing and insistent, drawing me in. I shifted slightly with an urge to move my feet.

"Please remain still," said the technician.

"She moved," said Griffin, excitement lacing his voice. "She hears the drum."

Griffin? No, it can't be. The change in the technician's tone was merely a crazy effect from the meds or a problem with the MRI's speaker. Definitely the speaker. I made a mental note to mention it to the tech after the scan finished.

Thump-tap-thump, thump-tap-thump.

The tempo surrounded me, and the inside of the tube glowed rosy pink.

"My lady, open your eyes," said Griffin.

Thump-tap-thump, thump-tap-thump.

"They're open," I mumbled. Why was Griffin shouting in my ear?

"Are you okay in there?" said the technician.

"In the pink." I snickered in a woozy haze. "Inside joke. I'm funny."

"Relax, Jess," said Melanie. "This will take a while."

"No problem. I'm good."

Thump-tap-thump, thump-tap-thump.

The rosy color coating the inside of the MRI tube deepened to crimson and then black.

"Cool," I said, shutting my eyes.

Chapter Four

Something warm and soft covered me. It was heavier than a hospital sheet, the weight of a blanket. I opened my eyes. The MRI unit was gone, and so was the hospital. I lay on a downy mattress underneath a patchwork quilt. A woman stood at the foot of a wooden bed. She wore intricately embroidered clothing, and her long hair hung in a braid down her back. Around her neck was a silver pendant enameled with the symbol of a rose. She held a small drum and struck it lightly, alternating between the heel of her hand and her fingers.

Thump-tap-thump, thump-tap-thump.

She stopped drumming and smiled at me. "Welcome back, Lady Jess. You see, Captain. I told you she was stronger than the carver's poison. She answered the call of the spirit drum."

The Rose Stone returns.

I looked above me. Racer perched on the headboard, peering at me with those crystalline eyes. Griffin stood next to him, lines of worry etched deep in his brow. He moved to the side of the bed, and my heart did a happy dance.

"Oh, hi," I said. "It's you again."

Griffin's worry lines disappeared as he flashed a broad smile. "How do you feel?"

"I'm okay." I sat up and looked around. Still

wearing the hospital scrubs, I was in a small room flooded with light from an open window. Outside was a garden, and delicate floral scents drifted in the air. A little warning bell rang. *This is a hallucination. Try to wake up.*

I stifled the bell. What was the rush? I was in the hospital, the safest place to be. If I had an unexpected medical emergency, Melanie and Dr. Turner would rush to the rescue. In the meantime, the presence of Griffin sent delicious flutters through me. Why not enjoy the fantasy while it lasted?

"Where am I this time?" I asked.

"Still in High Point Garrison but another chamber," said Griffin. He nodded at the older woman. "Danya is our chief drummer and a powerful healer. She treated you for carver poisoning. You should have told me it wounded you," he scolded gently. "Even a scratch from their claws is deadly."

"Now, Captain," said Danya. "How could Lady Jess have known? She is a stranger here, and her ways are not ours." Danya's piercing eyes captured and held my gaze. They seemed to peer right into me, weighing and measuring in a spiritual manner. I hoped her mental excavation didn't disappoint.

Danya smiled at me. "It doesn't."

I blinked. "How did you know what I was thinking?"

"Drummers have the ability to perceive hidden things," said Griffin.

Danya placed her palm against my forehead and then nodded with satisfaction. "Your body and spirit have traveled very far to rejoin us. Don't try to move quickly."

I rubbed a hand over the soft quilt and found it impossible to tell dream from reality. With a sudden impulse, I reached out and touched the rose on Griffin's tabard.

He smiled at me, and those pleasant flutters increased. "Am I real enough?"

I chuckled. "For now. I've decided not to question anything and merely go along with the story."

"I need to check the dressing," said Danya.

Danya unwrapped a bandage on my arm and aromatic leaves fell off. I stared at the barely visible pink lines, identical to the ones I saw in the loft. There was no pain. "I had the same marks at home, but they vanished the next morning."

"As will these and leave no scar," said Danya. Her eyes glinted with amusement. "If you wish to see me as a dream, I have no objection, but I hope you choose to remain with us a while this time. We didn't have a chance to talk."

"Since, apparently, I don't have control over how long I'm here, you better fill me in now on what happened. The last thing I remember was being in the dining hall and suddenly feeling blazing hot."

"A fever is the first sign of carver poisoning," said Griffin. "Fortunately, Danya arrived at that moment."

"Oh, right," I said. "You attended a birth. How'd it go?"

"I thought we were hallucinations," she said lightly.

I grinned. "You are, but I'm curious and want to fill in the details."

"Mother and daughter were both doing well. I treated your arm, but the poison sent you into a deep sleep from which few ever waken. Captain Griffin didn't leave your side."

"Naturally, I was concerned," he said gruffly. "Especially when Jess disappeared."

My eyes widened. "I did?"

"Yes," said Danya. "Your body vanished, but a link to your essence remained. It was strong enough for the beat of the drum to find you and show you the route back here. You returned a short while ago. However, your spirit did not anchor in place, being tugged in two directions."

"I thought I lost you," said Griffin softly.

Heat rose to my cheeks. "I heard you calling."

"I'm pleased you chose to answer."

Danya leaned toward me. "Is it true? You are the Rose Stone?"

"My *name* is Jessica Rose Stone. I don't know anything about the Rose Stone of yours."

Danya looked at Griffin. "Have you heard from Stone Keep?"

"I sent a warbird to Commander Tian with a message for the chancellor."

Racer cocked his head and then peered at the window. *A warbird returns.*

Danya rubbed her chin. "I expect Chancellor Emlyn will summon us to the council chamber. It can't be a coincidence that Lady Jess arrived as attacks from the darkling increase."

"Hang on a second," I said. "I have questions—" A knock at the door interrupted my protest, and Bram and Abril entered. Their expressions filled with wonder when they spotted me sitting up in bed.

"I'm glad to see you've recovered," said Bram.

"Carver poisoning is often fatal even when treated immediately."

"Indeed," said Abril, eyes twinkling. "The captain was so concerned we feared for both of you."

Griffin shot her a severe look, and she pressed her lips together. "Racer reported a warbird has returned," he said.

Abril straightened, all military business again. "Yes, sir. Commander Tian sent orders to bring Lady Jess to Stone Keep immediately. He also said drummers to the south have warned more breaches will occur at the boundary there."

Danya nodded. "It's as we feared. My people also received warnings from the spirit drums."

Griffin issued a flurry of commands to Bram and Abril to prepare for departure in the morning. "Lady Jess needs riding clothes," said Abril. "If she is well enough to stand, I can have her properly outfitted—"

"Stop!" I said. The room went silent. Racer flapped his wings. I threw off the covers and slid out of bed. "I'm not sure I want to go anywhere until I know what's going on. What is the Rose Stone, and why is it so important?"

"Lady Jess is quite right," said Danya. "She's a guest, not a Rose Guard under orders, and important decisions should never be made lightly. She needs to understand our world." Danya handed me a robe hanging over the foot of the bed and a pair of slippers and motioned to a door. "Why don't we sit in the garden and talk? Fresh air will do us both good."

I slipped on the robe. Griffin took the quilt from the bed and wrapped it around my shoulders. "Danya will answer your questions. I have duties to attend but will return shortly." As he tucked the quilt around me, I shot a sneaky glance at his hand. No wedding ring. Yay, my fantasy held tight.

Griffin left, and Danya beckoned me out a door. Off the chamber was a walled terrace with trees, neatly tended rows of herbs, and staked plants. A few stakes sat by themselves and had a T-shape at the top. I sat in a wicker chair by a table. Although the wall cut the wind, the air was chilly, and I pulled the quilt closer around me.

"This is my private garden where I grow medicinal herbs. Those who drum also heal," said Danya.

"It's lovely here."

"I've always found it soothing when I'm troubled. Time in the garden would have served Captain Griffin well." In an offhand manner, she said, "Concern for your health overshadowed his mind these past hours, and he is not a man to sit idly."

I avoided her sharp eyes. "He's been on my mind a lot, too."

"Has he? How interesting. I'll be back in a moment with tea."

Danya was right about her garden. The sun chased away the shadows, not a single cloud marred the perfect blue sky, and every scrap of tension melted away. It was hard to believe a towering wall of destruction recently blotted out the same sky. I closed my eyes, reveling in the warmth caressing my skin.

With a soft chirrup, Racer alit on the T-shaped stake nearest me and their true purpose as warbird perches became plain.

The legion is welcome in Danya's garden.

"So I see. Well, it's certainly a lovely place." He

peered at me with those unnervingly intelligent eyes as if expecting me to continue the conversation. "Um, been a warbird long?"

I bonded with Griffin when he reached full guard status. The hunting has been good. I received an impression of slashing talons, carvers lying dead, and a warbird's screech of victory.

"Uh-huh. Well, it's great to find fulfillment in one's work."

Yes. Fulfilled. I have a mate. I am fulfilled.

"Oh, um, that's nice. Is she here? I'd be happy to meet her." This was the strangest conversation I'd ever had.

Tempest and I have a fledgling, so she nests at Stone Keep for safety. Warbirds mate for life. The sky is empty without her.

A sudden wave of longing from Racer hit me. "I'm sorry," I said, moved by the heartfelt yearning of this creature. "Will she come home soon?"

She and the fledgling will join me shortly. He looked at the door. *Griffin's sky has always been empty. Griffin should find fulfillment, too. Tempest and I have told him so.*

"Racer!" Griffin strode outside, followed by Danya holding a tray. "Jess doesn't need her quiet disturbed by the idle ramblings of a warbird. We will leave on the morrow. Alert the legion."

As you wish. He launched from the stake and flew over the garden wall. I got the impression he was miffed Griffin interrupted our chat, and I stifled a snort of laughter at the thought of Griffin harangued by an impudent warbird.

Danya set down the tray containing mugs of

steaming liquid and a plate of cakes. "I have never found Racer's conversations to be either idle or rambling," she said innocently.

"You don't know him as well as I do," muttered Griffin.

She handed me a mug and offered cake. "Since our guest is new to this land, it's best to start at the beginning, whenever that might have been. It was so long ago no one alive today witnessed the origins of the Commonwealth. The tales that remain are mere fragmented records of the Great War."

"The world was once not as you see it now," said Griffin. "Humanity harnessed wave, wind, and sky. Powerful machines bit deep into the earth, sailed through the fiercest storms, and equaled warbirds in their mastery of the air. The stories say there were even machines that thought."

"I'm aware of them," I said. "In my world, they're commonplace and called computers. I even own one."

Griffin and Danya exchanged startled glances. "And the darkling hasn't attacked?" she murmured. "Then that portal is yet closed."

"Who is the darkling?"

Danya shrugged. "No one can say. We believe it lives beyond our space and time, but from its lair, the darkling can open a breach such as the one on the ridge and send carvers to do its bidding. They spread panic while the darkling hunts the spark."

"What's the spark?" I asked.

"We harness wind and water and use the fuel bricks for lamps, heat, and steam, but the old ways used the spark," said Griffin. "So wondrous, it is said, that their most powerful machines turned day into night and even rivaled the energy of the sun."

I startled. "You mean electricity? Nuclear power?"

He spread his hands in a helpless gesture. "I don't know those words, but the ancestors reached far and wide, questing for more knowledge, more powerful machines. They found methods to open portals to other worlds. Through them, it is said, came many wonders including lyrs and warbirds."

Griffin's jaw tightened. "One black day, the darkling arrived to hunt the spark. Breaches occurred in every quarter, spewing carvers and war machines that killed every living thing in sight. The darkling drained the spark from one area and moved to the next. Nothing slowed it. Nothing stopped it. The world fought, and the world died. The area that now encompasses the Commonwealth was the last free place."

"How was the darkling defeated?" I asked, hanging on every word.

"During the heat of the Great War, when all seemed lost, the Rose Stone arrived to save us. From where or how we do not know. The stone's power pushed back the darkling's army, sealed the breaches, and created the protective boundary."

"The boundary," I murmured. "You mean the shimmering curtain I saw on the ridge."

"Yes. It encircles the Commonwealth. The darkling hunts for weak spots in the boundary where breaches can occur. Fortunately, they have been small in number compared to those of the Great War when many occurred at once. The boundary also blocks the war machines. Carvers pass through the breaches, perhaps because unlike machines they are part living flesh, but until recently only one entered at a time—with the guard to stop them thanks to the Rose Stone's warnings."

Danya said, "The Rose Stone speaks to the drummers and taught us to hear the warnings and seal breaches to prevent the wind surge. Our people forbid the use of the spark in the Commonwealth as it draws the darkling and weakens the boundary. Eighteen years ago, the darkling's power rose again. Drummers sealed one breach, and another instantly formed. We feared the war machines would follow, but the Rose Guard and the drummers stood fast, and the attacks finally subsided. Since then, the darkling's assaults have remained steady, but not overwhelming, and continue to test our defenses." Her voice softened. "The Rose Stone is our salvation and as vital to our world as the sun in the sky."

"The recent increase in breaches worries me," said Griffin.

"You think the darkling plans another massive attack," I said. "I don't get it. What does it want here if there's no more spark to hunt?"

Griffin scowled. "The darkling covets the Rose Stone. It never stops probing for a way to weaken us, overrun the boundary, and take control. The darkling remains vigilant and realized an unknown had entered the Commonwealth. It sent the carvers, but instead of the spark, you appeared—a mystery. The darkling ordered your capture, hoping to control your power to seize the Rose Stone."

"Well, the darkling got its wires crossed," I said. "I don't have any power or a connection to a stone."

Danya gave me a questioning look. "Yet, Jessica Rose Stone, you are here."

I folded my arms and regarded them both sternly. "I hate to be the bearer of bad news, but I have no idea how I got here, and Rose Stone is just a name where I come from. There are probably dozens of women called Rose Stone."

"But you are the only one who had the courage to answer," said Danya. "Recently, drummers have noted a change in the Rose Stone. The messages are harder to comprehend, and breach warnings come suddenly with little time to prepare. More carvers have made it through, and we don't know why."

"I'm sorry," I said, truthfully. "I don't have answers for you."

Griffin leaned toward me. "The Rose Stone is at Stone Keep. Chancellor Emlyn is the leader of the ruling council for the Commonwealth. Please, come with us to speak to her. These are dire times. You've seen the carvers. The Commonwealth needs the wisdom of the Rose Stone more than ever."

"I told you," I said. "It's nothing but a name, and I'm only an artist. Nobody special." I rolled my eyes. "And certainly not wise."

"You are mistaken," said Griffin. His gently chiding tone caused my heart to skip a beat. "Artists have great insight. Others look at a bare sheet of paper and see nothing, but an artist's vision sees beyond and finds a whole world waiting to be brought to life."

"Perhaps that's why you were called and why you chose to answer," said Danya. "We sought you, but in your own manner, you also searched for us."

This world now had an intriguing backstory. I glanced at Griffin and felt a flush rise to my cheeks, so turned my head and pretended to gaze at the garden as I considered delving deeper into the Commonwealth of the Rose. What was the harm? After all, I had a painting to finish, and more inspiration was always helpful. Since I was stuck in an MRI tube under the influence of medication, I could enjoy this dream world until reality elbowed it aside.

And if I don't wake up?

I suppressed a shudder. Would it be so awful to pass away in an imaginary world during one last grand adventure instead of flat on my back staring at acoustic tiles on a hospital ceiling? I had a sudden determination to make every minute count while the clock ticked down. "I'll talk to Chancellor Emlyn." I leaned over and rubbed my leg.

"You are in pain," said Griffin.

"No, it's just a little stiff. I feel good and not wobbly which is helpful since I didn't pack my cane. Those new meds from Dr. Turner must be working."

Danya touched a hand to my cheek. "This is not the carver's doing. You have a deep-rooted illness."

I gave a bitter laugh. "Yeah, you'd think I'd be smart enough to hallucinate away the tumor once I got here."

"Tumor," she murmured. "Your healers can't help?"

"They're trying. In reality, I'm in an MRI tube right now. That's why I'm wearing hospital scrubs…" They stared at me blankly. "Never mind. It's not important, and I don't want to discuss it. Maybe we should leave immediately," I added with forced cheerfulness. "I could wake at any time."

Griffin's expression softened. "I was unaware of the depths of your illness."

"I'm fine for the moment and want to go."

"Rest now," said Griffin. "We'll leave at first light."

"I'll come with you, Captain, to see that Lady Jess is well-tended," said Danya. "The other drummers can handle my duties. We must make haste for time is against us. She may stay in my healing chamber tonight. I'll drum a message to the order at Stone Keep telling Chancellor Emlyn our plans to depart in the morning."

"Very well." Griffin turned to me and gave a slight bow. "I leave you in Danya's excellent care." He paused as if hunting for the right words. "I'm pleased you returned."

"Me, too." My gaze followed him as he left the garden.

"We are fortunate Griffin commands High Point Garrison," said Danya. "He's an exceptional captain. What do you think of him?"

Her tone hinted at hidden meaning. "Well, we've only met, but I'd say he's a strong leader."

"An honorable man, too. Interesting that his voice led you to the drumming path."

"Yes, well, go figure," I said in a hurry. "Speaking of drumming, may I watch while you send the message?"

"Of course."

To my relief, she didn't probe further about Griffin, but instead went inside and returned a moment later with a drum. Evidently, Danya noted my curiosity and held it out to me. "Touch it, if you wish."

The drum wasn't large, four inches deep, and the size of a dinner plate with a strap to sling it across a shoulder. The casing was wood, intricately carved and dyed with representations of lyrs, warbirds, and a variety of plant life. A tan leather skin stretched over the top. The color was lighter in the center, as if a hand struck the area many times. The surface was smooth to the touch, almost velvet, with a slight sensation of heat. I flicked my finger in the middle and it responded with a low reverberant *thrummm*. Goosebumps skittered along my spine.

"It's beautiful," I said. "Who made it?"

Danya looked pleased. "I did. Drummers build their instrument during training."

"You're an artist, too."

"Drummers have many skills." Danya took back the drum and ran a finger lovingly on the striking surface. Although I didn't hear a sound, my skin tingled as if in response to a static charge. "The act of creation forms a connection," she said. "When the design is right, the drum calls, and pathways to the mystic roads open. The drummer can then sense the formation of a breach, send messages to others in the order, or even harness the strength of the Rose Stone to aid a patient's healing."

"You carved a lyr and warbird on the casing."

"Yes. The drum didn't answer until I realized I was called to serve the Rose Guard. Since then, we have been bound to the order."

Danya went to the center of the garden. Her eyes closed, and her fingers began rhythmically tapping. She whispered a low, sing-song chant, and without conscious thought, my body swayed to the beat. Her hand moved slowly at first to one part of the drumskin, then the other. The beat quickened and slowed as if she searched for the right tempo. A rush of heat brushed against me, and the tap became a thump. Danya beat the drum with urgency that sent the vibrations to the tips of my toes. Light danced off her fingertips. Images and words flashed through my mind. Most went by in a blur, but I caught a few of me, Griffin, danger, and the Rose Stone.

The tapping ended abruptly, and the air stilled. Danya's shoulders sagged. Drumming obviously took a toll. "They have heard."

"Are you okay?"

"Yes, but I will go to my chambers now and prepare for tomorrow's journey. I'll have dinner sent, and then you should rest as well."

Danya left, and a servant arrived soon after with a tray. No stew this time, but cooked grain with roasted meat and vegetables. Hallucination or not, I enjoyed every bite. The servant returned to clear the dishes. "May I get you anything else, my lady?"

I flexed my fingers, pleased the pain remained at bay. "If it's not too much trouble, I have the urge to draw."

"Paper and ink?"

"Yes, thanks. That's perfect."

She left with the dishes and returned with sheets of paper, an inkpot, and a pen. Not a felt-tip or fountain pen, but one with a metal nib. Surface tension held the ink until released by gentle pressure. I hesitated considering my unsteady hand, but I was rock-solid at the moment and shoved misgivings aside, eager for the feel of the pen once more.

Enough light remained to draw so I sat at the table, enjoying the peaceful surroundings, and got to work. I roughed out Griffin and me on Cirrus. A comforting tactile sensation flowed into my fingers as the ink glided across the paper with smooth, controlled strokes. I'd forgotten what it was like to work without the shakes.

"You have a deft hand."

The pen jerked. So involved in the art, I didn't hear Griffin enter the garden.

"Forgive me," he said in a rush. "I didn't mean to startle you and ruin the drawing."

I looked down at the paper where a blot of ink had dripped from the nib. "You didn't." I felt a flush crawl up my neck. "It's only a study and nothing special."

His gaze went from the drawing to me. "You're wrong. It's beautiful and very special."

The flush reached my cheeks. They were scalding hot.

Griffin cleared his throat. "I wanted to make certain you were comfortable here."

"I'm fine, thanks."

"Well, then I'll leave you to your art."

"You can have it," I blurted, offering the drawing to him.

"Thank you," he said, taking it from me. "I'll treasure it."

My mind desperately searched for a topic to continue the conversation but froze at the penetrating gaze of his deep brown eyes. I jumped up and said, "It's kind of you to check on me."

Griffin smiled. "Abril will be by in the morning with attire suitable for the journey."

I chuckled and gave a little twirl with my hands on my hips. "What? You don't like these?"

He laughed. "Indeed, they are most becoming, but perhaps riding leathers will be more comfortable in a saddle."

"Hey, you laugh," I said lightly. "I didn't think you knew how. It's nice to hear."

"There has been little reason lately." The good humor faded from his expression. "This is a dangerous world, Jess. I'm sorry you were brought here."

My breath quickened. "I'm not. I want to help but have no idea what to do." The words stuck in my throat. "I-I'm afraid you expect too much of me, and I'm afraid of what will happen to you if I fail."

He took my hand between his. "This world is not yours. That you are willing to try to help is enough."

Say something clever! Keep him here. "Thanks." I gave an inner groan.

We stood there as seconds ticked away. Griffin seemed on the verge of speaking, but my mind went completely blank. He dropped my hand. "Goodnight, Jess. Sleep well."

I watched him leave, still searching for a logical way to call him back. Naturally, as soon as the door shut, a raft of clever, flirty phrases came to mind. I leaned against the table and this time, groaned aloud. "I am totally hopeless."

I doused the lamp, and slipped under the bedcovers, still feeling the sensation of Griffin's hand on mine. I shut my eyes, tired, ready to sleep, but anxiety clutched my heart. What if the dream ended, and I woke in the hospital? "Stay here," I murmured. "Don't go." It occurred to me then that's exactly what I should have said to Griffin.

Chapter Five

I opened my eyes at a knock. The surroundings were dark, and relief surged through me. The MRI tube was bright so I must still be in the Commonwealth.

Two servants entered, one with a breakfast tray and the other with burning tapers to light the lamps. As I finished eating, Abril arrived with an armload of clothing and leather saddlebags. "Good morning, Lady Jess. I hope you slept well."

"I did, thanks, and call me Jess. You're up early."

Abril winked. "The Rose Guard does not need to sleep according to our captain. Try these. I believe they will fit." She motioned to a door. "You can change in there."

It was a lavatory, complete with flush toilet. What a crazy place, so rustic in some respects, so modern in others. I tossed the hospital scrubs aside, idly wondering if I returned to the MRI at this moment would I be buck naked and, if so, how to explain it to Melanie and Dr. Turner. No, not possible. These clothes were part of the hallucination. I slipped into undergarments, pants, boots, a soft woven shirt, a leather jacket with a rose emblem, and a pair of buttery-soft leather gloves. I rejoined Abril and my thoughts turned to Griffin again.

"You're smiling," said Abril. "The clothes suit you?"

L. A. Kelley

"Was I?" I said, flustered. "Um, yes. They're great. Thanks."

She nodded with approval. "Now you look like a true guardian of the Rose Stone."

A servant came to the threshold. "Beg pardon, Corporal. Your father wishes to speak with you."

"Thank you. I'll be right there."

"Your father?" I said with surprise.

"Captain Griffin is my father, but also my commander." Abril chuckled. "He gives me no favor because of it as Bram receives no favor being the nephew of Chancellor Emlyn. All guards are equal in the eyes of the captain of High Point Garrison."

I gaped at her. Griffin was her father? He was so young. Or was he? Just because he looked early thirties didn't mean he wasn't a senior citizen. I had just worked up the nerve to ask Abril about her mother when Racer landed on the windowsill and cocked his head. *We wait.* He shifted from foot to foot. I got the impression he would have drummed his talons if he had the ability.

Abril grinned. "We must hurry. The captain is not known for patience."

She hustled me out the door and across the keep to the staging area in the front. The air had a frosty bite, and I was glad for the leather. Danya, Griffin, Abril, and Bram stood next to a group of a half dozen well-armed men and women in guard uniforms strapping packs and bedrolls to lyrs. Danya's drum hung over one of the saddles. Racer, Sojourn, and the rest of the warbirds sat on the pommels watching with interest. They flapped their wings as if eager to get underway.

Griffin came toward me leading a fawn-colored lyr

with large limpid eyes. "Her name is Alta. She is a gentle mount and will carry you well."

I scratched her nose. "Hi, Alta. You're a pretty thing." She made a melodic humming bleat, giving me the impression she approved of her new rider, too.

Abril secured my pack, and Griffin boosted me into the saddle. It was well-padded and comfortable with only a single rider this time. No protests from my rump either from the last wild ride—the benefits of a hallucination.

Griffin gave me the reins and then laid a hand on top of mine. "Are you rested enough? We can remain another day, but Danya insists time is of the essence."

"I take it Danya isn't one to argue with."

He grimaced. "You take it correctly, and she is wiser in such things than I am—as she often reminds me."

I swallowed back a smile and suspected not many people dared argue with the captain or swayed him if they did. "No problem. I've been inactive long enough." I inhaled deeply, taking in a lungful of sweet, clean air. With my new clothing, the bracing climate of the mountainous region was invigorating. "It feels great to be in the open. I've spent too much time indoors lately."

Griffin regarded me with interest. "I assumed you lived within city walls and were happiest there."

"I do, but at heart, I'd rather be outdoors. My place doesn't even have room for a garden. I used to hike and camp a lot and enjoyed roughing it. I even fantasized about eventually buying a home in the country—a real one, not a hallucination like this," I said with a teasing grin. I shifted in the saddle, surprised that a long-buried wish spilled so easily from my lips. "I haven't thought about that for a while. Not since I mentioned it once to Elliot, and he laughed it off."

"Elliot?"

"My last boyfriend. He was a city boy through and through and hated the country. I couldn't even get him to go on a hike."

Griffin gave me a questioning look. "He is no longer in your life?"

"No. He left."

"Then he was a fool, and you are well rid of him."

His heated words warmed me as much as the leather clothing. I had a sudden rush of awkwardness and gestured to Alta's pack. "This obviously won't be a quick jaunt. How far to Stone Keep?"

"A day's ride through a very fair hallucination," he gibed. "Nevertheless, promise to tell me if the need for rest arises."

"Ha," I teased. "Don't worry about me. You're the one who'll need a break first. Promise to tell me when you tire."

Griffin chuckled. "You have my word."

Out of the corner of my eye, I noted Abril follow our give and take with interest. She elbowed Bram and whispered in his ear, and Bram flashed a grin.

Griffin mounted Cirrus. With a shrill call, Racer launched from the pommel and soared into the air. The other warbirds followed, and Griffin signaled to the troop. They mounted, and we took off at an easy trot. I found the lyr's natural rhythm and relaxed into the gently swaying motion.

I had a better look at the garrison without a demon wave chasing me. The section in the center was surrounded by outbuildings. Several were plainly living quarters for the guard, and others offered services related to a military compound such as a stable, blacksmith, and armory. The amount of greenery surprised me, softening the roughness of a military outpost.

The inhabitants here were early risers. Although the sun barely peeked over the horizon, we passed groups of people who stopped their work to call goodbye. Several children huddled around their mother with bright smiles and waved as the troop passed. When the children spotted me, they gaped in open-mouthed wonder and whispered amongst themselves. I bit back a laugh. Gossip traveled fast in any community, even an imaginary one. I waved at them and received shy smiles in return.

"A lot of children live here," I said to Griffin.

"Yes," he said. "It's a hard place to keep a family, but harder yet for soldiers to be apart from their loved ones."

I discreetly studied the faces of the women we passed, wondering if one of them was his wife. I didn't pick out any family resemblance to Abril, and no one addressed Griffin directly. I shot a sly glance to double-check his hand. He wore riding gloves, but I hadn't seen a wedding band earlier. It might not be the custom, although I spotted them on others. I guessed Abril's age at sixteen or seventeen, and Griffin seemed far too young to be her father.

I shifted my weight in the saddle. Honestly, I had been seriously lax designing the Commonwealth of the Rose. My mind should have planned better and invented a richer history for the characters. It felt like an unfinished painting, and I didn't have enough color to add the extra polish.

Once we passed the garrison's outer walls, Griffin gave a hand signal to the troops, and the pace increased to a canter. He shot me a wary look, and I chuckled. "Don't worry. I won't fall off."

"You ride well."

"I rode a lot as a kid, and there's a stable in the hills an hour from where I live. I used to drive there on the weekends to rent a horse to ride the trails—not that you know what a horse is, or a weekend for that matter, but I haven't done that in a while." I paused and decided to take the plunge. "Abril told me she was your daughter. You don't look old enough to be a father."

"I was seventeen when Abril was born."

I blinked. "Wow, that's young. Or is that a normal age to be a parent here?"

The muscles in his jaw tensed slightly. "No, it is very young. I was not yet of age, but my father insisted a marriage take place before he gave permission for me to join the guard."

Ouch. I must have hit a touchy subject because Griffin prodded Cirrus to catch up to Bram and Abril, riding the point position. He spoke to them, and they galloped ahead. Griffin took their place, leaving me with nothing but more questions.

The garrison disappeared from view. We passed farmhouses and cultivated fields and eventually entered thick woods. The road was level and well-maintained. After several miles, we came upon Bram and Abril galloping toward us, and Griffin called the troop to a halt. "The wind surge not only downed trees, but also caused a landslide," said Bram. "The main route is blocked. Workers are trying to clear it, but it will take several hours."

Griffin rubbed his chin. "I have no wish to waste half a day. The trailhead?"

"I sent Sojourn to scout, sir. He reports it's passable."

"Then we'll take it."

We continued forward to a branch in the road. The trailhead wasn't much more than a footpath and so narrow the company had to ride single file. Even so, we made a steady descent down the ridge, the sure-footed lyrs easily finding hoof-holds on the rocky path.

The sun was high overhead when we reached the bottom of the rise. We entered a large meadow and beyond that was an expanse of lush green hills covered with trees. We stopped to rest and water the lyrs at a brook and eat a quick meal of jerky and dried fruit. As much as I enjoyed the ride, this hallucination had lasted much longer than the previous one. I expected to be back in the MRI tube by now, and as my gaze went to the hills an edgy feeling crept through me. Why didn't I wake up?

We continued to cross meadowlands. Around me was the soft creak of riding leathers, the jingle of metal fastenings on the saddles, the musky scent of the lyrs and soft *clip-clop* of their hooves on the ground. A gentle gust of wind ruffled my hair, and dazzling sunlight warmed my face. Sights, sounds, smells, touch, taste, the complete sensory package. So far, this had been an agreeable outing, yet I couldn't shake the uneasiness. I studied Griffin out of the corner of my eye. He was as real as any person I'd ever known, so was everybody else. What if this place wasn't a hallucination?

If so, then what was it?

"It can't be real," I muttered.

"You are unsettled, Lady Jess." I startled as Danya rode up beside me.

"I'm fine." I bit my lip.

"I think you are not fine. Something troubles you."

I made a face. "Griffin said you weren't one to argue with."

She winked. "I have always insisted the captain is a man of high intelligence. Now tell me."

"I expected to wake up by now."

"Ah, yes, the dream world. I fear I have no way to send you back to yours." She glanced at the spirit drum hanging off the saddle. "Unless you wish me to try…"

The idea of leaving brought an immediate protest to my lips. "No, that's okay. I guess I'll wake when I'm ready." Her comment hit me. "So, to you this is the real world, and the other is the dream. I hadn't thought of it that way."

Danya cocked her head. "Does that frighten you?"

"No."

"Good. I see more color in your cheeks, Lady Jess. You have no pain?"

"I feel fine. Also, please call me Jess." I grinned. "I'm no lady."

Danya chuckled. "That remains to be seen."

I looked around. "This sure is pretty country."

"It was a fair world until the darkling arrived."

"Tell me more about the darkling. You said the attacks have worsened recently."

Danya had a twinkle in her eye. "Why such interest in a dream world? Or do you believe this is something else?"

"Let's simply say I enjoy a good story."

"Over the past month, breaches have formed one after the other. The one on the ridge above High Point Garrison allowed three carvers to enter the Commonwealth, the most we've seen since the Great War. As each day passes, the Rose Stone's warnings are harder for drummers to hear." She scowled. "A rising tide of evil is building. I feel it like a band of pressure around my chest, squeezing tighter and tighter. My greatest fear is the darkling assembling a new war armada, gathering machines of destruction, and waiting for the chance to swarm the land once more."

I looked at Griffin. He'd throw himself into a fight to protect his people, no matter the odds. By the manner his troops regarded their captain, I had no doubt they'd follow him, if necessary, through the very gates of hell.

"After your arrival, I asked the spirit drum for clarity but only received another warning of danger," said Danya. Her voice dropped. "I believe a spreading menace threatens the abilities of the Rose Stone. If the Rose Stone fails, so does the boundary, so does the world."

Her words brought more chill than the mountain air. "Can the guard stop the carvers without the Rose Stone?" She remained silent, and my dread deepened. "Look, I want to help but don't have answers."

Danya gazed into the distance. "Nor do I. Perhaps the right questions haven't been asked, and the truth is yet to be revealed."

We reached the far side of the meadow, and the path led us into a forest of gently rolling hills. The wind turned harsh, whipping through the trees and shaking the limbs. The sun disappeared behind billowing gray clouds gusting across the sky in darkening swells. Griffin called a halt. He studied the sky and gave a shrill whistle. An instant later, Racer alit on the pommel. A flurry of communication passed between man and warbird. I received a brief image of a clearing before Racer took off again with an agitated shriek.

"A storm is coming, and we must seek shelter," said Griffin. "Racer reports the ruins nearby will provide suitable cover for the night." A few of the guards shot uneasy glances at each other. Griffin turned to me. "I had hoped to pass the hills by nightfall and secure more comfortable accommodations for you, but we have to make camp."

His somber tone clanged a warning bell. "You're worried. This area isn't safe?"

"Safe enough as it touches the boundary, but these hills saw one of the great battles. Our people find it difficult to rest easy here. The destruction is a stark reminder of the past."

"Racer wasn't crazy about the decision either."

"Warbirds prefer the safety of the aerie or flight in the open sky." He glanced around with wary eyes. One hand clutched the reins, the other rested lightly on his sword hilt.

"Like a certain Rose Guard captain who hates to be penned in," I said lightly.

"Perhaps." His visible tension eased. "Racer and I are both old warbirds."

"Not so old," I said without thinking and felt a flush creep up my neck.

Griffin signaled the group forward, but not before I caught the hint of a smile. We rode over uneven ground and past small ponds, oddly circular in shape as if scooped out by a giant hand. Alta pricked up her lop ears at a growling rumble of thunder. She must have sensed the coming storm and shelter ahead because she increased the pace, her hooves clattering over a hard surface. I looked at the ground, surprised to see broken pavement from an old road. Trees had taken root between the crumbled remains. They were much younger than the old growth we passed before and must have sprouted long after the others.

The lyrs slowed at the edge of a gully. It was a steep drop, but I had confidence in their sure-footedness as they trotted close to the edge. I peered down the side, and a shiver ran through me. This formation wasn't natural. Something had ripped into the earth and left a long narrow gash. The impact must have been powerful. Boulders were strewn on either side as if an explosive force sent them flying through the air. Chunks of metal, dull with age, protruded from the earth, their surfaces pitted with holes and warped from high heat. At the far end of the gully was a mass of rubble, blackened with scorch marks. I reined Alta to a halt and gawked in amazement at the shattered remains of a huge sweptback wing jammed between two boulders.

"You recognize it?" asked Abril.

"Yes. It's part of an airplane. A military jet, I think. They're machines that fly, common in my world."

"It must be a wondrous sight."

"I suppose, but I've always taken flying for granted."

Bram studied the wreckage with a glum look. "It is said the darkling's war machines could pluck them from the sky. Is it such in your world?"

"Not exactly. The jets have armament, but people on the ground use weapons to shoot them down."

Griffin shook his head. "No honor in that when a soldier can't see the eyes of the enemy." Thunder rumbled again. "Hurry, the storm is nearly upon us."

We reached a long, flat stretch of ground. Trees and bushes rooted between more scattered chunks of concrete and metallic wreckage, camouflaging the broken remains of a landing field. A crash of thunder made me flinch. Lightning ripped across the sky and raindrops spattered to the ground.

Racer and the warbird legion circled overhead. *Shelter this way!* We followed them past heaps of metal to a concrete structure with crumbling walls. Once, it might have been a command headquarters. Now, it made an imposing ruin. I glimpsed a shimmer beyond the surrounding trees. The boundary must pass next to this building, maybe even brush against it.

The warbird legion swooped inside. The narrow opening made it difficult to ride the lyrs, so we dismounted and led them in as the rain fell in earnest. Pillars, entwined with flowering vines, rose to the ceiling. Water dripped through holes, but enough of the roof remained intact in a back section for us to stay dry. A guard built a fire, which helped allay the eerie atmosphere. Others unpacked the lyrs, while Danya brewed spiced tea. I sat next to her by the fire and gratefully took a cup, sipping the hot drink to cut the cold and damp.

The warbirds had settled on exposed rafters. Their rasping chirps echoed, resembling gossipy neighbors chatting over a fence. Abril handed me another ration pack with jerky, dried fruit and nuts, and chewy bread. "How come you don't ride with a warbird?" I asked her as I ate.

"I hope to with the new clutch of fledglings." She shot a wistful glance at her father, seated next to me. "That is, if I successfully complete preliminary training and become a full member of the Rose Guard. No recruit is allowed to bond with a warbird before that time, and no warbird will accept an unqualified recruit."

"Then perhaps, Corporal, you should see to your captain's comfort and refresh his tea," said Griffin with a twinkle in his eye.

"Yes, sir." Abril jumped to her feet, took his cup, and hurried away.

I nudged him. "In my world, that's called throwing your weight around."

"Here, too," he said with amusement.

Abril returned with the cup, and then Bram called her over. A guard took out a flute and began to play. Another sang a wistful ballad of love and loss. Even the warbirds stilled their chittering to listen.

"I apologize for the rough surroundings," said Griffin.

"Don't," I said. "I'm comfortable, and I love camping." I rubbed my leg, massaging an aching muscle.

"Are you in pain?" said Griffin gently. "Danya will have a salve."

"I'm okay. It was a long day in the saddle, and I'm not used to riding. Perhaps I should move around and stretch my legs."

Griffin stood and offered a hand. "Allow me to accompany you, although I fear there isn't much to see." He added harshly, "This place doesn't reflect the best of our world."

I took a limping step, and he hurriedly crooked an arm around mine. I stiffened. "I don't need help—"

"But I do. It was a long day in the saddle." He jestingly threw my words back at me. "The Rose Guard will lose respect if they see their captain stumble and fall."

I chuckled. "Well, I can't have that." Griffin's grip was firm, but gentle, and it felt good to lean against him.

We meandered through the old ruin, avoiding drips from the ceiling, and stopped in a far corner where the sounds of the guards' laughter and singing muted. I ran my hands over a pockmarked wall. Bullet holes? The surface had the smoothness of concrete, yet there was a slight vibration. "It's throbbing, almost like a heartbeat," I said with surprise. "From the storm?"

"No. You feel the boundary. It touches the ruins."

"Have you ever been to the other side?"

"No. Nor do I know anyone who would dare pass and risk weakening the protective energy. We can see there is wilderness of course, but what lies farther than a few steps beyond no one can say."

The rain continued unabated, and the wind whistled with a vengeance through cracks in the building. "Listen to that," I said with a shiver. "I'm glad we're not outside."

"Storms in the heights are fierce, but generally last no more than a few hours. We're not far from the river, and Stone Keep is a short ride once we cross. The banks will be swollen with runoff and the current dangerous, but it will recede by morning. Tomorrow, I'll send a warbird ahead to alert the river folk. They'll have a barge at the landing waiting for us."

Griffin shifted his feet. "You make light of your illness, but I fear the effect is greater than you would have us believe. May I ask about it?" He spoke with both kindness and sympathy, and I didn't doubt he'd known his own share of pain.

"I'll tell you, if you tell me more about your marriage," I said, determined to satisfy my curiosity. "Why was your father so insistent that a wedding take place?"

Griffin hesitated a moment and then said, "Eighteen years ago, the darkling's attacks came with brutal force. Carvers wreaked havoc throughout the land. Drummers barely sealed one breach before the Rose Stone alerted to a new one. We feared the war machines would come again. The call went out for more to join the Rose Guard. The yearning to serve and protect this world burned inside me like a flame, but as an only child and barely seventeen, I was honor bound to my father. He agreed to give me permission if I married. Litha was two years older and heiress to the neighboring farm. Father had always coveted the land and wished our properties joined." Griffin paused. "Many enlisted in the guard, but few returned."

His meaning was clear as glass. "I get it. Your father wanted an heir, just in case. That's cold."

"Paxton is a practical man," Griffin said dryly.

"What about your mother?"

"She had died several years earlier. Litha and I agreed, and the wedding took place. Soon after, I received orders to report to the guard. By then, Litha was pregnant. The fighting was vicious, but the guard triumphed," he said with pride. "The carver attacks decreased, as if the darkling's power source had been spent. Fortunately, the war machines never came. To my father's surprise, I survived," he noted in a mocking tone. "To my surprise, the guard appealed to me more than farming ever did. I had found my true calling. My father wasn't pleased when I told him I decided to stay."

"And your wife?"

"Litha was content in her place. She wanted nothing more than to be mistress of a large holding and no wish to follow me from post to post. She was a good person, but we weren't suited to each other. I visited as often as duty allowed to see Abril. Litha never asked me to stay longer. She had no interest in garrison life, but Abril sat for hours listening to my stories and pummeling me with questions. She always begged to come with me, tears in her eyes, when I had to return to duty. When Abril was five, Litha died of a fever. I meant to keep Abril at the farm with my father when leave ended. She would have a safer life with him, and it was the logical choice. But when I held Abril in my arms to say goodbye, she begged again, and this time I listened to my heart instead of my head. I couldn't go without her. My father was angry, but I promised to send Abril back every harvest."

Griffin looked at his daughter sitting by the campfire, and his lips twisted in a wry smile. "He planned to make a farmer of her."

"Let me guess, it didn't work," I said, joking.

"Obviously not. Over the years, I tried to talk her into a secure life on the farm, but…"

"Your heart wasn't in it, and neither was hers.

She's her father's daughter. I admire you for taking sole charge of a child at such a young age. It couldn't have been easy."

"It wasn't, but there was joy, too, and I had help from other guard families. We support each other in difficult times. Although, many nights I'd lie awake wondering if I did the right thing by Abril."

"You did."

Griffin smiled. "You're so sure?"

"Yes, without a doubt. Abril is great. She's a smart, strong, happy young woman who found her true calling. My mother died when I was young," I said with an unexpected pang in my heart. "My father raised me alone, and we were close. He died several years ago, but I'll always be grateful to him for supporting my ambitions. You can't ask for more than that."

"You were fortunate." His words had a bitter ring.

"Your father never came to terms with Abril's choice?"

He grunted. "My father and I haven't spoken since Abril joined the guard. Now, enough of me. Tell me more of your illness."

I shrugged. "There's not much to tell. I have a brain tumor that's slowly killing me. It's responsible for the headaches, the weaknesses, and pain in my arms and legs."

For the first time since leaving the garrison, my hand trembled. Griffin took it in his and the movement stopped. "Is there nothing the healers can do?"

"At first, it was hopeless. My friend Melanie is a doctor, a healer. She found another who may be able to help. At this moment, I'm not here, but in a hospital getting tests for a new medical procedure," I said lightly. "If it works, I'll be able to have an operation to remove the tumor and be cured."

"Perhaps the Rose Stone will know of a treatment. It has done much for this world."

"If it had the power to make the tumor vanish, why hasn't it already? Hey, you worry about your daughter and your troops," I said, gently chiding him. "I see it in your eyes, so don't worry about me too. That's an order."

He gave a slight bow of his head in acknowledgment. "Your hallucination is at your command, but despite that your health will continue to be his concern."

The gentle pressure of Griffin's hand around mine relayed more than simple comfort. Subtle warmth flowed up my arm and wrapped around my heart, like a chain linking us together. "You are a stranger in this land, yet your presence feels so familiar, as if we've met in another place." Griffin gave a low chuckle. "Perhaps this dream is mine, and you are here to taunt me."

I smiled at him. "Since I have no clue what's going on, I can't argue that." The intensity of his gaze made my heart do flip-flops. Not even Elliot on our best days together ever managed that. I felt flushed and fluttery. Being with Griffin, my imaginary hero, brought comfort I'd never felt from a real man. It was also completely, totally, utterly insane. "I-I don't know what's happened to me. By the rules of logic, this world can't exist. Yet, it feels no different from my other life. I'm glad I'm here," I added in a rush.

"As am I. Perhaps you think too much," Griffin said.

I laughed. "No one has ever accused me of that."

"It's good to hear you laugh." Griffin's voice softened. "You face your trial with great courage, Jess."

I gave a shrug. "I simply take it day by day."

"I wish to help. It's not in my nature to stand by when another is in need."

"I'm afraid this is one battle I have to face alone."

"Not alone." He touched my cheek. "I will always be at your command, even if it is to merely hold your hand."

Will he kiss me? My heart beat faster at the thought.

In the dim light, a section of the wall behind Griffin shimmered. "What the…?" I stared in bewilderment as a bulge, a few inches in width, formed and then disappeared as if the concrete became rubber and a hard object had momentarily pressed into it from the other side.

Griffin gave me a questioning look. "Jess?"

"I thought I saw something." Weight settled on my shoulders. The voices from the campfire muffled as the air became thick and heavy, making it harder to breathe. Maybe it was an effect from the boundary. I edged past him and touched the wall.

I expected to feel cool, clammy concrete and the mild vibration from before, but jerked my hand back at a cutting sting, sharp as midwinter ice. I massaged my fingers, but the friction generated no warmth.

From high in the rafters, warbirds screeched a battle cry. Lyrs bleated and pawed the ground. The bulge reappeared, and this time a wave of stone-cold evil knocked me into Griffin's arms. The message couldn't be plainer. Something was hunting.

And it had found us.

Chapter Six

Griffin gave me a hard shove behind him. "Breach," he yelled, drawing his sword. "Jess, run."

I didn't. Instead, I stumbled back a few steps and watched the troop scramble to his side. They stood shoulder to shoulder, weapons at the ready, Griffin in the center. The bulge spread along the wall and formed a perfect rectangle, about nine feet high by six feet wide.

"Steady," he barked.

Behind me came resonant tapping from Danya's drum and the low murmur of her chant. For a few seconds, the bulge retracted and then it burst forth again, glistening with an oily sheen. "They're coming," she cried, sweat beading her forehead. "The breach is too powerful. The energy of the spirit drum can't close it."

A tiny black slit appeared in the center of the rectangle. I gaped in horror as it widened an inch and then two, creeping along from top to bottom, a jagged scar ripping through time and space. Wispy vapor trails oozed from the interior. I coughed at a burning electric stench reminiscent of shorting wires.

The slit began to draw apart like a malevolent curtain, revealing a hazy, glassy surface. Sparks crackled at the rim, wafting more of the pungent odor, and a low hum filled the air. The haze evaporated, and my heart sank to my knees. Five carvers crowded on the other side of the pane. Their claws opened and closed with an eerie clicking noise, as if anxious to begin their bloody task.

My pulse raced. I was no military strategist, but even I knew this was a terrible place to mount a defense. Nearly the height of the rectangle, carvers towered over the guards on foot. Lyrs provided an advantage, but they couldn't maneuver in this tight space. Neither could the warbirds, shrieking in frustration from the rafters.

A stinging blast of air gusted from the slit and bit at my skin. Behind the carvers, dim lights flickered. An object in the background moved with subtle clanks and an eerie mechanical hiss, but their massive bodies blocked a clear view.

The carvers' hands bent and flexed. Five sets of claws pressed against the transparent opening. Sparks spewed from the tips as they began to force their way through the breach. They threw back their heads and emitted an unearthly howl of triumph. A shrill command resounded in my head. *Kill them.*

The darkling.

"Kill them," echoed the rasping cry of the carvers.

"No!" I shouted. A fiery ember sprouted deep within me and fanned out through my limbs. My hands burned like smoldering coals, and a crimson glow bathed the breach. The carvers bellowed with rage and fell back to the other side.

Kill them, shrieked the darkling.

"No," I said again. "Leave them alone."

I see you, the darkling spoke in my mind. Paralyzing fear stole my breath.

A second voice whispered, *I am here for you*. It wasn't harsh, but melodic and forceful. More heat built in my hands. I gawked in disbelief as my skin glowed with crimson fire. Liquid light poured from my fingertips, slamming into the breach. Color washed across the transparent surface, deepening the tint from crimson to blood-red, and the glassy pane clouded over. The monsters' blurry shapes bent double, howling in torment. The haze thickened, obscuring the view on the other side.

The stone! The darkling shrieked in frustrated rage.

"Jess, the Rose Stone calls to you," cried Danya. "Seal the breach."

"How?" I said, panicking. As if in answer to my will, the light diffused across the entire rectangle. The edges began to pull toward the center, knitting together the two sides. My arms and legs trembled with the strain of holding onto the power.

Open, screamed the darkling. The carvers were mere shadows now, pounding on the glassy surface.

Bang, bang, bang.

The ground under my feet vibrated with each hammering blow.

"Jess," said Melanie.

I looked around. "Melanie?"

"The MRI is finished."

The cascade of crimson light spilling from my hands decreased from a flood to a broken stream, but one third of the breach remained. "No, I'm not ready," I shouted. "Griffin needs me. The guard is in danger." A final blast of light shot from my fingertips and struck the wall.

"Jess, open your eyes," said Melanie. Her voice

sounded closer now.

Rose light surrounded me, filling my mind, clouding my vision. My body felt light. The ground dropped beneath my feet, and I flailed my arms to keep from falling. "No, please, not yet. I can't go."

"Jess!" shouted Griffin. He barreled past the guards and lunged for me. I touched his hand. "Hold on," he said, but my fingers slipped away, and I fell, fell, fell into the dark.

No sights, no sounds, no smells, just dark. In the distance sparked a flashing wire.

You cannot run. You cannot hide. I will follow.

****

"Hey, sleepyhead. Wake up."

My eyelids shot open, and my stomach churned with a whirling sensation as if I rode a roller coaster at breakneck speed. After a deep breath, the nausea settled. The rose light had disappeared, and everything around me was white and shiny. "Where am I?" I sputtered. "Griffin is in trouble."

"Griffin? It's Melanie. I'm sorry to spook you. The scan is finished. Don't move yet, the table hasn't retracted."

I fought a swell of panic, trying to focus my muddy thoughts. "Wait," I babbled. "The breach, carvers…" The table slid from the MRI tube into the high-tech surroundings. Reality crashed in on me, followed by the frigid clutch of despair. I was back.

Melanie ran into the room with the technician. "Hey, it's okay. Do you know where you are?"

"What? Yes, the MRI." I inhaled slowly to still my pounding heart and sat up. "You woke me in the middle of a nightmare."

"Take it slow," the technician cautioned. "You might feel a little dizzy."

"I'm okay now."

Melanie didn't seem convinced. "You don't look okay. You're very pale."

"Really, I'm fine." I forced a smile. How could I explain what happened when I didn't understand myself? "What did the scan show?" Melanie shot a glance at the booth, and a sinking feeling enveloped me. "That bad?"

"Get dressed, and I'll meet you outside. Owen will talk to us in his office."

I nodded numbly and went to the changing room. A mirror hung on the wall, and I stared at my reflection. "The Commonwealth is fiction," I whispered. "It didn't happen. Griffin can't get hurt. He isn't real. Neither are the others. Look at your clothes." I ran my hands down the sides of the hospital scrubs. "The riding gear is gone. Explain that, if it's not a fantasy."

I couldn't. Nothing made sense. The claw marks had vanished from my arm as if they'd never been, as if they were part of a dream. Then I closed my eyes and recalled the sensation of unchained power, the touch of Griffin's hand, the fear in his voice as I slipped away.

Determination grabbed hold of me. Every doubt fled, and I shoved the world of logic aside. So what if the trip to another world seemed like the crazy delusion of a damaged brain. No rational answers existed for what happened, but I didn't care and embraced a new truth. My truth and no one else's. The Commonwealth of the Rose was no hallucination. It existed as surely as the hospital's sterile confines, and a wondrous thing happened when the breach tried to open. The Rose

Stone spoke to me, and a mysterious force responded to my command. I clenched my fists. I had to return. I had to see Griffin again.

I sagged against the mirror. I had no clue how.

Melanie waited in the hallway. "No hints?" I said with a weak smile.

She took my arm, and for once I didn't complain about needing a steadying hand. "Let's hear what he has to say."

Dr. Turner stood in his office. He motioned me to a chair and pulled up the scan on the laptop. I had zero desire to look but forced myself to peer at the monitor. The tumor's shape had been burned into my memory. It was round in the center with tendril-like offshoots, bringing to mind a mutant starfish from a campy 1950s science fiction film. "I don't need to be a doctor to see the tumor has gotten bigger since the last MRI."

"Yes, and faster than expected, which explains the severity of symptoms," said Dr. Turner. "The location isn't the best." With his finger, he made a circle on the screen inside the tumor, cutting off the tendrils. "However, if the medication can remove these parts and reduce the mass in size to no greater than this, then we can operate. I won't lie, it's high risk. In order to get there, I have to use a much higher dosage. The aftereffects at such a concentration are unknown. This is a harsh drug, and since the procedure is in the testing stage, you'd be the worst-case patient…" His voice trailed away, and he shot a sympathetic look at Melanie.

"And the meds may kill me," I said. "Or the tumor may kill me before the meds shrink it or I could die on the operating table. I understand. It's a longshot, and no guarantees, but I'll take it."

"I'll be with you every step of the way," said Melanie.

"The good news is if the medication works, the results are immediate," said Dr. Turner. "Within a few days, we'll know one way or the other."

"When do we start?"

"The day after tomorrow. The drug must be given intravenously in the hospital. The dose takes several hours, so you'll be there for a while."

I stared at my hands. "I have a painting to finish."

"After this is over, you'll have all the time in the world to paint," said Melanie kindly. "Have you had any more hallucinations?"

"No." I lied.

Melanie eyed me askance. "You were talking to Griffin again."

I forced a smile. "Mel, it was a dream, and then I woke up and he disappeared."

She folded her arms and eyed me askance.

"Okay," I admitted hesitantly. "I saw a rose tint inside the tube. No big deal."

"Do you see it now?" asked Dr. Turner.

I gazed around. The room was normal, and I hid my disappointment. "No."

"Don't look so disappointed," teased Melanie.

Dang.

"From the location of the tumor, I expect hallucinations more complex than color changes," mused Dr. Turner. "No voices? No objects or people suddenly appearing and disappearing. I can give you additional medication for that."

"I'm good."

Melanie narrowed her eyes. " 'I can't wake up yet. Griffin needs help.' " She mimicked my panicked urgency. "That sounded pretty intense for a dream."

Dr. Turner gave me a sharp look, and I shifted in the chair. "Okay, yes, I have been seeing things."

"That concerns me. I'll increase the dosage of the anti-hallucinogen."

"Is that necessary?" I said, alarmed.

Melanie rolled her eyes. "Do you prefer to run into traffic because you thought you were being chased by a bear?"

"I see your point."

Dr. Turner patted my hand. "We're in this together, Jess, and I'll fight for you. I'll copy Mel with the appointment details and send the new prescription to the pharmacy."

"Thanks, Doc. I appreciate everything you've done." We left his office, and I nudged Melanie. "He called you Mel."

She blushed. "It doesn't mean anything."

"The clerk said he was single. Did you ask him if he was seeing anyone?"

"That hardly entered our conversations. The focus is on you, remember?"

"I'll ask him and say you're interested."

Melanie gaped at me in open-mouthed horror. "Don't you dare."

"You look out for me. I'll look out for you. We've been doing that since we were kids. Don't expect me to stop now."

"Don't hassle Owen. We concentrate on your health, not my love life. Deal?"

I hooked my arm around hers. "Deal." *Until the*

time is right, and then I'm hassling you instead.

We stopped at the pharmacy for the medication, and then Melanie dropped me at the loft. I declined her offer of lunch, using the excuse that I wanted to work on the painting. In truth, I wasn't hungry. After all, I filled up on camp rations a short while ago.

I placed the new anti-hallucinatory pills in the medicine cabinet. I needed to be alone with my thoughts and had no intention of taking drugs that interfered with whatever tenuous connection I had with the Commonwealth of the Rose. I massaged an aching twinge in my legs. The weakness had crawled back in, but despite the limp, I paced the floor, and ignored the pain medication, too. I needed a clear head to process what I'd seen and felt in the MRI tube.

The Commonwealth was real, and so was Griffin. Somehow, someway, I bounced between worlds, but the belief did nothing to ease my mind. Was it an alternate universe, a different dimension, an alien landscape? What did it matter? I had no way to return.

I limped to the easel and touched the rose on Griffin's chest. "Are you okay?" I whispered to him. "I left you in quite a spot."

The only voices were muted and coming from the open window as pedestrians on the street below mingled with the traffic blare. I selected a brush, but my hand refused to hold steady. I closed my eyes and exhaled, recalling Griffin's touch. The pain dulled; the shaking eased. I dipped the bristles in black and slashed an angry line down the canvas. My own breach. I dabbed more paint, outlining the shadows. The darkling had seen me, I was sure, and marked me as a threat.

You cannot run. You cannot hide. I will follow.

Despite being warm and dry, I shivered. Here, sturdy walls surrounded me. But what about Griffin and the others? The carvers fell back, but they'd try again unless the breach completely sealed. The voice of the Rose Stone spoke to me and activated a wondrous power. I could almost feel it again, surging from my fingertips. I rubbed my palms together. Almost, but not quite.

I shook my head. No, what happened in the ruin was different. That extraordinary ability didn't flow *from* me. It flowed *through* me as if I were a conduit. I scraped the canvas and slathered paint over the crack, obliterating it completely. With a brush, I added a delicate crimson rose. "Hah! Try to force a way through that."

I rubbed my eyes and stepped back to study my work. The new addition felt right, unlike my head which pounded. "Tumor, tumor, go away," I muttered, massaging my temples. "Kill me on another day."

Even the small amount of energy needed to clean the brushes was an effort. I got a bottle of water from the fridge and hobbled to the sofa, easing my legs onto the cushions with a groan. A yawn escaped my lips. "Nap time." I swallowed a pain pill and then leaned back and closed my eyes, my mind drifting. With no surprise, my thoughts landed on Griffin. I pictured him in the ruin, but for some reason his face peered down at me from a different angle. Lines of worry etched his brow.

"You're safe," I whispered.

"Safe," he echoed, and the lines eased. "And you?"

"I'm okay. Don't worry about me."

"It's my duty to worry."

"I release you from that burden."

"I refuse—and it is no burden, Jess. It is an honor."

Griffin's image dissolved, and my body grew heavy with the lethargy of sleep. The headache vanished. I was warm and relaxed and felt better than I had in ages. I had a painting to complete, Dr. Turner offered hope, and the image of Griffin lifted my spirits. I was certain the Commonwealth of the Rose hadn't fallen in my absence. Would it stay safe as long as my mind gave it life? If so, I'd fight for that.

I drifted into peaceful slumber. No thoughts, no questions, no pain.

A sparking wire snaked through the blackness, bobbing and weaving, testing the surroundings with unflinching intent. *Where? Where?* it called, pressing forward in a relentless march. The wire halted, and the tip swung toward me. I tried to run, but my legs turned traitor and refused to move.

There! The sparking tip shot forward, stabbing me between the eyes. *I know you now.*

The world exploded in flames.

My eyes shot open, and I bolted upright on the couch, heart hammering against my ribs. I clutched my shirt, damp with sweat, and drew in a deep lungful of air. "Just a dream," I gasped out. "I'm home. I'm safe." The sunlight through the windows had faded, I'd slept for several hours. I switched on the lamp on the end table and rubbed the back of my neck, waiting for my heartbeat to slow to a respectable thump. That was scary, the worst nightmare I'd ever had.

I jumped at a knock on the door and then steadied myself and called a shaky, "Come in."

Melanie entered holding a pizza box. "You refused

lunch, so I brought dinner. You look a little groggy. I'm sorry, did I wake you?"

"No, I just got up. I worked on the painting and then took a nap."

Melanie put the pizza box on the kitchen table and set out plates and glassware. I sat in a chair, and she poured me an iced tea. "Tony's Pizzeria?" I said, opening the box. "That's new. You always go to Angelo's." I took a deep appreciative whiff. "Wow, it smells good."

"Owen mentioned it."

"See, he's attracted to you. A man doesn't share his favorite pizza place with just anybody."

"Zip it and eat."

I took a bite. "Much better than Angelo's. Send Dr. Turner my regards."

We polished off most of the pie, and Melanie cleared the table. "I'll call you tomorrow," she said as I walked her to the door. "Oh, by the way, I remembered where I heard of Griffin and the Rose Stone. They were both in your book."

Chapter Seven

I gawked at her. "My book?"

"Uh-huh. Don't you remember? Well, it was years ago during a sleepover at my house. One of our first, I think, because I have the impression we were really young. We were looking at an old book of fairytales; all the drawings were boring black and white. The girls in the stories were lame and mostly hung around waiting for rescue. We were both budding feminists and not impressed. I said you could do better."

A hazy recollection formed. "I-I had a drawing tablet with me," I stammered in shock.

"That's right. Even back then you were always scribbling away." Melanie chuckled. "You were very bossy. I remember I wanted to call the hero Kyle because I had a crush on a boy at school named Kyle, but you insisted the name had to be Griffin. It stuck in my head because it was a funny name, and I'd never heard it before."

I tried desperately to summon the details of that night but could only bring to mind a blank sheet of paper and my hand holding a pencil. "I remember drawing, but I can't visualize the pictures. Did I tell you the story?"

"No. I'm not sure we got that far. You told me the title was *The Rose Stone*, but maybe you worked on the pictures later. We were kids and got distracted easily. I don't think we talked about it again. I'm surprised I even remember that much, since it happened so many years ago." Melanie gave me the once over. "You look a little pale. Are you feeling worse?"

I straightened up and forced a smile. "No, I'm fine. I had a long day. I'll take the rest of my meds and relax."

We said goodnight. I shut the door and then leaned against the wall, swamped by an overwhelming flood of emotions. My legs shook, but not from any illness this time. Had a half-remembered story from my childhood spearheaded an elaborate mental ruse to convince me the Commonwealth was real? If so, I had no reason to return. Griffin was merely a figment of my youthful imagination. Perhaps a desperate yearning for love buried in my subconscious.

I squared my shoulders. No—the Commonwealth of the Rose was real. I would find the way again to Griffin and the others, and Melanie had unknowingly opened another door. I needed to search my old sketchbooks.

Along the back wall was a row of screens hiding a pile of dusty storage cartons. I dragged them to the couch. They were filled with odds and ends from my childhood, including sketchbooks I could never bear to toss away. Melanie was right when she said I was always drawing. I don't remember a time without a pencil or crayon in my hand. I even doodled borders on math tests, much to my teachers' amusement.

Over the years, I discarded random sketches, but always kept the wire-bound notebooks. They felt like a part of me, but I hadn't examined them in years. Now I pawed through the pages in a frenzy. Few had dates, but by the skill level, I worked out a rough approximation of my age for each sketch. Apparently, my younger self also loved to draw boys emphasizing their faults. In the last carton, I pounced on a notebook with a caricature on the front page of a kid named Wesley. I had considered him particularly poopy-headed because he refused to pay any attention to me. Wesley had transferred to our school about the time of my first sleepover at Melanie's house. I hurriedly thumbed through the pages, but they held nothing of interest.

On the bottom of the bin was the final sketchbook, different from the others. The cover had no idle scribblings. I opened it, and a flutter of excitement raced through me. There was a title page done in my childish hand, *The Rose Stone*. I had printed the words with a flourish, lots of curlicues and fancy embellishments.

I turned the page to the first sketch and sucked in a breath. A boy sat in a saddle holding the reins of his mount. The creature he rode had lop-ears and was, most definitely, not a horse. The details were crude, but the shape of the boy's face had an uncanny familiarity. I ran my fingertips over the paper. "Griffin," I whispered. This was hardly a polished portrait, I didn't have the skill back then, but hair and eye color were the right shade of brown and the scar on his face in the same location. It was more pronounced though, as if recently inflicted. The perspective was off, too. The lyr was much bigger or, perhaps, Griffin much smaller. He must have been young. The lyr's coat mimicked Cirrus' tawny shade, but I was no expert in lyrs and had no clue if that animal was the same. Not a single rose was present, but the lyr stood among clusters of blue flowers with dabs of white in the center.

Griffin's outfit bore no resemblance to a guard's uniform. He had on a long sleeve shirt, no tabard, no sword or bow at hand, just simple, everyday rustic clothing. Exactly what Griffin would have worn as a child on the family farm.

Other differences were apparent, too, such as the saddle. The pommel was rounded rather than T-shaped and not nearly wide enough to make a fitting perch for a warbird. Griffin's head was slightly turned, and his eyes looked to the side. Now that was unusual. Kids that age always drew people facing front, but Griffin seemed to peer out from the page. I had a strange impression he searched for something.

Nothing was written on the drawing to give a clue to the story. With mounting frustration, I scoured my mind for hints but came up empty. Any original plot points were muddied by the other books devoured in my youth, waiting for poopy-headed boys such as Wesley to pay attention. For the first time in my life, I regretted being such a voracious reader.

The next page had a pencil sketch of an oval standing on end, the interior filled with little jagged marks. Spiky lines protruded from the sides, the way a child would portray the rays of the sun. Was this my interpretation of the Rose Stone? I wished I had bothered to add color.

I studied the drawing when it dawned on me that I'd never seen the actual Rose Stone, but assumed it was a crystal. This one had a multitude of crisscrosses and straight lines that may have been my representation of facets. I'd obviously spent a lot of time on them and the whole composition gave the impression of a carefully constructed pattern, surprisingly complex for a child. A single blur in the center distorted the clarity of the whole. I wondered why I hadn't bothered to clean a pencil smudge. I peered closer. The blur had a strangely familiar shape. It wasn't an animal or a flower, but I was certain I'd seen something identical recently.

The answer eluded me, so I flipped to the next page and experienced another letdown. Here, artistic inspiration took a completely different track. The sketch was a house. It was either white, or I'd decided not to add color, but the door and the shutters on the windows were bright turquoise. In the background were rolling green hills and long-stemmed plants with spiky yellow poofs on top, perhaps a fanciful representation of grain growing in the field. Was it a farm? I had included animals in the yard, although drawn with imaginative flair. Since when did a pig have a mane and zebra stripes?

The next page was also a disappointment. A blue line snaked across the paper past a scattering of concentric circles, brown chevrons, and green blotches. A series of black dots, one big and several small, clustered in the corner. Near to them at the top of the page was a red rose in the middle of one of the concentric circles.

No matter which way I turned the picture, none of it made any sense, at least not a pattern I recognized. I thumbed through the rest of the sketchbook but found only blank pages. That was oddest of all. My sketchbooks filled in short order, but it was as if I finished these drawings and then shoved them aside and forgot them. I don't even remember packing the book away.

I blew out my cheeks in disgust. Apparently, I hadn't been taken enough with the story of the Rose Stone to draw more and, unfortunately, didn't leave any notes. My fingers trembled again, and I rubbed my hands against my jeans in frustration. I was muddle-headed and tired, and a thread of anxiety took root. I had been handed a perfectly logical explanation for a hallucination. My mind recreated the Commonwealth of the Rose from childhood imaginings, but I chose to dismiss it because I wanted Griffin to be real. That was close to the ramblings of a nutcase.

"A fresh start in the morning," I muttered.

I ignored the anti-hallucinatory pills and took the meds that knocked back the dull ache and muscle weakness. I crawled into bed and stared at the ceiling, mind whirling, body spent. If I mentioned my belief that I visited another reality to either Melanie or Dr. Turner, they'd point at the notebook and conclude my subconscious latched onto sketches from childhood and formed a vivid hallucination, so solid it imbued life into a fantasy.

I imagined Dr. Turner folding his arms and shaking his head. "I warned you. Why didn't you take the meds?" Melanie would study me with large anxious eyes.

Of course, they were right. Any sensible person would head to the hospital to be pumped full of drugs to end the visions. Anyone who disagreed with the diagnosis was too far gone to make rational decisions and should be hospitalized at once.

I ran a hand through my hair. Storybook be damned. I had formed a connection to another world as a child and then lost it. Only a void in my heart remained. I tried to fill it with work and then I thought I could fill it with Elliot, but that itch for more remained. I wanted desperately to visit the Commonwealth of the Rose again.

I squirmed under the covers. It wasn't the Commonwealth, but Griffin I needed to see. I had left him and the guard in danger, yanked away by forces I didn't understand. I closed my eyes and relaxed, focusing my thoughts on Griffin.

My breathing became shallow. Comforting warmth seeped through me. My mind drifted away as sleep encroached. "Where are you?" I mumbled.

A soft whisper filled my head. "Searching for you."

With a smile, I tumbled headfirst into the deep empty well of sleep.

****

Tap, tap, tap.

"Danya's drum!" My eyes shot open, and I was instantly letdown. Danya's drum didn't wake me. Instead, the gentle patter of rain beat against the skylight. I sank into the pillow. The intense longing to return to the Commonwealth proved fruitless.

I got out of bed, a little wobbly on my feet. The medication for the muscle weakness had begun to wear off, but it wasn't time for another dose. The day was gray and dismal, dark enough for the streetlights to stay on. It matched my mood to a T. I peered out the window. Bobbing umbrellas sheltered a river of pedestrians flowing down the street. The traffic light at the corner blinked out, and I flinched at squealing brakes. An instant later technology triumphed, the light shone bright, and the traffic moved. Yippee. Civilization reasserted itself.

Even a breakfast of the remaining slice of leftover pizza (usually an attitude enhancer) didn't help. I stood in front of the painting of Griffin, searching for inspiration but haunted by the image of the sparking wire. I chose a paintbrush, touched the tip to the canvas and put it down with a shudder. I didn't want to draw that horrible thing. It didn't belong in my Commonwealth. Thoughts of the eerie wire kept a damper on my spirits.

A cloud obscured my artistic vision, leaving me with no distinct idea where to begin. "Did the carvers break through?" I murmured. "Is your daughter safe? Are you?" My portrait of Griffin made no reply. Only returning to the Commonwealth would provide answers and, for the moment, that seemed beyond my ability.

Usually a walk cleared my head, but I'd done little of that lately. My life had been consumed with medical tests and worry. The pain had eased for the moment, but the muscle weakness in my legs also gave me a staggering lurch that attracted unwanted stares. I glared at the hated cane propped against the door—a symbol that control over my life had slipped away.

"It's only a hunk of metal," I said to myself.

I threw on a jacket and leaned on the cane. The handhold had a T-shaped grip identical to the warbird perch on Griffin's saddle and the feel was strangely comforting. I hated to admit it, but the cane helped my balance and allowed me to carefully ease down the stairs. By the time I reached the entrance, the rain had decreased to a drizzle, but the cloudy sky remained ominous. I had decided against an umbrella; the cane was cumbersome enough to lug around. I pulled the hood over my head and stood in the doorway wondering which way to go. Each direction was equally wet.

The coffee shop two blocks away had excellent pastry, so I headed there. The streetlight in front of my building flickered and then flared back to brilliance. I passed underneath the next one, and it did the same thing. Evidently, technology was having an off day, too.

I arrived at the coffee shop thankful the daily commuters hadn't scarfed the last of the blueberry scones. I ordered a latte, too. A crooning, high-pitched hum filled the air. The lights dimmed and an instant later returned to brightness. The woman behind the counter rolled her eyes. "It's been doing that all morning."

The rain began again, pouring down in buckets, and I decided to wait it out and rest my legs before going home. I took my order to a booth. A previous customer had left that day's newspaper at the table and the headline reported scattered outages in the city. I read the article as I ate. The reporter quoted an official at the power company insisting the trouble was an "indeterminate drain." I snorted. "That means they don't have a clue."

By the time I finished the latte and scone, the rain had slackened to a drizzle again. I left the coffeeshop and ambled to the loft. Maybe it was the fresh air or the blueberry scone, but as I navigated the stairs, I had another stirring of creative juices. As soon as I got inside, I propped the cane by the door and went right to the easel. The mostly blank canvas called me to find the story.

I roughed in a pencil sketch of Danya, Abril, and Bram in the background behind Griffin. Racer and Sojourn soared overhead. I grabbed a brush and paint and worked until my hand ached. My stomach rumbled, too, so I took a break to make a sandwich and eat in front of the TV. The news continued to report scattered outages.

"The power company is working to maintain the grid," said the newscaster. "Currently, the problem is concentrated in several areas of the central business district."

The lightbulb in the lamp on the end table made a fizzing sound and then *pop*! The light went out. I replaced the bulb.

Flash-flash-flash-pause. Flash-flash-flash-pause.

Strange blinking lights from outside flickered a pattern on the wall. Curious, I went to the window, lifted the sash, and peered down at the street. The rain had stopped. Below, two workers from the power company stood by a lift truck deep in conversation. The streetlight next to them was stuck in a repetitive loop.

Flash-flash-flash-pause.

My lips twitched in a smile. The power company needed to replace a light bulb, too, albeit larger. The light continued to flash the mysterious sequence. One man got in the lift truck and called to kill the power.

The other scratched his head. "I did, but it turned on again."

The streetlight bulb exploded, showering the ground with glass. The shattered bulb exposed a snapped wire. It dangled from the post, jumping to and fro. In the half-light, tiny sparks streamed from the tip.

Flash-flash-flash-pause. Flash-flash-flash-pause.

The wire stopped its jerky dance and stiffened. The tip rose and pointed directly at me. *The path is marked*, said the darkling. *Slowly now, I test the portals. Soon they will open to me.*

I gripped the sill, blood turning to ice water. Neither of the two utility workers looked at the sparking wire. They hadn't heard a thing. My hands shook, and not because of muscle weakness.

The wire jerked again and then dropped to hang limply. The sparks sputtered out. "Okay," yelled the man on the ground. "The power is off this time."

Mouth dry with fear, I shut the window, hurried to the bathroom, and fumbled in my medicine cabinet for Dr. Turner's new anti-hallucinatory prescription. I opened the bottle and shook a pill into my hand. I stared at it, my thoughts in a whirl. Was my mind lost in an ever-deepening hallucination? If I didn't take this now, would death come knocking sooner?

"This is it," I said, heart thumping. "Decide once and for all what is real and what isn't."

I dropped the pill in the bottle and returned it to the cabinet. I didn't need any medication. This was no dreamworld, no hallucination. The darkling was real and hunting me. Time was running out, and I wouldn't do anything to prevent finding the way to Griffin again.

As the afternoon wore on, I continued to paint, the need to add more details pressing on me. Eventually, the light faded, and the clouds emptied again. The rain sent rivulets washing down the street. Every so often, I paused to look out the window. I tensed each time, but only heard normal city sounds and the patter of the droplets against the glass. The streetlight below burned steady and bright.

Early in the evening, Melanie called to confirm our departure time for tomorrow morning. I waved off her invitation for dinner as I wanted to be alone. My muscles ached again. I'd stood way too long and rejected the pain pills as they made me groggy. I needed to be sharp to paint. My gaze went to the window, and I shuddered. I needed to be sharp to hear, but the voice of the darkling didn't return. At bedtime, I surrendered to the constant hurt and took the meds. Drowsiness conquered me in nothing flat.

I slept fitfully and kept jerking awake. No nightmares that I recalled, but my nerves sparked like that dancing wire. Rising anxiety over the first treatment didn't help either. I woke the next morning to sun streaming through the skylight over my bed and the hefty weight of disappointment. Despite my consistent yearning to return to the Commonwealth, I hadn't budged an inch or dreamt of Griffin once.

As I waited for Melanie, I scrutinized the painting. I had accomplished a lot with my burst of creativity the day before but had mixed emotions. The artist in me was thrilled. This composition had more energy than anything I'd ever done. The woman in me was unsettled. It was merely a static picture. I hadn't brought my desires to life. The Commonwealth of the Rose remained frustratingly out of reach.

I flexed my fingers. The urge to paint came again, but the canvas was too big to lug to the hospital, plus I had to be flat on my back when they transfused the drug. On a whim, I tossed the old tablet with the Rose Stone drawings in my purse. It had plenty of empty pages. If I couldn't paint, maybe I'd feel strong enough to draw.

Melanie was right on time. I took the cane with no argument, checked into the hospital, and was shown to a treatment room. While Melanie stayed outside to wait for Dr. Turner, I propped the cane against the wall and settled on the bed. I dug out the sketchpad and put it within arm's reach on the nightstand next to me. In the hallway came the indistinct murmur of voices.

"I hear you and Dr. Turner," I shouted. "No secrets behind the patient's back. That's rude."

The door opened, and they entered. "It's no secret," huffed Melanie. "We were discussing the procedure and there's obviously nothing wrong with your hearing."

A nurse came in behind them. She pushed an IV stand attached to a tray with an assortment of small vials.

"Make yourself comfortable," said Dr. Turner. "One of the side-effects is drowsiness, so don't fight sleep. We'll have you hooked to monitors, but the nurses and I will check on you frequently. How is your pain level?"

I shifted on the bed and winced. "Getting worse."

He motioned to the tray. "I've added extra medications to control the pain and tremors." The nurse attached me to several beeping machines. She inserted the IV, and I flinched at the momentary sting.

One by one, Dr. Turner injected the contents of the little vials into the IV. Within a few minutes, a slight burning sensation centered in my arm where the needle entered the vein. Warmth flowed from the injection point throughout my body, and I became lightheaded. The pain disappeared, and my cares drifted away. "Hey, this isn't awful." I yawned. "Don't bother to stay, Mel. I'll probably doze off."

She patted my hand. "I'll be back after work."

"I'll walk out with you," said Dr. Turner. "I realize this is stressful, Jess, but try to relax," he said kindly.

"How soon will you learn if it's successful?"

"That's the good part. Within forty-eight hours of the first treatment, we should see a change in the tumor's size."

Or nothing at all. I pushed the dismal thought aside. As Dr. Turner headed to the door, I mouthed to Melanie, "He likes you." She rolled her eyes and followed him.

The nurse put the call button on the bed within easy reach of my hand. "Can I get you anything?" she asked. "A cold drink, perhaps? Do you want the TV on?"

"No thanks, but you can hand me the sketchbook."

She gave it to me and said, "I'll check on you in a little bit, and so will Dr. Turner. If you need me in the meantime, push the button."

The door shut behind her, and I was alone. I thumbed through the tablet and stopped at the final bizarre drawing. It still resembled nothing but silly scrawls across the page. I'd never been an abstract artist. What idea was supposed to be conveyed by those dots and whirls? With a sigh, I leaned back and shut my eyes. The sensation of warmth in my arm vanished. I floated, heart at ease, and then began to fall.

Down.

Down.

Down.

The window was shut, the single noise in the room was the soft rhythmic tone of a medical monitor. *Beep-beep, beep-beep.* My breathing unconsciously echoed the beat, in and out, in and out.

Beep-beep, beep-beep.

Thump-thump, thump-thump.

Thump-thump, thump-thump.

I shifted in the bed. The abrupt change to rhythmic tapping became louder, drowning out the machine.

"Jess," Griffin shouted with excitement. "Can you hear me?"

"I hear you, Griffin," I murmured sleepily. "Where are you? How do I find the way?"

"Follow the drum…" His voice faded to a whisper then disappeared.

Thump-thump, thump-thump.

Thump-thump-thump-thump.

Thumpthumpthumpthump.

Louder and faster came the call, urging me on. "This way," said Danya. "Hurry. The path is closing."

My mind reached out to touch a gentle presence and then I chased it along a mystic trail. In the distance, a spark flared to sudden brilliance and sped toward me. It was fire, but also ice. It was merciless hate. The touch of death.

I taste the power of this world. When every path is marked, its spark is mine.

I latched onto the drumbeat, and it pulled me to safety. The spark flickered and faded into the darkness.

Chapter Eight

"Jess."

I opened my eyes. Griffin knelt at my side. At the sight of his smile, a flood of happiness rushed into my heart. "I'm back. I found you again."

He brushed my cheek with gentle fingers. "You called, and I answered."

"The breach, the carvers," I blurted. "Is anyone hurt?" I moved to sit.

Griffin put a supportive hand behind my back. "Be at peace, Jess. The breach sealed. No carvers entered, and a wind surge never formed. We are safe, thanks to you."

I looked around at the ruins overhead, that much was the same, but rain no longer dripped from holes in the roof and no wind howled through the cracks. Danya stood behind Griffin, holding the drum. The rest of the guard were in the background, speaking in hushed whispers.

"How are you feeling?" asked Danya.

"Good. A little groggy." I had a crick in my back as if I had rested on a lumpy surface but otherwise felt fine. I stretched my legs. No tremors and no pain. My hand was steady, too. "How long was I gone this time?"

"A few hours. It's nearly morning."

"Oh. It was days in my world. Time sure is different between here and there."

Abril knelt beside me, eyes round with wonder. "How did you close the breach?"

"I-I don't know. I think the Rose Stone spoke to me, and then I felt this power. Thank goodness the breach sealed in time. I was pulled away before I was sure. I didn't want to go but couldn't stop."

"Danya used the drum to search for you," said Abril. "Your body appeared a short time ago, breathing so slowly the rest of us feared for your life, but Father insisted your spirit was strong and would find the way."

I smiled at Griffin. "I heard you call. I followed your voice, and here I am."

"The tumor is healing?" said Griffin. "Are you still in the emma ray?"

I chuckled. "It's MRI and no. I'm out of the tube, but back at the hospital, starting a new treatment. It's too soon to tell if it will work, but the doctor gave me medication. For the moment, the muscle aches and shaking are gone." My cheeks grew hot. "I was afraid I'd never return."

"You kept your heart and mind open, and the drum was able to track your spirit," said Danya.

Griffin smiled and helped me to my feet. "I'm glad you didn't stop searching."

The heat in my cheeks deepened. "Me, too."

"Are you well enough to travel?" said Griffin. "The storm passed. We can be on our way and arrive at Stone Keep before nightfall."

I looked toward the wall and shuddered. "Are you sure the breach won't return?"

"Yes. The darkling never uses the same route after it's been sealed by the Rose Stone. It must hunt for another weakness in the boundary." He eyed the ruins with a scowl. "Being confined makes me uneasy. We should leave now."

"Fine with me," I said. "I'm eager to meet Chancellor Emlyn. She might have answers."

"I sent a warbird ahead to inform her of our arrival. She and the council are expecting us."

"What's that?" asked Abril, motioning to the ground.

I followed her gaze and my mouth dropped open. "It's my drawing tablet." I snatched it up and ran my fingers across the cover. The tablet was real, all right. "I took it to the hospital. It has pictures I drew when I was a child." I looked at Griffin. "There's one you should see." I flipped to the page with the boy. "Is that you and Cirrus?"

His eyes widened. "Yes, but much younger. Cirrus had a temper when he arrived on the farm. He refused the saddle, so my father decided to use him as a draft animal. I thought it wrong to hitch such a fighting spirit to a plow and determined to ride him. The first time I tried to sit on his back, Cirrus threw me into a fence and gave me this." He touched the scar on his cheek. "I didn't give up, and we soon became friends. When did you draw the picture?"

"Years ago. I'd completely forgotten about it until my friend, Melanie, reminded me of a story I invented as a kid about a Rose Stone and a man named Griffin. At least at the time I thought it was a story. I-I can't explain." I turned to Danya. "Can you? How did I know about him?"

"You had a bond to this place even then." She gave Griffin an appraising look. "Stronger than I presumed."

"But how? Why?" I asked.

132

"That I cannot say." She patted my hand. "Perhaps the Rose Stone will have answers."

Griffin ordered the guard to break camp. I was lighthearted, overjoyed to be back, and eager to start the adventure ahead. Thanks to the medication pumping through my veins, I looked forward to the journey and sent a mental blessing to Dr. Turner and his wonder drugs. As the guards stowed gear and saddled the lyrs, my gaze drifted to the far wall, and I shuddered at the memory of the carvers' howls.

"Jess, are you ready to go?" said Griffin.

I peered at the back wall, hesitant to leave. "Not yet. I need to take one last look at the place where the carvers nearly broke through."

"Why?"

I struggled to give him a logical answer. "I can't explain what happened to me there, so let's just say, I want to make sure the breach sealed."

Griffin said nothing but motioned me ahead. We walked to the wall, his hand resting lightly on the sword hilt, prepared for trouble. I faced the wall, heart pounding. No rose tint, no claws ripping through reality. Everything was perfectly normal. I ran my fingers on the scarred, pitted surface. There was a slight vibration but nothing sinister, and I relaxed with a nervous chuckle. "I don't know what else I expected to find."

"Proof you are more than you believe?"

"I'm only an artist."

His eyes glittered with amusement. "Speaking as your creation, I find you exceptional."

I laughed. "Thanks, but don't get your hopes up." My smile faded. "I glimpsed some kind of machines moving on the other side."

"War machines. They cannot pass and wait for the boundary to fall."

A shiver ran through me. "There was also a presence. It was dark and hateful."

His jaw tensed. "The darkling."

"Yes. Have you ever seen it?"

"No, nor do the ancient tales have a description. The darkling's form is a mystery." He scowled at the wall. "The breaches are more powerful each time. I fear larger ones will soon allow the darkling's war machines to enter. We have no defense against such weapons. You've seen the devastation they caused."

"I sensed the darkling's hate," I murmured. "It was enraged I ruined its plans. It certainly didn't expect to see the Rose Guard prepared to meet the carvers on the other side of the breach."

"The darkling's preferred method of attack is stealth. Breaches open far from settlements so carvers can slip into the Commonwealth unnoticed. It's fortunate you were here. If five carvers broke through our lines, they would have ravaged the countryside before troops arrived. The danger is mounting, Jess."

"In my reality, too. Power outages are everywhere, and I heard the voice of the darkling again. It took the form of a spark and spoke to me. I'm afraid, Griffin. The darkling found the route to my world."

"We must hurry to Stone Keep, then. Time for both our realities grows short." Griffin took my hand, and my breath froze as the simple touch turned my knees to water. "My heart is torn, Jess," he said in a hushed tone. "I rejoice at your safe return, and yet there is no safety here. My desires are selfish. Part of me wishes you remained in the other life far from harm."

"I'm not safe there either, not with this tumor eating away at my brain. If I have a choice, it's to be here with you, so don't think you can get rid of me. I'll fight to stay." His smile warmed me from head to toe.

"We're ready, Captain," called Bram.

With a sharp screech from Racer, the warbird legion launched from the rafters. We mounted the lyrs and exited the building into gray dawn light. The storm scrubbed the air clean and left a fresh invigorating scent. "You look tired," I said to Danya as the ruins of the old airfield disappeared behind us. "Did you drum the entire night?"

She chuckled. "There are worse ways to spend an evening. Fighting carvers that have broken through the boundary is one of them."

Abril's eyes twinkled. "Our captain is not a patient man, yet he stayed at Danya's side, watching her drum. Perhaps with rapidly advancing years, the patience of the elderly becomes greater."

"Age certainly hasn't improved his disposition," said Bram jovially.

"Or he simply forgot why he was there," added Abril with an innocent expression. "The elderly can be afflicted with memory loss." From the guards came an eruption of laughter.

"I am still young enough to note certain Rose Guards require extra duties to keep them mindful of authority—cleaning the stables perhaps," Griffin said dryly.

"In that case, Captain," said Bram. "I volunteer the corporal and myself to ride point to Stone Keep." He spurred his lyr, and he and Abril galloped ahead.

The troop followed, riding at a brisk canter. As the morning wore on, the woods thinned out, the path widened and emptied onto a true road. Griffin reined in Cirrus beside me. "Do you need to rest?"

"No, thanks. The muscle weakness is gone for the moment, and I want to get to Stone Keep as soon as possible. I could be flung home again at any time."

"The new medication from the healers is working on the tumor?"

"I hope so. It's supposed to shrink small enough for an operation to remove it."

Griffin raised an eyebrow. "This operation is dangerous?"

I shrugged. "Yes, but so is the tumor. I don't have a choice."

"One always has a choice," said Danya, who rode on my other side. "The trick is to make sure it is the right one."

"How do I know the right one?" I asked.

"Simple." She winked. "The wrong one kills you."

"Just what I need," I said dryly to Griffin. "A hallucination with a twisted sense of humor."

We exited the woods and came to a flat plain, dotted with clumps of trees between rolling hills. It was a weird landscape unlike any I'd ever seen. A strange sense of dread hung over the place. Something went very wrong here. "What are those?" I asked, motioning to the hills.

"Burial mounds," said Griffin, solemnly. "The ancient tales say entire cities and their wonders are entombed underneath. The war machines caused massive destruction, spitting fire and burning everything in their paths. The remaining survivors gathered in Stone Keep, consolidating defenses to rebuild our world. Eventually, people spread out again in towns and villages to the edge of the Rose Stone's protective boundary. The forest reclaimed the broken land. We maintain the roads but avoid settling near those places."

"Have your people explored them?" I asked.

Danya wrinkled her nose. "We've scavenged metal bits that remained on the surface, but the hills still hold the stench of death."

"Have you ever wondered what lies beyond the Rose Stone's boundary?"

"For many idle hours especially in my youth," Griffin said. The smile returned. "My father often accused me of thinking of little else. For now, the boundary is closed, but, perhaps, someday…"

A dot in the sky plummeted toward earth and Sojourn circled overhead. *Bram and Abril arrived at Stone Keep.* He beat his wings and then flew off again to the east.

We increased the pace. Tension knotted my shoulders as we rode among the low, eerie hills, and I didn't relax until the last of them were behind me. Finally, we arrived at the river. Along the shore, great waterwheels turned. The storm had passed, but the current danced with churning ripples, and the presence of muddy vegetation high on the banks gave evidence of recent runoff from the storm.

We reached a bustling community lined with piers where men and women worked on barges. As we approached, one man shouted a greeting and called out, "We've been waiting, Captain. Two Rose guards passed through early today and told us of your arrival."

He lowered a gangway, and we rode the lyrs aboard. The craft had a mast and sails, but also an engine in the prow.

"Steam power?" I asked.

"Yes," said Griffin. "The river folk use steam when sailing against the current. Our people make power from water, wind, and fire, but not the spark." He scowled. "Never the spark. Its presence draws the darkling."

A woman hoisted the sails, and the barge got underway, sailing downriver with the current. I found a quiet place at the railing to watch the scenery go by, delicate spray hitting my face. The river was a busy place. We passed other craft of different sizes and shapes laden with goods and people. A few chugged upstream, smokestacks sending white puffs into the air. I leaned on Alta, steadying myself against the rhythmic rise and fall of the deck. Griffin approached me with a questioning look.

"I'm okay," I said, joking. "I walk this way all the time. You're the one who needs sea legs."

"It's not that. I see a change in you, no more doubt in your eyes. You believe we are real now?"

"Yes, I do. Of course, that doesn't mean you are," I said teasing. "Everyone at home would think I'm crazy, so I'll keep the Commonwealth of the Rose and her inhabitants to myself."

"So you spied on me in childhood," he said with good humor. "Had I known I would have behaved better."

I chuckled. "Don't worry. Apparently, I didn't see much except you on a lyr." A sudden rush of awkwardness made me stammer. "I-I can't explain it,

Griffin, but I must have made a tenuous connection to this place long ago."

His hand rested on mine. "Or to me?"

I breathed out a single word. "Yes."

I hardly knew this man, yet my life was suddenly a jigsaw puzzle with the final missing piece slipping into place. The completed picture was perfect. Griffin was at the center and made my heart sing. *I've fallen for him.* It was crazy. It was illogical. It was unarguably the truth.

"Ours is a fair world, Jess," said Griffin. "Or will be once the boundary is secure. It would please me to show you its gentle beauty one day."

"I'd love nothing more, but I can disappear at any moment and never return." A sweet, sad yearning tugged at me. "I wish with my whole heart that wasn't so."

Griffin gazed thoughtfully across the water to the far bank. "Your world has healers skilled with treatment of your disease. You must return to get well."

"I don't want to go until I've helped here but don't even know what I'm meant to do. I don't understand how I sealed the breach. Maybe it was a fluke—"

"We have a saying here," he said, chiding gently. "Do not let the problems of tomorrow interfere with the pleasures of today."

"We've got one similar. Don't worry. Be happy."

Griffin chuckled. "I like that." He took my hand and touched my fingers to his lips. "Don't worry, Jess. Be happy."

The barge hit a wavelet. The deck lurched, and I stumbled. Griffin put an arm around me and held tight. "For as long as you are here, I am at your side."

I leaned against him. "And I'm at yours."

We journeyed downstream past more villages, fields, and waterwheels. Griffin stayed with me. I never wanted the trip to end, but eventually, the barge turned toward the opposite shore. We disembarked at another settlement and took an inland road. Soon, more settlements appeared with sturdy cottages made of wood and stone, set between tidy fields, lush with grain. The houses had doors and shutters painted vibrant shades, giving them a quaint storybook appearance. Although similar to the one in my drawing tablet, none were white with a turquoise door.

Animals abounded, too, but no maned pigs with zebra stripes. Farmers in the fields waved as we went by. Word must have spread concerning the strange woman that appeared out of nowhere. They watched me pass with a mixture of curiosity and excitement as if they hoped I had come to save them. I had a rush of guilt. I couldn't even save myself.

The road led to a high wall encasing the massive Stone Keep. A heavy gate hung open. Men and women in Rose Guard uniforms peered from a walkway on top, shouting welcomes as we galloped underneath. By the wide-eyed excitement on their faces, they'd heard the story of the woman from another world, too.

We rode to a central structure with several turrets. One must have been an aerie for the warbirds, their sleek forms darted in and out of openings at the top. Another turret was higher than the rest, glistening pure white in the sun. It looked older, too, as if the people built Stone Keep around it. A series of windows led to the top, following what must have been an internal spiral staircase. A cupola with a gold roof capped the tower, the windows underneath tinted a delicate rose color with the added sparkle of leaded glass.

Bram and Abril met us at the bottom of the stairway in the main structure. Several people waited with them, including a woman with a silver circlet on her head inset with a rose-colored gem. Her tunic and leggings sported bright colors and a silken sheen, but as with the other inhabitants of the Commonwealth, the outfit suggested underlying practicality. None of those silly poofy outfits of fairytale queens. This woman didn't park her butt on a throne planning balls but got important work done.

We dismounted, and she shook my hand with an iron grip. "Welcome, Jessica Rose Stone. I'm Emlyn, Chancellor of the Commonwealth of the Rose."

"Thank you. Frankly, Chancellor, I'm at a loss here. I'm sure Bram and Abril told you I sealed a breach, but how is beyond me."

"I believe the Rose Stone called you to this world for a purpose, Lady Jess. Until we determine why, you are an honored guest at Stone Keep. Allow me to offer food and drink and then I will take you to the Rose Stone."

I stared at the highest turret where the windows had a faint crimson tint. "It's up there, isn't it?"

"Yes," she said. "Do you sense something?"

"No, but if it's all right with you, I want to see it first."

"As you wish."

I turned to Griffin. "Will you come with me?"

Griffin bowed his head. "It would be my honor."

"You are welcome, too, Danya," said Lady Emlyn. She turned to Bram. "I know you and Abril have duties to attend but join me for a meal afterward. I wish to hear reports from the field firsthand." She winked at Bram. "And I promised your parents to keep an eye on you."

Bram kissed her cheek. "Thank you, Aunt. We'd be happy to come. A meal at your table is always better than a meal in the barracks."

"And yet you continue to insist that you're not wise enough to be chancellor," Lady Emlyn said with a laugh.

He grimaced. "Please, spare me from such punishment."

We headed into the heart of Stone Keep. Despite the name, it projected a warm, welcome atmosphere. "Abril told me Bram is your nephew," I said to Lady Emlyn.

"Yes. His parents both serve in the guard and are stationed in the southern plains. Since childhood, I have threatened to cede the mantle of the chancellorship to him if he didn't behave." She chuckled. "It kept him from mischief."

"Is the chancellorship inherited?" I asked.

"No, the truth is the Rose Stone seems to sense the right candidates and communicates their identities to the drummers. They make the choice. That method has served us well. No one is ever selected with personal ambitions that outweigh the good of the Commonwealth. I certainly didn't volunteer to be chancellor. I was a teacher and happy to remain so." She shrugged. "But when duty calls, we answer."

"Bram would be an excellent chancellor, but everyone in the Commonwealth wishes your leadership to continue for many years to come," said Griffin.

Lady Emlyn's eyes sparkled in amusement. "Captain Griffin doesn't want the job either."

Paintings and tapestries covered the walls in the corridor leading to the tower, depicting, I assumed, the flora and fauna of the Commonwealth. They were skillfully done, and I admired them with an artistic eye. We passed a painting of the countryside, and I stopped and did a double take. Rooting under a tree was a zebra-striped pig with a ruff of black hair. "A striped pig?" I asked.

"The stripers are a specialty of the eastern heights," said Griffin. "My father raises them on his farm."

"Excellent eating," added Danya.

At the entrance to the tower was a landing with a large wooden door, polished to a high gloss. Over the lintel was an elaborate mosaic done with the touch of a master artisan. Delicately crafted handiwork formed a jeweled rose set in the center of brilliantly colored enamel tiles.

An armed man and woman stood guard outside the door, the emblems on their uniforms identifying them as members of the Rose Guard. They stepped aside and bowed with deference as Lady Emlyn approached. She retrieved a shiny gold key from the folds of her tunic and unlocked the door to reveal another staircase. I sent a silent thank you to Dr. Turner for the meds as we started to climb. Sunlight beamed through the windows, illuminating the steps. The added height allowed for sweeping vistas of the countryside beyond the walls. Not far was the faint glimmer of the boundary. It was closer here than at High Point Garrison, not more than a few miles away.

As I neared the top of the turret, the atmosphere

changed. Staticky prickles danced against my skin. Each inhaled breath held a charge that coursed through my body. At first, I thought the stones constructing the walls emitted a soft glow, but then realized the rose light spilled from a doorway above. My heart raced, and not from exertion. The chamber of the Rose Stone was dead ahead.

One last step and a circular room opened in front of me. I stood still to catch my breath. A row of windows ringed the chamber. Between the windows were elaborately carved panels and elegant tapestries, but my attention was immediately drawn to an object on a rotating pedestal in the middle of the room.

The Rose Stone was larger than I expected, nearly the size of my fist, and stunningly beautiful. A multitude of facets shone as in my childhood imaginings, but no drawing did justice to the real thing. The Rose Stone not only reflected light but also absorbed it. Tiny flashes of incandescent fire danced inside, ricocheting between the facets, and emitting prickles of energy that rippled up my arms. I realized now the leaded glass panes in the turret windows were clear, not tinted. The soft pink illumination I'd seen below came from the Rose Stone. At any time of day, it was a shining lighthouse bringing comfort to everyone in the city.

I gaped in wonder. "It's magnificent."

"It is, indeed," said the chancellor. "The Rose Stone secured the boundary of the Commonwealth, and the power has protected us for many years."

I regarded Lady Emlyn with dismay. "Now that I'm here, I don't know what to do next. I've never seen anything like it."

Danya patted my arm. "The Rose Stone called, and you answered. Let it speak to you again."

Griffin nodded at me. Words were unnecessary, his message clear. *If you need me, I am here.*

I nervously licked my lips and approached the pedestal, then stopped and stared in wonder. The pedestal was fixed in place. The Rose Stone didn't rest on top but hovered a few centimeters over the surface, spinning slowly. This close, the energy beat against me in waves. If this were a new form of radiation, it wasn't unpleasant or frightening, and no mental warning bells cautioned me against getting closer to the billowing warmth. The people of Stone Keep had lived here for years and never been harmed. It wouldn't hurt me either.

The Rose Stone stopped spinning. I drew in a breath and cupped my hands underneath. It dropped into my open palms as if waiting for me. Maybe for that reason, an introduction seemed in order. "Hello to you, too. My name is Jessica Rose Stone. I think you sent me a message a long time ago. I only got it recently and here I am. You've kept the Commonwealth safe for many years, but something has changed. The breaches are more frequent. I've heard the voice of the darkling, and frankly, it scares the pants off me. The people here worry about the safety of this world." I shot a glance at Griffin. "I do, too. So as one Rose Stone to another, how can I help?"

The pulses in the crystal were mesmerizing, bright flashes with a steady rhythm, as if controlled by an intelligent hand. They reminded me of a message in Morse code, waiting for someone with the ability to unlock the secret.

"Let me in," I whispered. "I'm ready."

The facets moved. Images capered through my mind, too fast to sort them out. The power behind the Rose Stone had accepted me, and suddenly, I felt a beneficent essence. The Rose Stone beckoned, and my mind happily followed.

I was falling but unafraid. Pathways of pure energy flowed through a crystalline matrix, and I laughed as they danced against me, warm and welcoming. More powerful than any energy source I imagined, they aligned and balanced the forces of this world and bound everyone together. In a way I'd never understand, the Rose Stone was life.

"Perfect," I murmured, and a chill gripped me. Perfection had a flaw. In the heart of the Rose Stone was a black knot, studded with tiny protuberances, identical to the waving tentacles on a carver's head. It had a strangely familiar shape, but before I could recall where I'd seen it, a tendril brushed against me, and I understood what it meant to touch evil. This thing was an invader from outside and had no place in perfection. A tentacle wormed into the Rose Stone's facet and blocked the flow of energy to the rest of the matrix.

"No," I shouted. "Leave her alone."

As if my challenge were a blow, the tentacle flinched and retreated, but a bulge in the knot formed, and another sprouted from a different section. I noted others, spreading, growing, sending their fleshy tendrils deep into the heart of the stone.

The Rose Stone fought back, slowing their advance. I reached for the knot and felt ravenous, gnawing greed that lapped at my strength.

Feed me. I hunger.

Nothing but streams of raw power nourished its rapacious desire. This was the crux of the darkling, kept at bay only by the dwindling life force of the Rose Stone. Deeper and deeper, I searched for the cause of the unquenchable craving. Buried inside the knot was a barely visible black wire, clouds of inky mist seeping from a tiny spark at the tip.

In that instant, I realized the awful underlying truth. Sick at heart, my mind retreated. The Rose Stone drifted away from me to float, once more, over the pedestal.

The mental release was like being dropped from a ledge, and I swayed on my feet. Griffin jumped to my side and put out a hand to steady me. "Jess, what did you see?"

I leaned against him. "The Rose Stone is dying."

Chapter Nine

The chancellor paled. "The drummers perceived fluctuations in power, an unexplained weakness, but complete failure? How can you be certain?"

"I-I can only describe what I felt." I struggled to put into words the uncanny experience. "Pathways of energy drew my mind inside to where a black knot is spreading poisonous tendrils. The Rose Stone is fighting back, but they multiply too fast. If the tendrils block enough of those pathways…" I couldn't say it.

Griffin's jaw tightened. "The Rose Stone dies."

"Yes." My shoulders sagged. "Before that happens, the darkling will attempt to take control, but the Rose Stone would rather die than allow that to happen. There's more you should know. The darkling is responsible for the knot binding them together. I think it's been inside a long time, maybe from the beginning. Growth must have been slow, so it only recently caused trouble. The heart of the connection between them has to be destroyed, but it's hidden inside the knot and the Rose Stone's power can't reach it. I-I don't know how to help." Their expressions reflected shock and dismay, and my stomach clenched. They didn't know either.

Griffin put an arm around my shoulders. "Jess is exhausted," he said firmly. "We've asked much of her today."

The chancellor straightened. "Quite right. She had

a long journey and needs to rest before any further discussion. Meanwhile, I'll summon the council."

"And I must report these findings to my order," said Danya.

"Dinner awaits in your quarters, Lady Jess," said the chancellor. "Rest now, and leave any troubling thoughts here."

I nodded numbly, too tired to argue. Griffin took my arm, and we left Lady Emlyn and Danya in the chamber, speaking in hushed tones. I slowly descended the stairs, Griffin at my side to lend support. Physically, I didn't need it. The pain meds from Dr. Turner continued to work, but I was loathed to reject the comfort of his touch.

"Your thoughts are deep," said Griffin.

I gave him a wry smile. "Not that deep. I'm having a hard time coming to terms with what happened in that room. I want to help her."

"Her?"

"Yes. The darkling is definitely an 'it,' but the Rose Stone is alive, although not like any lifeform I've ever come across. I can't explain it, but I got a sensation of welcome from a female friend." A thought occurred to me. "What if she originated in another place?"

"You mean through a portal created by the old ones."

"It's possible. Would that knowledge upset your people?"

"No, not everything that comes through a portal means us harm. The ancient tales say lyrs and warbirds arrived before the start of the Great War. So did other creatures. Yet they are part of the Commonwealth now." He gazed at me with a slight smile. "You came from afar, although the bridge that led you here is different. We've never found the Rose Stone's like in the Commonwealth, but no matter her origin, she is one of us and cares for this world." His smile widened. "I have never found the like of Jessica Rose Stone here, either."

I chuckled. "Is that good or bad?"

"Very good."

We returned to the main keep and entered a long hallway. Griffin stopped at an open door. Inside was a table set with dishes, and a mouthwatering scent drifted toward me. "I hope you find your quarters comfortable," he said. "There's a view of the gardens and the Rose Stone's turret from here."

I felt the blood rush to my cheeks. "Will you join me for dinner?"

"Nothing would please me more, but I have duties to attend. I must speak with Commander Tian, my superior officer. He's also a council member. Do you need anything before I leave? I can summon a servant for you."

"No. I'm fine." I gazed into the room, hesitant to let go of Griffin's arm. "I don't want to sleep. I'm afraid I'll wake at home and won't find my way back here."

"Have no fear," he said gently. "If you disappear, I'll sound the drum myself and call until you answer me."

I smiled. "Are you allowed to do that? I have a feeling Danya would squawk if you touched her drum."

"I have been known to break a rule or two."

"Not according to your daughter."

"Abril doesn't know everything."

My heart raced. *Say something clever.* "Thank you. I'll be fine."

"It is my honor. I'll join you at the council meeting." Griffin bowed then turned and walked down the hall.

Tell him how you feel.

What if he doesn't feel the same?

Words to call him back froze in my mind. I shut the door and sagged against it, blowing out my cheeks in disgust. "Unbelievable. No matter where you go, your love life sucks. Why can't you ever think of anything clever to say?"

At least my new room was lovely. Paintings decorated the walls. A thick, silky area rug lay on the floor in front of the bed. Against one wall was a large armoire with a mirror. Inside hung changes of clothing, the contents of my pack, and the drawing tablet.

Along with the covered dishes, the table had a vase of fresh flowers, a basket of fruit, and a clay teapot with steam curling from the spout. This room also had an attached bath. Someone had filled the bathtub with hot water and rose petals perfumed the air. After a hard ride on the trail, that might be a subtle hint I smelled, but the tub was definitely inviting. I stripped off my clothes and then poured a cup of tea, chose a piece of fruit, and sank blissfully into the water.

The fruit was delicious, with a flavor between a pineapple and a mango. Next to the tub was a delicate porcelain jar filled with fragrant gel. I slathered on a handful, and it made bubbly foam. I pushed worries from my mind and soaked and scrubbed. By the time the teacup was empty, I was Jessica Rose not only in name but also in color, my skin tinted warm pink.

After drying off, I wrapped up in a towel, examined the clothing in the armoire, and selected a silky green tunic, pants, and an elaborately embroidered sash. The shoes were soft beaded leather moccasins with sturdy cushioned soles, similar to those worn by the chancellor.

I scrutinized myself in the mirror and nodded with approval. The outfit had an Arabian Nights flair. Although the Commonwealth had vestiges of a fairytale land, complete with rampaging monsters, it also contained an air of sophistication lacking in those stories. Many different skin tones were present. Why bother with ethnic squabbling when an entire civilization was bound together by a common threat? The women had equal status, too. Clothing revealed a lot about a culture. Females here were free to move: no corsets, girdles, veils, or imprisoning laces and ties. No silly shoes to keep them from leading an active life. They charted their own destiny. Take that, Hans Christian Andersen. If mermaids inhabited the Commonwealth of the Rose, they'd never waste their time moping on the rocks for a dumb prince.

I sat at the table by the window to eat. Griffin was right, the view of the garden below was lovely. The Rose Stone's tower stood sentinel in the middle, keeping watch over the inhabitants of the Commonwealth. But for how much longer? I sighed and pushed the morbid thoughts away.

After eating my fill, I retrieved the drawing tablet from the armoire, fluffed the pillows against the headboard, and stretched out with the tablet propped on my lap. The bath and meal refreshed me, but I refused to sleep and risk being whisked away again. The lack of control was maddening but all wasn't lost. The Rose Stone sent a summons, and I answered. Why bring me here only to discover the Commonwealth was doomed? There must be a way to help.

I turned the pages to the sketch of the Rose Stone. The blurred pencil mark that marred the interior facets stood out even more to me. I thought it had been a mistake made by a childish hand, but now...

The truth hit hard, and I sucked in a breath. I'd seen it a short while ago in the interior of the Rose Stone. Not only that, but this was the second time in a few days I came across the same shape. The other had been on the picture from the MRI. The tumor killing me was identical to the poisonous knot imbedded in the Rose Stone. My connection to her was mental and physical, and we both fought a terminal illness. I leaned back on the pillows and gazed out the window at the turret. Even though I couldn't see the Rose Stone from the bed, I was convinced she knew I was here.

The delicate crimson light shining from the turret brought unexpected comfort. "Okay," I said with a smile. "We're in this together. Don't worry, I'll hang tough."

I flipped to the page with the strange abstract markings, but their meaning continued to elude me. The drawing of Griffin brought a chuckle. "So, you've been buried in my subconscious all these years. Nice to finally meet you face to face. The real Griffin is far better than a childish dream."

A servant entered and announced Chancellor Emlyn and the council requested my presence. I made a move to put the sketchbook aside and then had second thoughts and tucked it under my arm. I followed her down several hallways. Griffin waited in a corridor outside a chamber with an open door. His gaze traveled from my head to my toes, and his smile of approval showcased those dimples. My heart gave a happy skip.

"You look rested," he said.

"I am, thanks." I peered inside the room. Chancellor Emlyn and Danya sat with a dozen others at a long table. Behind them was a window with a view of the Rose Stone's tower. "They're all council members?"

"Yes, each represents a separate order or district. Danya will speak for the drummers. The man in uniform next to the chancellor is Commander Tian, head of the Rose Guard and my commanding officer."

"Your boss doesn't look happy."

"He's concerned with the health of the Rose Stone, as we all are."

"Which one?" I said with a grin. "I'm sure you gave him a full report on me. Did you tell him I was big trouble?"

Griffin's eyes twinkled. "Assuredly, but the most interesting trouble I've ever dealt with."

Chancellor Emlyn waved us to the table. We took the last two empty seats, and she made introductions.

"Is it true?" barked Commander Tian. "Captain Griffin says the Rose Stone is dying." He scowled at me. "He said you have special abilities and received a message, but how can you be certain of the meaning?"

I shifted in the chair under his penetrating gaze. "The Rose Stone and I are connected in more than one way. I have a tumor identical in shape to the knot interfering with the energy flow. Mine weakens me as the other weakens the Rose Stone. Soon, the boundary will collapse. I feel it. I know it." I desperately searched for comforting words but had none to offer.

Griffin tensed. "How long?"

"A few weeks, maybe a few days..." I bit my lip. "Not long." Council members exchanged fearful looks.

"The breaches in the boundary already arrive with frightening regularity," said Commander Tian with a scowl. "Reports flow from every district. Carvers don't appear singly any longer but in groups of three, four, and five and in places that have always been secure. Drummers barely give one warning before sounding another. So far, the Rose Guard have been able to keep them at bay. Drummers seal breaches and prevent wind surges, but if the frequency of attacks increases, that won't last."

An anxious murmur went around the table. "Jess speaks the truth," said Danya, raising her voice above the others. "Those in my order suspected as much and her vision confirmed our worst fears. Warnings sent to the drummers by the Rose Stone have become harder for us to hear. At first, we were afraid our connection was fading, along with the power of the drums, but now the reason is plain. The spreading poison muffles the Rose Stone's voice."

"Isn't there anything we can do?" asked one of the council members.

Danya lifted her hands in a helpless gesture. "The drummers call for clarity from the Rose Stone as we speak, but the answers are still hidden from us." She turned to me. "The Rose Stone spoke to you."

"I got a warning and saw the problem, but not a solution," I said.

"Even if we had months, the picture is bleak," said Commander Tian. "We are running out of time. My guards will fight to the end, but there aren't enough to stop the darkling if the boundary fails. The carvers will overrun us, and the war machines will follow. Once the Rose Stone is taken, we are doomed. The darkling will strip the Commonwealth of life. Everyone at the table knows that. Forgive me, Lady Jess, but looking death in the face without a plan of action does not sit well with me," he said gruffly.

"I understand," I said. "And, believe me, I want to help."

A flutter of wings and muted chirrups came from the windows. Warbirds crowded onto the ledges, and Racer craned his neck into the room. *The aerie wishes to see the Rose Stone.*

"Humph," the commander grunted. "I see you're the talk of the legion, Lady Jess."

"They are curious about her, sir," said Griffin. "They sense the connection she has with the Rose Stone."

"Come then," shouted the commander to the warbirds. "Satisfy your curiosity." A flurry of wings dove into the room. Racer settled on the back of Griffin's chair. Another, I assumed partnered with Commander Tian, alit on his. The rest perched in the rafters.

The chancellor nodded at the sketchbook. "What have you brought, Lady Jess?"

"Oh, drawings I made when I was a child." I flipped to the page with the Rose Stone. "Long ago, the Rose Stone must have reached out to me, and we made a connection. The dark spot inside is the same size and shape as my tumor."

I studied the drawing with a frown. "I thought these jagged lines were facets, but now that I look at them again, they resemble a reading from an EKG." They gave me blank stares. "An EKG is a machine," I hurriedly added. "It measures the heart's electrical activity. I was hooked up to one at the hospital before I returned here."

"The internal spark of life," murmured Danya.

"Yes, you could call it that…" My eyes widened. "These little up and down marks are exactly the same as several EKG strips lying on top of each other as if we have the same heartbeat. What does that mean?"

"That you and the Rose Stone are bound tighter than you believed."

"No, that can't be right," I sputtered. "The Rose Stone has been around since long before I was born."

"The rivers of time between your world and ours do not run straight and true, but bend and stretch," said Danya. "You said so yourself. Time in your world passes at a different rate."

"If we're connected that closely, I won't do you much good," I said softly. "I'm not well."

Griffin took my hand. "Don't say that, Jess. Don't even think it. Your healers will find a cure."

"What else did you draw?" asked the chancellor.

I flushed and skipped past the one with Griffin and flipped to the last drawing. "Um, a few people and animals and a farm…there's another one that's abstract. I can't figure out what it means."

Griffin took the sketchbook from me and studied the picture. He traced a finger along the blue line. "This might be a stream or a river."

"A map?" said Commander Tian, raising an eyebrow. "It's unlike any I have ever used. What's the purpose of these winding circles within circles?"

Racer hopped off the back of Griffin's chair and onto the table, his brilliant blue eyes studied the drawing. *A warbird's view from above.* He stabbed his beak at the paper. *Here are hills, here are valleys.*

I gasped. "This is a contour map. The circular lines represent height around a flatter plain. The closer the lines, the higher the elevation."

"Yes," murmured Griffin. "I see it now. Racer, do you know the area?"

Yes. You do not?

Griffin gave Racer a curious look and examined the map again. His shoulders stiffened. "These are the hills and eastern plains that border the Last Stand River. The dots in the center are the location of my father's farm and the outbuildings." He rubbed his chin and frowned. "Jess, what did you mean by drawing this little rose at the top of the picture? From the location, it appears to lie just within the boundary set by the Rose Stone."

"Beats me. I figured the flower was a decoration." I added dryly, "It's a strange thing to add though considering it's not very decorative."

"These wilds are where the people of the Commonwealth put aside their differences and banded together to stop the darkling," said Griffin. "It's the scene of the last great battle."

"Last Stand River," I murmured. "You mean, if the darkling's army had broken through the line in these hills…"

"The river was the last stand. Fortunately, although

many gave their lives, the Rose Stone prevented our annihilation."

"So this is a kind of treasure map where X marks the spot," I said, excitement rising. "Griffin, I need to go there."

He looked doubtful. "All that remains are the ruins of the great battle now long buried."

"That's entirely possible, but I can't shake the feeling it's important for me to see this place."

"Very well. Commander Tian, with your permission, I will take Jess and a squad and leave in the morning. We can journey upriver as far as the settlement of River's Edge and then ride to my father's farm, make camp there, and explore the area."

"I will accompany them," said Danya. "I also wish to see what may be buried in the hills."

"So granted," said the commander. "Captain Griffin, leave at first light and keep me informed of your progress."

I felt a gentle tug and looked out the window at the turret. "What is it?" asked Griffin.

"I'm not sure."

Danya followed my gaze. "The Rose Stone wishes to go with Jess."

"Impossible," sputtered Commander Tian. "It has never left the turret."

The chancellor's gaze went from me to the window. "The Rose Stone has decided the time is right."

"Chancellor, Stone Keep is the strongest fortification in the Commonwealth," barked Commander Tian. "Protection of the Rose Stone has never failed us here, but removing it from the turret…"

"Thick walls will do no good if the Rose Stone dies," said Lady Emlyn. "The Rose Stone should go with her."

"Wait," I said. "I can't be sure the answer is in those hills. What if the power that protects this place weakens once we leave?"

"The Rose Stone spoke to you, not to me or any of us here," said the chancellor. "Not even the drummers and they have always been able to interpret the messages. If the solution to our dilemma exists, then the Rose Stone believes you are the one to find it."

Commander Tian turned to Griffin. "I trust your judgment, Captain. You believe this, too?"

"I do," he said without hesitation.

"Very well, then. The guard will remain on alert and prepare for war."

My hand shook. I hurriedly placed it in my lap, but not before Griffin noticed. "The tremors have returned. You're not strong enough for another journey so soon."

"I'm okay. The medicine is wearing off, but no headaches. At present, I'm able to travel. I'm sure Dr. Turner will give me a second dose any time now." I wasn't sure that was true, but it didn't matter. I had to go. "We should leave as soon as possible though. I might be snatched back to my reality at any moment."

"I will tend to Jess during the trip," said Danya. "Meanwhile, she should return to her quarters. There is nothing more for her to do here."

I rose to leave, uncomfortably aware the council members watched me go with hopeful eyes.

Griffin accompanied me to my chamber. "You are troubled," he said.

"The answer might be in those hills, but I wish I

knew what to look for."

"We will find it."

"I hope so," I said and added lightly. "Well, well, I get to meet your father. I can't wait."

Griffin made a sour face. "I have considered the issue and see no way to avoid it."

"It's been a while since you've seen him. Maybe a reunion won't be so awful. Are you sure he'll welcome Rose Guards camping on his doorstep?"

Griffin snorted. "He'll have no problem with the arrival of Rose Guards, only their captain, and as I serve the wishes of the Council, he can hardly refuse. I'll send Racer ahead with a message informing him of our arrival."

We reached the door to my chamber, and I was suddenly overcome by awkwardness. "I'll see you in the morning then."

He brushed an errant strand of hair from my face and his touch brought a delicious feeling. "I'm pleased to hear you'll be here in the morning."

"I'll fight to remain."

"Eventually, you must return to your world. The one hope of a cure is with your people."

I couldn't argue with that but made no move to open the door. Griffin shifted his feet. Was it as difficult for him to say goodbye as it was for me? "Hard times are upon us, Jess. War looms. Even as we speak, Rose Guards battle the enemy."

I squared my shoulders. "So will I."

"You are not a soldier."

"No, but I belong on the battlefield as much as you. Maybe more. Danya said the Rose Stone called to me years ago. The child didn't understand the message, but the woman does. A way for me to help her exists, and I have to find it."

"Everyone in the Commonwealth is grateful."

My breath quickened. "And you?"

Did I read wistfulness in his eyes? "Part of me wishes you'd never heard of the Rose Stone," he said. "My duty as a member of the guard is to keep you safe and the only certainty is for you to leave this place and never return."

The steadiness of his voice gave no hint to any underlying emotions, but mine were a roiling sea. I whispered, "If you never saw me again, would that put your heart at rest?"

The intensity of his gaze stole my breath away. "I'm merely a common soldier, more used to action than words," Griffin said.

"There's nothing common about you, Griffin, but I understand," I said, chiding gently. "I've always been better with pictures than words myself." It was hard to think clearly when his eyes peered so deeply into mine. "You were much easier to talk to when I thought you were a hallucination," I blurted.

He chuckled. "Then, perhaps, it's best if we don't speak of such things now. It's late, and we leave before dawn. Good night, Jess."

"Good night, Griffin. I'll be here in the morning. You won't get rid of me that easily."

"I have no wish to be rid of you at all." Griffin took my hand. He touched it gently to his lips, then turned and left.

I shut the door and leaned against it. My legs shook, and it wasn't from the tumor. "Well, that went well," I snorted in disgust. "You resolved absolutely nothing."

Griffin obviously didn't want to discuss his feelings. I wasn't sure I did either, but, perhaps, for different reasons. Griffin may feel a sense of duty, but not the same attraction to me as I had to him. On the other hand, if more than that bound us together, we faced an impossible situation. Griffin couldn't live in my world, and I didn't know how to stay in his.

I went to the window and leaned on the sill, gazing at the turret. The sun had set. From the window, the Rose Stone's radiance was a beacon in the night washing over the land, falling like a comforting blanket to ease the cares of this world.

"Sorry, I wasn't much help today," I whispered. "Any words of wisdom for me?"

Instead of answers, the tenseness in my body relaxed, replaced by a sensation of peace. "Thanks," I chuckled. "I needed that."

I got ready for bed and crawled between the sheets. A troubling thought kept me awake. What if I disappeared again before I found a way to help? Then an image of Griffin rose to my mind. He called for me once and I answered. He'd call for me again, of that I was sure. I closed my eyes and welcomed sleep.

****

I entered the Rose Stone and reached into the void for the black knot at the center. It brushed my fingers, leaving a slimy trail and then slipped from my grasp. The knot zigged and zagged, weaving a sinuous course, but I stuck to the chase until at last, I had my elusive quarry cornered against a facet.

"Nowhere to go," I taunted. "You can hide from others, but not from me."

Sparks exploded from the interior and struck me with burning torment. *The stone is mine!*

"Not a chance," I snapped, standing fast despite the pain. "I'll never let you take control of the Rose Stone."

I grabbed the knot with both hands. It struggled to escape, first fire then ice lashing at my skin. Then came hate. I reeled against something that wasn't an emotion, but virulent poison, wrapping me entirely in its filth.

No, not quite. There was a tiny gap in the onslaught, a hidden flaw, a vulnerability buried deep inside. If only I could touch it…

With a crackle of static, the knot burst from my grasp. *You are dying. The spark that remains is fleeting.*

"I'm not dead yet, but you're not as strong as you think either. Everything has a weakness. It's only a matter of time before I find yours and destroy you."

Not if I destroy you first.

Chapter Ten

The rap at the door jarred me awake, and my heart raced. I bolted upright, clutching the sheet, searching for the malevolent spark. The faint rosy glow from the turret cast the only light in the room. The moment of disorientation passed, and I sagged against the headboard, weak with relief. I was at Stone Keep and hadn't been yanked back to the hospital. There was a second knock, louder this time.

"Come in," I called.

The door opened, and Abril entered with a breakfast tray and leather saddlebags slung over her arm. "Hi," I said. "You're up early."

Abril placed the tray on the table and lit one of the lamps. "I volunteered to wake you. Father wishes to get underway before dawn. Lady Emlyn will meet us downstairs with the Rose Stone." She went straight to the armoire. "I'll pack for you."

"I can do that. I don't want to make extra work."

Abril gave a careless wave. "Have no concern. Preparing a proper kit for travel is part of guard training. I'll be done before you dress and finish breakfast."

While I ate, Abril took the clothes from the armoire. She set aside the riding gear on the bed and then began to fold the others and place them neatly into the saddlebags. Now and again, she shot me a hesitant glance as if wanting to speak and then thinking better of it. She filled one bag and buckled the fastening. "Father is concerned with your comfort."

"He's been very kind to me."

"It is more than kindness. I have not seen him show such tender regard for another as he has for you."

Sudden awkwardness overcame me, and I cleared my throat. "Oh?"

"Yes. You haven't spoken much of your life. Do you have someone pledged?"

"Pledged? Oh, you mean a man. No, I'm not involved with anyone. There was a guy recently," I stammered. "But we parted ways. We didn't suit each other."

"There have been women in my father's life, but he's never pledged his heart to another," Abril said. "He insists the life of a guard is enough, but I don't believe him." She folded a shirt and tucked it neatly into the saddlebag. "It's a wonder to me you saw a vision of him as a child."

"I can't explain it either."

"If Father wished to pledge to another, I'd have no objection," she said cheerfully.

"Uh, I'm sure he appreciates your support." The conversation had taken a sharp turn from awkward and nosedived into really-really-awkward. Time to make a hasty exit. Discussing my feelings for Griffin with his daughter was beyond weird. "I'll get changed now."

I grabbed the riding gear and hurried into the bathroom. By the time I finished dressing, Abril was stowing the last few items. I poured a cup of tea and offered her one, but she declined, saying she ate in the aerie.

"With the warbirds?"

"Yes. I wanted to visit the new clutch. Racer's mate, Tempest, has a female fledgling with a friendly manner toward me. She even takes meat from my hand. We are similar in mind, and I hope to offer a pleasing name when I reach full guard status."

"A name?"

"The guard offers a name and if the warbird approves and accepts then the partnership is sealed. I believe we'll be well-suited to each other. Sojourn says she has a fighting spirit."

"Spirit is a fitting name for a warbird."

Abril's eyes lit up. "Indeed. I shall remember that. Now, if only I can complete my training and become a full member of the Rose Guard." She sighed. "At times, it feels as if the last bit takes forever."

"I'm sure your father is proud of your progress."

"It's difficult for me to tell. He is not quick to offer compliments, but Bram insists Father is pleased."

"Bram must be a good friend."

"He is. He's only a year older, and we've known each other since childhood. His mother and father both serve in the guard, and we were often stationed at the same post. They are at the southern boundary now."

I gave her a playful nudge. "I'm sure your father wouldn't mind if you two were closer. Bram wouldn't either."

"You think so?" She smiled shyly.

"I know so. I've seen the way Bram looks at you. It isn't just a buddy-in-arms thing."

"I've always found Bram pleasant company, but for now I must keep my mind on duty," she said with a serious expression. "At times, I feel Father worries about me too much and slows down my training to keep me near him."

"Aw, cut him some slack. It's a father's prerogative to worry, but he didn't stop you from joining the guard, right?"

"That's true. When I turned sixteen, I applied for training at High Point Garrison. Recruits must have permission from the captain in charge." She had a thoughtful look. "Father could have sent me to Stone Keep and Commander Tian or any of the other districts."

"See? He approves and enjoys having you around. How long is the rest of your training period?"

"A few weeks, unless there's a delay." Abril's expression clouded over.

A delay like a war?

"Father has always understood how much the guard means to me. I never wanted more than this life." Abril shook her head. "I pity poor Grandfather. He tried to make farmers of Father and me and failed miserably. I love them both dearly, but I don't wish to be in the middle when they meet again." She snickered, put her hands together, and then jerked them apart making a noise like an explosion. I got the picture.

We went downstairs. A dozen guards, including Bram and Danya, were in front of the keep, checking the packs and cinches on the lyrs. Racer wasn't there, but the other warbirds shifted their talons on the pommels as if they were eager to be aloft. Griffin held the reins of Cirrus and Alta, and Abril hurried over and secured my saddlebags to the latter.

"This long to pack two saddlebags, Corporal?" Griffin's tone was jesting rather than harsh. "Perhaps you need additional instruction on the proper method to prepare a travel kit."

"No sir," said Abril.

"Blame me, Captain," I said. "I made Abril stop working to tell me your faults. The list was extensive. I'd be happy to share it with you on the way." A ripple of amusement went through the soldiers.

"That won't be necessary," said Griffin with a twitch of his lips. "I've already heard them in great detail."

Lady Emlyn exited the keep with Commander Tian. He looked even grimmer than usual. Griffin stiffened. "Something's amiss."

"A breach report in the southern district arrived this morning," said the commander. "Drummers had difficulty pinpointing the location, and five carvers made it through." His jaw tightened. "Twelve dead before they were stopped, and drummers report more weakening in the boundary and fear other breaches will follow. I'm sending reinforcements. Take Bram and Abril with you, Captain, but I need the rest."

The chancellor carried a velvet bag and handed it to me. The cloth was warm to the touch. I opened the drawstring top and looked inside. The Rose Stone lay nestled in the bottom, emitting a soft glow. "Comfy in there?" The light flickered as if in response.

"This is the first time the Rose Stone has left the turret," said Lady Emlyn. "I'll expect to feel a certain emptiness without the light shining over us."

"She'll be back soon. I promise."

Commander Tian frowned. "She?"

"Yes. Maybe the feeling comes from the connection we have, but to me the Rose Stone is 'she,' like a sister, one I haven't seen in a long time. I'll take excellent care of her."

He nodded and turned to Griffin. "If help exists for us in those hills, Captain, you must find it without delay. If nothing is there…" He shot a meaningful glance at the chancellor.

"Find a way to take the Rose Stone to your world," she said softly to me.

My eyes widened. "I can't leave the Commonwealth unprotected."

"If this is our last stand, so be it, but keep her out of the enemy's hands. The Rose Stone's power must never fall to the darkling. Promise me."

I swallowed. "I promise to protect her with my life."

She smiled at me. "I know you will. Good luck."

The velvet bag had a long strap, and I slung it across my chest. The gentle heat was pleasant but did little to ease my rising anxiety. The Commonwealth didn't have weeks. Time was swiftly running out.

Sojourn launched from Bram's pommel and soared overhead as we galloped from the keep. Racer was still AWOL, and then I remembered Griffin planned to send him with a message for his father. Dawn broke as we neared the river. I squinted as the first bright rays of the sun streamed over the horizon. A sharp pain burrowed behind my eyes, likely the meds wearing off. I pushed those thoughts aside. There was nothing I could do about it.

A barge waited at the pier with sails lashed, the steam engine puffing white smoke from the stack. We rode the lyrs onto the deck. I slipped off Alta and nearly stumbled from the weakness in my legs. Yep, Dr.

Turner's medicine was rapidly diminishing. I glanced around, and to my relief, Griffin spoke to Bram and hadn't seen my near fall. He laid a comforting hand on the young man's shoulder and said a few words that eased the tenseness in Bram's stance.

"The weakness has returned."

I startled and turned to face Danya's sharp eyes.

"Yes, but please don't say anything to Griffin."

"You should rest."

"I can't, not yet."

"Being torn between two worlds wears on your body. I have a tonic for pain, but the weakness is growing, and my medicine won't help. We have several hours' journey before landfall. Perhaps if you slept…"

"I don't want to. Not now. I promise to take it easy at the farm."

"I understand. Once your healer's treatment wears off, the call to your world might be too strong to overcome."

I looked at Griffin. "Yes. I need to keep my wits about me and fight to stay here as long as possible."

She patted my arm. "I will make tea with an herbal remedy to mitigate your pain but keep your mind alert."

Danya left to root through her saddlebags, and I leaned against the railing to steady my legs. The river folk shoved off, and the barge headed upstream, engine chugging, as we plowed steadily against the current. A man tossed a brick-shaped object into the burner from a large pile on the deck. It was similar others I'd seen at High Point Garrison, but bigger.

Griffin came to my side and inhaled a deep breath. "Even in troubled times, one can find a measure of peace on the water."

"Don't tell me you've decided to trade Cirrus for a barge."

He grinned. "Cirrus would never forgive me, nor would Racer."

I motioned to Bram. "He's worried about his parents."

"Concern for their safety is natural. A few encouraging words helps a soldier stay focused. Too much is at stake for personal issues to distract from duty."

For you, too? I swallowed the question and changed the subject. "What's burning in the engine? It's not wood. Are they the same things I've seen people use for light and heat?"

"Yes. They're packets made from a mixture of plants and lyr droppings. The river folk use them to boil the water powering the barge's steam engine."

"Manure?" I said, eyes wide. "It doesn't smell."

"Lyr droppings are highly valued, as fertilizer and fuel, and carry little scent."

"Pity horse manure isn't as nice. We never would have switched to cars."

"Cars?"

"Machines that carry us around."

Griffin shook his head. "Strange to think of a world where people do not have such a bond with animals."

"You can't miss what you don't know exists."

"In the old days, our people were bound to the spark. I would not wish to return to that life if it meant severing ties with warbirds and lyrs."

"I understand why." I patted Alta, and she rubbed her head against me. Her little nicker had a comforting undertone, and I laughed and scratched her neck. "I know, sweet thing. I miss you when I'm gone, too." She nickered again and nosed me toward Griffin. "Of course," I sputtered, feeling my cheeks grow ten degrees warmer. "I miss Griffin, too." I hissed, "Butt out," in Alta's ear and received a definite impression of amusement. That's one advantage of driving. My car never offered an opinion on my love life.

I return.

Racer streaked from the north to join Sojourn who continued to circle overhead. Griffin held out a gloved hand. Racer and Sojourn dove toward the barge. Sojourn landed on Bram's pommel while Racer pulled up sharply and alit with grace on Griffin's wrist.

The letter of our arrival is delivered to Paxton.

"Any word in return?"

None.

Griffin snorted. "Exactly what I expected."

Danya brought me a cup of spiced tea, this time with an extra ingredient that added sweetness to the taste. After a few sips, my headache went from a biting sting to dull pounding.

Griffin regarded my drink with suspicion. "That's one of Danya's healing brews. You are in pain."

I waved off his concern. "A slight headache. It's practically gone." My hand shook. I clasped the mug in a double-handed grip, but my subterfuge didn't work.

"Your hand is trembling, too," said Griffin. "You should have said—"

"Don't start. I had the same argument with Danya, and she didn't get any further than you will. We're not turning the barge around, and I won't take a nap. I may not wake up here, and I can't risk that."

Griffin clenched his teeth. He left me at the rail,

and I watched him go with a heavy heart. I braced for a scene if Griffin attempted to turn the barge around, but instead he returned shortly with Abril and Bram. They each carried sacks of grain that the barge transported upriver and stacked them near the rail. They returned for several more and constructed a rudimentary bench.

"Sit," ordered Griffin.

I sat. It was surprisingly comfortable. "Thank you. Are you going to glower at me for the rest of the trip?"

"Perhaps." His expression softened. "Perhaps not. I should save the fiercest of them for my father."

I patted the spot next to me. "Have a seat. I don't want to think about my health now, so I'd appreciate a distraction. Let's talk about anything else."

Griffin sat down and said no more about my condition. Instead, he pointed out birds on the shore. Danya returned for the empty cup. I gave it to her and then placed my shaking hand in my lap. Without a word, Griffin took it in his. The shaking didn't ease this time, yet comfort remained. Was it the warmth of his hand or the warmth from the Rose Stone as her ever-present heat seeped into my body? Either way, I was content.

We sat by the rail holding hands, and I listened as he described life in the Commonwealth. It wasn't an easy place to put down roots. The people worked hard and lived under a constant death threat. Yet that also gave them a singular purpose and pride. Only the strong survived here.

"The boundary protects us yet also constrains us," Griffin said. "Bit by bit, the population increases. Soon, the resources at hand will not be enough. Even now, the amount of arable land in the northern heights is at the limit. Other areas will follow. Eventually, we must move beyond the boundary or face starvation."

"But if you do that, the protective power weakens. The darkling will come anyway."

He gave me a resigned look. "Another problem for another day."

We stopped talking and simply sat quietly, each in our own thoughts. The barge plowed steadily through the water, the soft *chuf-chuf* of the engine mingled with the slap of rivulets against the keel. The peaceful, hypnotic rhythm almost made me forget the gnawing pain in my limbs.

Almost.

How long were we on the river? The passage of time was difficult for me to judge without a clock, but the sun was high in the sky when Abril broke out rations and Danya offered me another cup of tea. Griffin asked questions about my life in the "other world," and I laughed at the incredulous look on his face as I tried to explain microwaves and television, UPC codes, traffic lights, and cellphones. When I got to computer dating, his mouth dropped open.

"A machine picks a mate?" He practically choked on the words.

"Not exactly. You answer a bunch of questions and the machine sorts through the answers and then gives you the name of a person who's compatible."

"That means nothing." Griffin snorted in disgust. "How can a machine see into a human heart and read the truth?"

"It can't, obviously, or it wouldn't have matched me to my last boyfriend."

"A machine selected him for you?"

"Yes, and at first it was good. I thought it would become great, but after a while I realized our lives were out of sync. He loved the city and had zero interest in moving to the country where I always yearned to be. He loved parties and the latest gadgets, and I loved quiet time at my easel. Little by little, his dreams for the future overshadowed mine. One day, Elliot got a big promotion. He had planned his career track to the minutia. He'd climb the corporate ladder from one job to another, one big city to another and, naturally, I'd follow. I told him I didn't want to leave."

I chuckled. "Elliot didn't listen and kept blathering on, planning out our lives. We'd get married right away because it was time. Time…" I murmured. "Not because he was madly in love with me, but because he was comfortable with our arrangement and it was time. It hit me. I couldn't envision us growing old together. Poor Elliot. It was quite a shock when I turned him down. I think I was the first plan he ever had in his life that fell through."

"Love should never be a struggle," said Griffin.

My heart skipped a beat. "Even if you're from two different worlds?"

Griffin tucked a wind-whipped hair behind my ear. "Even so." He gazed at the river. "I fear for this world. I cannot see my future or that of anyone else."

Despite the gusts off the water, my cheeks felt flushed and warm. "What if the Rose Stone is healed?"

For a second, an undefined emotion flashed across his face. Hope? Desire? Or was that merely wishful thinking on my part?

A deckhand called out, "River's Edge landing dead ahead."

The moment vanished. Griffin stood and helped me to my feet. As the barge docked, the warbirds took to the skies and soon disappeared from sight. Griffin boosted me onto Alta, and we rode through the settlement to a country lane. Fields on each side bloomed with ripening grain. The long stalks had yellow poofs at the top, mimicking my childhood sketch. They rippled in the stiff breeze like the wavelets on the river.

In the distance, at the edge of the plains, was a ring of craggy hills. Some low, some high with odd asymmetrical shapes. When I looked at them, a shiver ran down my backbone.

Griffin followed my gaze. "Burial grounds for those who gave their lives in the final battle of the Great War," he said. "The death toll was high. Then the Rose Stone appeared, and the tide turned in our favor."

"What happened that day?"

"No one is certain. Suddenly, the Rose Stone was among us, and a miraculous upheaval followed on the battleground. The soldiers who were there described it as a wind surge in reverse. The ground trembled, hills collapsed burying everything under mounds of debris, dust clouds obscured the hordes of carvers and their war machines. When it subsided, the land had been scoured clean, any structures and the bodies of the dead had been entombed in the rubble. They discovered the protective boundary in place." Griffin pointed to a far crest. "Look there."

I squinted and caught the faint glimmer of the boundary before it disappeared on the other side of a ridge. Abril had placed my sketchbook in a saddlebag, and with a rush of excitement I took it out. The distinctive contours of the hills precisely matched the map's layout. The location of the tiny rose was definitely to the north, but from my position it was impossible to determine the exact spot. Wondering what secrets lie buried caused an unexpected shiver and I stuffed the notebook back in the saddlebag.

We rode from one dirt road to another, passing more fields on either side, until we reached a long winding lane. "Our farm begins here," said Abril. "It's the largest in the district."

I stifled a sigh, relieved rest was at hand. The sun sank low on the horizon, dragging the temperature down with it. I had no wish to navigate lonely country roads in the dark. We passed pens with livestock, and my eyes widened at the sight of a litter of black and white piglets with tiny ruffs around their necks and little zebra stripes.

Griffin hadn't spoken since we entered the lane. His lips set in a thin tight line. I could practically see the tension building inside him, and I didn't feel so hot myself. Danya's brew had helped, but now my limbs had a constant ache. I bit back a groan at every bounce in the saddle, and my headache beat a rhythmic hammer blow. Without warning, my vision blurred in a crimson haze. I clutched the pommel, blinking hard, and it disappeared—just momentary weakness, nothing to worry about.

Beep, beep, beep.

The noise was strange, very different from the steam engine on the barge, and I assumed it came from some type of farm equipment hidden from sight in the fields. The lyrs passed a row of fruit trees. Ahead was a farmhouse, and unconsciously, I smiled. My childhood drawing had been crude, but here was the turquoise door and the right number of windows. In the front yard were the same blue and white flowers. The whitewashed walls had a slight pink tint from the rays of the setting sun.

Near the main house were several structures I hadn't drawn including a barn and stable, more outbuildings, and a tidy fenced vegetable garden. I took the drawing pad from the saddlebag again and thumbed through the pages. Yes! The dots on the contour map matched the locations of each one. We had to be on the right track.

The lyrs stopped, and Racer and Sojourn alit on the pommels. People working in the garden waved hello and shouted greetings as they ran toward us. Abril and Griffin waved back.

Beep, beep, beep.

I frowned and rubbed the back of my neck. The annoying chirp was louder and nearer this time. Funny how it reminded me of a medical monitor in the hospital.

My pulse raced. I stared at the wall of the farmhouse and blinked hard, willing the rosy tint to disappear. Instead, it deepened in color. I clutched the velvet sack and the sketchpad tight to my chest. Warmth trickled through my fingers from the Rose Stone, and I sent a silent plea. *I can't go. Help me stay.*

The door to the house whipped open. The servants stopped in their tracks, casting nervous glances at each other. A man strode onto the porch, his resemblance to Griffin plain. Paxton was as tall as his son with the same powerful physique. He did not wear a happy face. The thought crossed my mind he might not have one.

"Father," said Griffin, coolly. "Racer reported he delivered my message."

"I received it," he grunted. "The stable is ready for the lyrs."

"Is the stable ready for us, too, Grandfather?" Abril asked, obviously teasing.

Paxton's face lit up. He held out his arms. "Come here, girl." She slid off the lyr and ran into his arms. He hugged her tight. "Your room is just as you left it."

The rest of us dismounted. My feet touched the ground, and I bit my lip to stifle a groan. With the full weight on my legs, the pain was intense, and I leaned against Alta for support. She let out a soft nicker, and I patted her neck. "I'm okay," I whispered. "I'll ask Danya for more tea as soon as we're settled."

Griffin strode to his father and Abril. "Is there room for us, too, or do we quarter in the barn?" he asked without a flicker of emotion.

Paxton scowled and motioned to the house. "Inside. I see it took official orders for you to pay a visit."

"The last one hardly came with an invitation to return."

Paxton snorted. "How would you know? You didn't stay long enough for a decent conversation."

Griffin's jaw tightened. "All our conversations end in shouting. I wanted no more of it, although it's the language you understand best."

"It wouldn't be this way, if you hadn't stolen my granddaughter from me."

"That's not true. Abril was old enough to make her own choice and joined the guard willingly."

"You could have stopped her."

"Jess?" said Melanie. "How are you feeling?"

I jumped at the touch of a ghostly hand on my arm. "I'm fine," I blurted, rubbing away the sensation. "Come back later. I'm not ready to leave."

"What did you say?" said Melanie. "Speak up, I can't hear you."

The haze deepened, clouding my vision of the house and Griffin. "I said, I'm fine," I shouted. I blinked repeatedly, but instead of fading the haze began to glow as if charged with spectral light. "I have to stay. Griffin needs my help."

"Jess!" called Griffin.

I looked around, but he had disappeared from sight. "I can't see you. The haze is too thick." I reached out my hand and touched another. My grip tightened. "Griffin, I'm here. I don't want to go."

"Go where?" said Melanie. "You're in the hospital. Owen, she's not waking up."

"Jess," said Dr. Turner. "Open your eyes now."

As if yanked by a cord, my body tore away from Griffin and into a void. Light on one side, shadow on the other, me in the middle.

A spark loomed in front of me, dancing between light and dark. *I am waiting,* the darkling said. *The stone was mine once and will be again.* Without warning, the spark lunged, but the light instantly formed a protective barrier around me, and it fell back, howling in pain.

"Ha!" I shouted in triumph. "You're not omnipotent. That hurt."

Mine! the darkling screamed. *Give me what is mine, or I will destroy you all.*

L. A. Kelley

"Never." I turned my back on the spark and embraced the light.

Chapter Eleven

My eyelids fluttered open.

"It's about time," said Melanie. She stood next to Dr. Turner. Her face, creased with worry lines, hovered over mine.

My hand was empty, fingers crooked as if still holding onto Griffin. "I'm back."

Melanie grinned. "Don't sound so disappointed."

Dr. Turner patted my shoulder. "Technically, you never left."

"Right." I licked my lips. "Is it…is it over?"

"Yes. Feel like sitting?"

"Sure."

Dr. Turner elevated the head of the hospital bed, and without thinking, I reached for the velvet bag with the Rose Stone, but only found the sketchbook at my side. The wave of disorientation from flitting between worlds quickly passed. The nurse unhooked the beeping monitor, but the IV remained in my arm. I flexed my fingers and winced at a muscle spasm. My legs ached, too. "How long was I under?"

"Six hours," said Melanie.

"Really?" I said, trying hard to mute any flippancy. "I could have sworn it was days."

Melanie sat on the edge of the bed and took my hand. "You were talking about Griffin again."

"I know he's imaginary," I said in a rush. "I'm

trying to finish the painting, so he's been on my mind a lot." I turned to Dr. Turner. "Can I get out of here now?"

He and Melanie exchanged a look. "Not yet. I want to hear more about Griffin."

I leered at him. "I'm not comfortable sharing my sexual fantasies with you."

Melanie glared at me. "She's kidding."

"I checked on you several times and you seemed to be having a conversation about a stone," said Dr. Turner. "Are you hearing voices again? Did you see more of that pink haze?"

I forced a smile. "Well, yes, but it was obviously a dream."

"Your eyes opened," said Melanie, sternly. "You called for Griffin and said he was lost in a haze. I don't believe you were dreaming."

"We need to treat this, Jess," said Dr. Turner gently. "I'll prescribe meds to keep them at bay."

I fought to quash a swell of rising panic. "Really, I'm fine. How do I know you're not a hallucination?"

"That isn't funny," said Melanie. "You need to be honest with us. How's your pain level? And don't tell me it's fine. You've been making that face since you woke, and your hands and legs are shaking."

I blew out my cheeks in resignation. "They hurt."

"I have something for that, too," said Dr. Turner. "With the IV, the effect will be almost immediate."

The panic crested to a tidal wave. "I-I don't want to be doped up. Okay, you're right. I have been hearing voices, but I know they're not real. I can function and need to work on my painting."

"If anything, the medication will help," Dr. Turner

said in a soothing voice. "You'll be sharper without pain as a distraction. Are you sure I can't check you into the hospital? You have to return tomorrow anyway for the second treatment."

"No, I'd rather go home. Painting relaxes me, and besides, I sleep better in my own bed."

Dr. Turner hesitated a moment and then said, "All right. I'll be back with the meds."

He left the room and Melanie gave me what my grandmother used to call the old fisheye. "I don't buy your 'I'm totally in control and know it's not real' story," she said in a huff. "You were way out of it."

"I couldn't have been too far gone. I heard you call my name and woke up."

"You didn't seem as if you wanted to. Tell me more about Griffin."

"Why?"

"The way you spoke to him, I'd swear he has a strange hold on you. When you called out his name, you closed your fingers as if you actually touched his hand. There was genuine fear in your voice."

I forced a grin. "Well, he obviously doesn't exist, because I'm here and not in dreamland."

"That isn't the point." Melanie leaned toward me. "Jess, I'm worried."

"Dr. Turner isn't."

"Owen doesn't know you like I do. You've focused more and more on a man who isn't real. He's invaded your mind. This obsession to get back to the painting, for instance. Would it be so bad if you didn't work on it for a few days?"

"Melanie, painting keeps my mind preoccupied and not obsessing over my health as you are. Maybe you should take up painting."

"Jess—"

"Don't worry. I'll take my meds, be a good girl, and do nothing but work on the canvas. Deal?"

"All right," she said with obvious reluctance. "But I'm going to keep an eye on you."

Dr. Turner entered with a tray holding two syringes and two vials. "The first is for the tremors and aches. The other will block the hallucinations." He loaded the syringes and injected them directly into the IV tube.

I watched anxiously, forcing myself to relax, as the liquids seeped into my body. *The meds can't keep me from Griffin. They prevent hallucinations and he's real.* Within a few minutes, the pain disappeared, and my limbs stopped trembling.

Dr. Turner patted my shoulder. "How do you feel now?"

I wiggled my toes without so much as a twinge of discomfort. "Much better, thank you. I'm sorry to be such a baby."

"I understand. Despite living a healthy life, your body betrayed you, and being a test case for a radical new procedure is scary. This treatment requires giving up complete control, and that's tough for anyone. Just remember, Melanie and I are on your side."

That was the truth. They had nothing but kindness in their eyes and sympathy in their voices. Dr. Turner and Melanie were good people who wanted to help me, and I had no way to push them aside without sounding crazy.

"The medication should last until you return tomorrow," said Dr. Turner. "I'll give another dose then. You'll have one more treatment, and then I've scheduled an MRI for the following day to check the tumor's response rate."

"Thank you, Dr. Turner. I appreciate what you're trying to do for me." Despite any apprehension the medication would cut me off from the Commonwealth, I meant every word.

"I'll wait in the hall," said Melanie, jumping off the bed. "I want a word with Owen."

The nurse unhooked the IV. I put on my shoes and jacket. Although I had no pain, my arms and legs were leaden as if I had overtaxed the muscles. "Well, it was a long trip to Paxton's farm from Stone Keep," I muttered with a grin.

Were Griffin and his father still arguing? I left in the middle of a doozy but collapsing in front of them probably put a damper on the conversation. I drew in a deep breath and quieted my thoughts, straining to hear the beat of Danya's drum. Nothing came but the sound of muted voices in in the hall. I slipped the sketchpad into my bag and grabbed the cane.

Melanie poked her head in the room. "Ready to go or are you hungry? Maybe you should eat first."

I made a sour face. "Hospital food? No thanks, but I could go for a meal. It's been hours since we broke out rations."

"Rations?" Melanie eyed me with amusement. "Did you enlist in the army and forget to tell me?"

"No," I sputtered. "I mean, I meant…oh, never mind. Let's get something to eat."

We stopped for Chinese takeout on the way home, but Melanie made me sit in the car, so I didn't exert myself. I had no desire to argue and no wish for exercise. Although my legs were pain free, and I didn't need the cane to steady myself, my body was limp and nearly drained of energy. I felt like a run-down, battery-operated toy that worked in fits and starts.

The wind blew hard, generating a high-pitched whine as it whipped across the powerlines. The lights in the Chinese restaurant winked on and off. A man talking on a cellphone walked to the car parked in the next spot. "You're breaking up," he shouted. "I can barely hear—" He yelped as a spark shot from the display. He let out a curse and dropped the cellphone on the ground, shaking his hand.

I leaned out the window. "Are you okay?"

"Fine," he said retrieving the phone. "Damn batteries. Cellphone companies swear nothing is wrong, but they've been catching fire without warning. It happened to my girlfriend yesterday. Pieces of junk." He tore off the back panel, and a wisp of smoke rose in the air. "Look at that, fried to a crisp."

A cold chill raced up my spine as he got into his car and drove away. I stared at the powerline. It continued to sing in the gusty breeze, an eerie high-pitched tuneless melody. "Calm down," I murmured. "It's just the wind."

Melanie returned carrying several bags. "The lights flickered on the street," I said. "Has that happened a lot?"

"All over town, and they've gotten worse since yesterday. They pop up and disappear, no rhyme or reason."

My hands went cold and clammy, and I rubbed them against my jeans. "As if someone is testing the grid?"

"That doesn't make sense. No one would run a test

on the grid except the power company, and they deny causing the outages." Melanie's brow creased in a puzzled frown. "Although now that you mention it, while you were under one of the nurses at the hospital told me her husband works at the plant and they can't find anything wrong. The engineers first thought a hacker was responsible, but they didn't find any signs of breached security."

My mouth went dry. "Did you say breach?"

"That's what he called it, a breach. Anyway, he insisted it can't be a hacker because the outages are happening everywhere now, not only here but abroad and the grids aren't connected. Power fluctuations start and then stop. Cellphone service has been wonky, too, and that's a completely different system. The latest news reports suggest a relation to atmospheric conditions, sunspots or cosmic rays or whatever."

We reached my building. Melanie offered an arm to help me climb the stairs, but I shooed her ahead and took my time. When I got to the loft, she had dinner laid out on the coffee table. I sank into the couch with a grateful sigh. While she doled out plates of cashew chicken, I turned on the TV. The top stories on the news were the scattered outages on the electric and cellphone grids. Each lasted no more than a few seconds at a time, mysteriously appearing and disappearing, as Melanie had said. Even remote locations experienced odd fluctuations.

A spokesperson for the power company stated they were monitoring the situation and expected no long-term negative effects. I snorted in disgust and turned off the TV. "That means they're keeping their fingers crossed it doesn't get worse." The uneasy feeling that burrowed inside me since I saw the man with the cellphone remained.

"I'm not worried," said Melanie. "It's more annoyance than anything. A few minor outages occurred at the hospital today while you were under, and it was no big deal. They have a powerful generator, and it kicked in immediately." She cleared away the leftovers. "I can spend the night on the couch."

"That's sweet, but not necessary. I'm much better. Besides you don't have any of your lady things with you, and I don't want your cootie fingers touching my stuff."

"Very funny. Can I get you anything before I go? Another cup of hot tea?"

"Tea would be nice."

Melanie poured me a cup and then wandered over to the painting, peered at it, and gave me a funny look. "You added yourself to the story."

I choked mid-sip and hurriedly set down the tea.

"Are you okay?" she asked.

"Fine," I sputtered, getting to my feet. "Swallowed too fast." I hurried to the easel and gawked at the painting. Sure enough, my image sat atop Alta, riding at Griffin's side. The setting had the same perspective as the drawing I did in Danya's garden. However, that had been more of a rough sketch. This new addition was in colorful oils with the extra little details I would surely have added, including creases in the riding leathers and shadows on the ground. Even a glistening Rose Stone rested in my hand. Every bit duplicated my touch and style as if the composition had been plucked from my mind.

"Why did you add yourself?" asked Melanie.

"Don't read anything into it," I insisted. "It's pure escapism. Reality hasn't been much fun for me lately, so I thought I'd plunk myself in the middle of a fairytale."

"I like the leather outfit," said Melanie. "It's practical and sexy. What's the pink, shiny thing? Is that the Rose Stone?"

"Yes." I couldn't tear my gaze away. The color had a glossy photographic sheen and seemed to emit a soft glow.

"The effect on the stone is so cool," said Melanie. "How'd you do that?"

"Um, I'm experimenting with a new technique."

"It's great. Keep at it. So, what's the plot? You and Griffin look dead set on a mission."

"I'm working out the details, but the Rose Stone is dying and can't protect the Commonwealth much longer. Griffin and I are on a journey to find a way to heal her."

"The Rose Stone is female, not just a rock?"

"Yeah." I smiled. "She speaks to me and definitely has a feminine attitude and a mind of her own."

Melanie nudged me. "This is a fairytale quest with a romance. No wonder you've been obsessed with the hero."

"I'm not obsessed with Griffin, but you know me. I think every story needs a little romance."

"Do you?"

I looked at her, puzzled. "Do I what?"

"Ever find a way to heal the Rose Stone?"

"Oh," I stammered. "I don't know. I haven't finished yet."

Melanie hugged me. "Well, be sure to give the

romance a happy ending. What's the point otherwise?"

"Right," I murmured. "What's the point?"

Melanie said goodnight and left. As soon as the door shut behind her, I dug the sketchbook from my bag and flipped through the pages. My heart skipped a beat. I had made the drawing on a separate sheet of paper and given it to Griffin at Highpoint Garrison, but somehow it remained in my sketchbook. I held it up to compare with the painting. The composition was identical except for the addition of the Rose Stone. Even an untrained eye could see it was done by the same hand. Except I didn't do it.

Or did I?

Did my connection to the Commonwealth run deeper than I thought? Had my thoughts and actions in that place been transferred to a canvas here? I absentmindedly rubbed a fingertip over the Rose Stone on the painting. Was it merely friction, wishful thinking, or did I detect a slight sensation of heat? Either way, it was warm and comforting and not one bit scary.

"Keeping an eye on me?" I whispered. "Or are you trying to remind me about our link? I won't fight it. Please, if you know, tell me how to access the power from here so I can return."

No answer came from staring at the canvas, so I put down the sketchbook on the worktable and took a brush, the tip poised in front of the surface, seeking inspiration. "Not Griffin and me or the Rose Stone," I murmured. "They're done, but the painting needs more."

I closed my eyes and recalled the map and the landscape surrounding Paxton's holdings. Ringing the fields were craggy hills, looking as if they had sprung from the ground with no discernable pattern. Which were natural and which held buried secrets?

I opened my eyes and flipped the pages to the contour map. To get a real sense of the hills, I needed to draw them, but not from a warbird's perspective. I grabbed the pallet and squeezed out dabs of primary colors—blue, yellow, red. Mix the blue and yellow for green, red and green for brown. A spot of blue here to deepen shadows, a bit of white and yellow for brightness.

When I was in the zone, the brush acted like a part of my hand, directly wired to my brain, a conduit for inspiration. The images practically flowed from me to the canvas. How long I worked at the easel was a mystery, but I finally stepped back, completely spent. I put down the palette and studied the painting. It was perfect—no, not quite. I dabbed bright crimson halfway up one of the hills, the mark of the rose, and the message came through loud and clear.

"That's the spot on the contour map." I said. "We have to head northeast from the farm and find that hill." But the distance and route remained a question. The map didn't show a road.

My shoulders sagged. I peered at Griffin. His facial features, so stalwart, yet comforting, now appeared to display a gently chiding manner. "Rest for now," he seemed to say. "You've done enough."

"You're a painting," I said with a smile. "Quit nagging me."

I was too tired to do anything else except clean my brushes and palette. I staggered to bed, shedding my clothes on the floor along the way, and crawled between the sheets with the feeling I accomplished an important task. I opened my mind to Griffin's call, but nothing invaded the silence of the night.

****

I woke the next morning to disappointment. This wasn't where I wanted to be. Instead of Paxton's farm, I was in the loft. I sat up and threw off the covers and then rubbed a painful spasm from my calves. Dr. Turner's medication gave me a good night's sleep but had started wearing off. To add to my gloom, I had a dull headache and didn't dream of Griffin. No drumbeats from Danya, no calls from the warbirds either.

The painting was as I left it yesterday, no additions or subtractions, but gazing at the canvas gave me renewed strength. "I'm waiting," Griffin's expression seemed to say. "You have the courage to find the way back to me."

"I will," I said. "I won't stop searching."

I ate breakfast in front of the TV. Again, the power outages were the top story. They had spread but not worsened, lasting only seconds at a time. Even so, they left me anxious, and I turned off the report.

Melanie arrived. I put the sketchbook in my purse, and we headed to the hospital. We were early, so I sat in the waiting area while she went to get us coffee.

"It was so weird," said a hushed voice. "The whole thing gave me the creeps." I looked around. Two nurses chatted at the counter. Neither noticed me listening.

"What happened?" asked the other one, eyes wide.

"They wheeled the patient out of surgery and hooked him to the monitors in the ICU. I made my rounds and checked on him last. He was doing well, vital signs normal, but on a drip for pain. As I stood there reading the chart, the lights flickered and then…" She snapped her fingers. "Like that, the machine cut out, and the painkiller stopped. He groaned. It started and then cut out. Off, then on, back and forth, as if someone flipped a switch, toying with the patient to see how much pain he could stand."

She shuddered. "Then everything went back to normal. The machine's readout didn't show any interruption in medication. It happened so fast, I wondered if I imagined it. I checked on the other patients in ICU and asked at the desk. No one on duty noticed anything unusual, and none of the monitors showed problems."

"What did you do?" asked the other nurse.

"To be on the safe side, I swapped out machines and called the med tech. He ran a diagnostic. The machine was functioning normally. He called it a false reading due to the power fluctuations, but I swear it happened. That's not the only strange thing." She leaned over the counter. Her voice dropped, and I strained to hear. "One of the EMTs told me the number of burn calls has skyrocketed over the past few days. Appliances and electronic devices have been emitting crazy sparks for no reason."

My blood ran cold.

"At first, they were annoyances, but now they're doing real harm to people," she said. "We're treating more second-degree burns."

The other nurse shivered and hugged herself, rubbing her arms up and down. "What's gotten into the world lately? I've had problems getting my car started, too."

"I heard it's sunspots. Let's hope those in the know develop a fix. I can't imagine living without my cellphone."

"Yeah, with no technology, this whole place falls apart."

"Your room is ready," said Melanie, plopping down beside me.

My heart skipped a beat. "Geez, give me a little warning next time."

"Were you snooping?" she asked, in a mock scolding tone. "Don't you know that's rude? What were they talking about? If it's hospital gossip, I want to know."

"The power outages."

Melanie gave a nonchalant wave of the hand. "That's boring stuff. Put them out of your mind. I told you, the hospital has an excellent generator. Any power interruptions are momentary. I hardly notice them."

I went into the treatment room and stretched out on the bed, clutching the sketchbook tight. A nurse attached me to the monitors. Dr. Turner entered, and we exchanged pleasantries. Although I hadn't returned to the Commonwealth last night, the anticipation of a second dose of medication brought rising excitement and quelled my anxiety. Surely, I'd find the way back today.

"Your heart rate is up," he said. "Worried?"

"No, I'm good, eager to begin."

"I'm glad to hear that. Any hallucinations?"

"None."

Melanie chuckled. "Don't look so disappointed. That Griffin must be hot stuff. Hoping to run into him?"

I shot a sly look at Melanie and Dr. Turner. "Well,

he's not a single doctor in case either of you have an interest in single doctors." I was pleased to see both of them flush. "By the way, Dr. Turner, Mel is free for lunch."

"Please put her under before she says anything else," said Melanie tartly.

"My pleasure," said Dr. Turner. He gave Melanie a shy smile, but she was watching me and didn't notice.

Dr. Turner injected the medications for hallucinations, pain, and muscle weakness first and then the dose to shrink the tumor. Again, I had slight burning at the IV site and then slow lethargy advanced through my body.

"I'll see you this afternoon," said Melanie, giving my arm a squeeze.

A nurse stuck her head in the room. "You're wanted at the desk, Dr. Turner."

"Thanks. I'll be back to check on you soon, Jess." He and Melanie left together.

The nurse came over to me and placed the call button next to my hand. "How are you feeling, hon? Can I get you anything? How about a bottle of water?"

"Sure." I yawned. "But I may be asleep by the time you get back."

"No problem. I'll put it on the nightstand. It'll be there if you need it."

She left the room. I settled into the pillow, lulled by the comforting beep of the medical monitor. Soon the meds would take effect and I'd drift away to dreamland. This time I'd surely find my way again to the Commonwealth of the Rose. I would listen for the drum and Griffin's voice and then take a leap of faith. He promised he'd be there for me, and he was a man who never broke his word.

Beep, beep, beep.

"Anytime now," I mumbled, sinking into pleasant drowsiness.

Beep, beep, beep… sissss.

"What the…?" My eyes opened, and I turned my head to the readout keeping track of my heart rate. The screen showed the normal series of regular spikes. Up and down, up and down.

Above them, from peak to peak, danced a tiny spark.

The hissing increased, drowning the beep. The spark melded into the display line. The spikes flatlined and then shivered. A peak became a whirl, twisting around and around to form a series of big and small loops joined together with lines. My heart hammered as the loops and lines became words.

I see you.

I gripped the sheet. "No, you can't be here."

The nurse entered with the bottle. The words collapsed, and the steady beep resumed. She moved to the side of the bed and blocked the screen. "I told you I'd be back soon. Do you want me to open the water?"

I forced a smile. "No, thanks. Leave it on table. Do you…is that monitor working?"

She stepped aside and glanced at the machine. It showed the regular series of spikes and valleys. "It's fine, hon, although your heart rate is slightly elevated. Feeling all right? I can have Dr. Turner take a look."

"No. I'm okay." I swallowed again. "A bit anxious, though."

The line on the monitor behind her shimmered again. *Let's play.* The words dissolved back into normal spikes.

"Perfectly understandable," said the nurse. "Now, you relax. The drugs will kick in soon and you'll fall asleep. I'm surprised you haven't already."

The lights in the ceiling flickered. From the hallway came the sound of running footsteps. A voice over the intercom called, "Code blue," and the nurse stiffened.

"What happened?" I asked.

"Medical emergency. I have to go, but I'll be back to check on you." She hurried out the door.

Sissss.

A spark flitted across the monitor's screen. It left a trail of words like a child trying to write their name with a sparkler, but these stayed suspended long enough to read before fading to black.

One machine, then another. Soon they will fall to me.

"What are you?" I demanded. "Where did you come from?"

I am I. More footsteps ran past the door. From the hallway came muffled voices imbued with a sense of urgency. *The spark beats inside your people. Those here need machines to live but take away the spark and death comes. Soon, all paths laid bare. Breaches open. Carvers attack. Life dies. The spark is mine.*

Helpless rage swelled inside me. "We'll fight."

Fight then lose then die. Easy. The lights flickered again. *When this world's spark is mine, the world is mine. Unlesss...* The threat ended in a hiss.

"Unless what?" I spit out.

The stone is mine. I jumped as a spark flew from the machine. It landed on the end table and then sputtered out, leaving a tiny singe mark. *If the stone is mine, breaches will never open. This world is safe.*

"Liar."

Truth.

"What about the Commonwealth?"

They took the stone and will pay the price. One world lives or both worlds die. Carvers mass even now, ready to swarm, eager to kill at my command. You choose.

I narrowed my eyes. Something stunk about this offer, and suspicion crept into my mind. "Why the big rush and the sudden increase in attacks? Why not wait? The Rose Stone weakens. The barrier will fall soon, and no one in the Commonwealth can stand against your army."

Bring the stone now.

"Do I sense a hint of desperation?" I mocked. "Is your power weakening, too? You expected to have the Rose Stone in your grasp long before now. You're running out of time."

The line quivered as if the darkling's rage was barely contained. *Strong enough to take this world, feast on this spark. It will sustain me while the fight continues.* The display spit and crackled. *Days, weeks, years. Time means nothing to me. Eventually, the stone will be mine. Choose before both worlds fall.*

The line flattened and then resumed the steady peaks and valleys. I sank into the pillow, shaking, gaze fixed to the display, but the spark had vanished. I drew long, deep breaths, in and out. The spiky jumps of the readout slowed as my heart settled into a normal rhythm. I had a funny feeling the medical personnel would never note anything in the readout but a regular heartbeat. The darkling would see to that and give no one else in this world a warning of what was to come.

The burning sensation in my arm returned. My limbs went numb as the medication took effect. I dropped my free hand to the sketchbook at my side. "Griffin," I whispered. "Are you there? I need your help to find the way back."

Beep, beep, beep.

I shut my eyes.

Beep, beep, beep.

Tap, tap, tap.

"Jess," called Griffin. "Follow the drum."

A hand closed around my fingers. I latched on and chased the beat along the mystic trail.

Chapter Twelve

I opened my eyes, stifling a cry of relief. Griffin peered down at me with an anxious expression, and I laughed with joy. "We've got to stop meeting this way."

He took my hand and held it to his cheek. "Welcome back."

Danya stood behind him, holding the drum. "How do you feel?"

"No pain or headache. The doctor gave me more medication, so I'm good for a while." I lay in bed, covered with a blanket. "How long was I gone?"

"Through the night and into the day. You returned an hour ago."

I sat up straight. "The Rose Stone?"

"Safe at your side," said Griffin.

I dropped Griffin's hand and threw back the covers. The velvet bag lay next to me. I opened it and breathed a sigh of relief at the rosy glow from within. "We have to get going," I said in a rush, swinging my legs to the floor. "We're running out of time. The darkling followed me into my world and is inching through the systems. I have to stop it before it controls the power grid and the carvers come—"

"Where exactly do you wish to go?" said Griffin with a smile.

I froze. "I-I know the general direction.

Somewhere in the hills."

"Peace, Jess." Griffin helped me to my feet. "You have new information. That's good, but we can't rush blindly into the wilderness. First, we need a plan. Tell us what happened."

I described the addition of the tiny rose to the painting and the confrontation with the spark. "I'm sure we have to head to the same spot as the rose on the contour map."

Danya said, "Before anything is done you must keep up your strength. Breakfast will be ready by now. I'll make tea, and we'll discuss our plans." She left the room, and Griffin and I were alone.

"Actually, breakfast sounds good," I said. "I'm hungry and Danya's tea is as charged as a cup of strong coffee."

"You've spoken of coffee at other times. Is it a medicine?"

"Not really, but it sure gets me going in the morning." I felt a draft on my legs and looked down. I was barefoot and wearing nightclothes. "Um, something's different."

"After you returned, I brought you here. Abril and Danya dressed you in one of Abril's old gowns. Your clothes are on the chair."

"Thanks. Sorry to be such a bother."

"You aren't."

There were shadows under Griffin's eyes. "You must have been awake the entire night," I said. "Did you eat anything?"

He shrugged. "I had little appetite."

My heart beat faster. Despite wearing a nightshift, I wasn't cold. The surrounding air even seemed to grow warmer. "I heard you calling."

"And you answered," he said.

"Yes." Awkward silence stretched to several seconds and then I said, "I take it I'm in the farmhouse."

"This is my old room. I'll wait for you downstairs in the kitchen." He stepped into the hallway and shut the door.

The thought of sleeping in Griffin's bed brought a smile to my face and a tingle in parts of me that hadn't tingled in a while. I hurriedly dressed and then sat on the bed to pull on my shoes and felt a nudge at my side. The sack with the Rose Stone had rolled next to me. I took her out and rubbed my finger over the surface.

In outward appearance, the stone had the same warmth and glow, yet something seemed different. Frowning, I peered into the facets, hunting what hid beneath. A sensation of falling enveloped me, and then I spotted the black knot buried deep inside her. The location had shifted. No—the location was the same, the facets were identical in size and shape, only the knot differed. The tendrils remained, but some were stunted and wizened. As I watched, one broke off and faded to nothing.

I blinked and found myself rising to the surface again, but this time with renewed hope. "If the darkling's knot shrunk and some tendrils have disappeared, does that mean the same for my tumor?" I asked. In answer, a sense of encouragement filled me. That was good enough for now. "So before I toss you back in the bag, any thoughts on Griffin's feelings?" I asked with a grin.

The Rose Stone deepened in color. I laughed and

slung the sack over my shoulder. "Yeah, my feelings about him to a T."

I went downstairs to the kitchen, and Griffin pulled out the chair next to him for me. Danya tended a kettle of water at the stove, while a servant bustled about setting the table. "Will there be anything else?" she asked Danya, putting down the last plate.

"No, thank you." Danya took the kettle off the stove.

The woman grabbed a basket from the floor and opened the back door. Paxton stood on the stoop, knocking mud off his boots against a scraper. Apparently, having a strange woman collapse and vanish in his front yard and then reappear hadn't altered his work schedule. The servant edged past and scampered away as if eager to go.

Paxton grunted. "I see she's awake."

"*She* has a name," I said. "It's Jessica Rose Stone, but please call me Jess." Griffin turned his head away, but not before I caught the hint of a smile.

"Paxton. But I suppose you know that already," he muttered.

"I do, and it's a pleasure to meet you."

"Is it now?" He narrowed his eyes at his son and then strode past to wash his hands in the sink.

"Yes," I said. "Your farm is beautiful. I love the blue door."

"My late wife's idea. She had an eye for such things."

"She saw beauty everywhere," said Griffin in a low voice.

"She loved the farm," said Paxton. His expression softened and then hardened again. "Unlike others who saw fit to leave."

Griffin rolled his eyes, and the muscles in his jaw clenched. I braced for another argument, but the door opened, and Abril and Bram entered. "We did a circuit of the farm, Captain, and rode to the base of the hills, but did not venture farther as you ordered," said Bram. "The perimeter is secure."

Abril went to a drawer in a sideboard, took out the sketchbook, and handed it to me. "I hope you don't mind, but I showed the map to Grandfather." Her eyes sparkled. "You had a vision of Father as a child and drew him, too."

"Yes, well, not exactly a vision," I stammered. "I mean, I thought it was my imagination, but, obviously, it wasn't." *Stop babbling.* "Wow, that smells good."

"Breakfast is ready," said Danya, pouring the tea.

As we ate, I explained what happened at home. Paxton's gaze stayed fixed on the bag holding the Rose Stone. "Do you want to see?" I asked. Without waiting for an answer, I took her out, and she glowed softly in my hand.

Paxton's eyes widened, and he drew in a sharp breath. "It's magnificent."

"She," I corrected lightly. "Do you want to hold her?"

He seemed to regard the suggestion with horror and shrunk back in his seat. "I don't dare."

"She won't bite." Before he uttered a protest, I grabbed his hand and placed the Rose Stone on it.

"I-it, I mean, she is warm," he stammered.

"The Rose Stone lives in her own way," said Danya. "She's a loving mother who watches out for her children, even sending messages to other worlds for help."

Paxton stroked the Rose Stone with a gentle touch, and a slight smile twitched his lips. The first one I'd seen today. It vanished in a flash, but not before I marked dimples in his cheeks, too. Like father, like son.

He handed her back to me. "Thank you, Lady Jess."

"Anytime." I returned the Rose Stone to the bag. "And call me Jess."

Danya cocked her head and studied me with sharp eyes. "The darkling followed you. That is troubling news. I'm sorry, Jess. Linking to the Commonwealth brought danger to your world, and if we cannot heal the Rose Stone, worse will come."

"It's not your fault," I said. "The darkling hunts the spark and may have found its way to my time and place, eventually. At least we have warning, although no one will believe me." I made a face. "They think I'm having hallucinations."

Bram chuckled. "I understand their concern completely."

"The darkling is weakening," mused Griffin, rubbing his chin. "Now, that's interesting. We believed its power intensified, but the increased frequency of the attacks is merely a sign of desperation."

"I don't see how that helps us, Father," said Abril.

"A desperate enemy makes mistakes. We have always thought the darkling unstoppable. The Rose Stone is our most powerful defense, but even with the boundary in place, she can only keep its evil at bay. Jess discovered a hidden truth. The darkling has a link to the Rose Stone and infected her with poison. The purpose is not destruction but to weaken the boundary enough to forge through, capture the Rose Stone, and bind her power. Sever the link, and perhaps the Rose Stone will be able to halt the final confrontation before it begins."

Paxton's eyes widened, and he turned to me. "Killing the darkling is possible? The breaches will end?"

"I can't say for sure," I said. "I have just bits and pieces of information and a sense from the Rose Stone we're on the right track. I only know I have to find a way to help her." I pushed the sketchbook to him. "Check out the map. Maybe you'll see something familiar."

Paxton opened the sketchbook and slowly turned the pages, pausing to peer at the ones of Griffin and the farmhouse. "You drew these as a child?"

"Yes. Strange, huh? I'd forgotten about them until a short time ago. Even now the memory is hazy, but that must have been the day I formed the link with the Rose Stone."

"Or with Father," said Abril with a cheeky grin.

Paxton shot me a curious look and then flipped to the map and pointed to the little rose. "This is on the easternmost trailhead along the foot of the hills, an unusual location to mark."

"Why?" I asked.

"As a boy, I'd go with my father to search for metal scrap to sell. Pieces were common then and fetched a good price, but over the years, the land shifted and became unstable. Landslides killed scavengers. No one goes there now. It's not worth the risk."

"Boulders block the end of the path, but the warbirds might find a way around or the rocks may have shifted again and cleared the route," said Griffin.

Paxton narrowed his eyes. "How do you know that?"

"I explored on a hunting trip but wasn't able to get that far."

He stiffened. "I ordered you not to take the trail to the hills. The ground was too treacherous."

"I told the deer, but they didn't listen, so Cirrus and I followed them," Griffin said coolly.

"You could have been killed," he snapped.

"I was careful and returned when Cirrus decided the route was too unstable." Griffin leaned forward, the muscles in his neck tightening. "You should have trusted me to make the right decision. After all, I am your son. You taught me to hunt and tread carefully, not wander blindly into danger."

I decided this was no time to hash out old family issues and jumped in. "So, these are burial mounds from the old days. What did you see?"

"Not all hold the dead," said Paxton. "Most are barren, craggy hills, but the ones with bits of metal had an eerie feel to them. There were cracks and crevices with deep shadows that appeared to lead underground. We camped at the base, and my father forbade me to explore them because of the danger." He glowered at Griffin. "I obeyed him."

If he expected an argument, Griffin refused. He pushed back his chair and stood up. "I'll send Racer and Sojourn to sweep the area and hunt for the best passage."

Paxton's face reddened. "I suppose you'll take my granddaughter, too. It's foolish to risk her life."

"He's my captain," said Abril sharply. "I'm proud

to follow him. I trust his judgment as you trusted your own father's."

Paxton swung his head toward me. "How can you be certain you'll find something there?"

"I'm not, but I drew the rose in that location for a reason, and I agree with Griffin. We have to go."

Griffin strode to the door. "Sergeant, Corporal, with me." They rose and followed him, so did Danya.

Paxton watched them go. His expression twisted in a scowl, but I caught more than that—fear welling in his eyes.

"I get it," I said. "You're more afraid for them than angry but too stubborn to admit it."

"You know nothing of me."

"I know it's a good thing Griffin was on patrol when I arrived in the Commonwealth. If he hadn't been in the guard and killed the carver, I wouldn't be here today. No one would know the darkling is poisoning the Rose Stone. She might even be under its control by now." My exasperation rose with his silence. "Your son is a brave man, an exceptional warrior, respected by his troops, his commander, and the chancellor. Do you think they would have sent him on this mission otherwise? That's quite an accomplishment for a man who started as a farmer's son. Stop being angry at him."

He gritted his teeth. "You are free with advice, Lady Jess. My family is not your concern."

"I told you to call me Jess," I said. "Let's not be so formal, if we're going to yell at each other." He merely grunted, but the tense lines on his face eased. "I haven't known your family long, but they mean a lot to me. Make your peace with Griffin now. Because if the worst happens, and he doesn't return from this mission, you'll never forgive yourself." I added in a joking manner, "Besides, Abril's young. She'll eventually marry and have kids. Maybe you can turn one of them into a farmer, but that won't happen if your attitude chases her away."

Paxton turned his piercing gaze from the window to me. "The same can be said of Griffin."

I felt a flush rise to my cheeks and decided it was time for me to exit. Griffin was in the yard, standing in front of a low fence ringing the garden. Racer and Sojourn perched on the top rail, cocking their heads as Griffin spoke to them. Racer screeched, flapping his wings. He launched into the air, and Sojourn followed. I stood next to Griffin and watched with him as the warbirds caught a rising thermal and then banked toward the hills.

"I see you survived your first conversation with my father," he said dryly.

"Aw, Paxton's not so scary. He's still miffed at you though, for taking Abril away and allowing her to join the guard. He can't see she has a will of her own and would have left eventually, the same as you."

Griffin shot a dour look at the farmhouse. "The world turns, seasons change, but my father's mind remains rooted in place."

"Paxton is more afraid than angry. He understands the danger faced by the guard. He loves you and Abril. What comes across as anger is actually fear for your lives."

"You are so sure."

"No doubt about it." I gave him a playful nudge. "Don't forget, he's my hallucination."

I was pleased to see a smile. Griffin shaded his

eyes from the sun, following the track of Racer and Sojourn as they shot toward the hills. "The path we need to follow is thick with undergrowth. The warbirds may not be able to spot an easy passage from the air."

"Oh, I was hoping they'd find a direct route."

"Their eyesight is keen, but warbirds can't see through trees. Danya may have better luck."

"Danya?"

"She has her own methods. She took her drum and went in search of a quiet place." Griffin snorted. "She said adverse vibrations near the house blocked her perceptions. I sent Bram and Abril along to keep watch. Do you feel up to a walk?"

"Yes, thanks." He offered his arm, and I took it. The medication Dr. Turner shot into my veins did the trick, no pain and not a single tremor, but it crossed my mind the support I enjoyed was more emotional than physical. The sun shone brighter with Griffin at my side.

We strolled past the garden, bordered by the same blue and white flowers as in the sketchbook drawing of the farm. They emitted a delicate lemony scent, and I gazed around with a smile. So much was similar to my world. Bees and butterflies danced around the blossoms, but many of the vegetables had unfamiliar shapes and sizes and resembled an assortment of exotic legumes and squashes. I didn't have enough of a green thumb to guess at the herbs, but nothing screamed, "This isn't real. You don't belong here." Except for the zebra-striped pigs and the lyrs, even the livestock wasn't totally out of place. Although, what Griffin called chickens swam in a pond and resembled a weird mashup between a cardinal and a duck.

We followed a footpath and then stopped at a plot of land ringed by trees and blooming with wildflowers. "My mother, my grandparents, and their parents are buried here along with Litha. My father will join them one day."

"It's a peaceful spot."

"When the war first began, panic set in, families were separated. Soldiers died far from their loved ones. Their bodies were buried where they fell. We sowed seeds on the graves and watched new life spring from the old. It brought some comfort to believe their spirits were bound with the earth. In this way, lost friends and relatives have remained connected to the Commonwealth. Do you have such beliefs?"

"We have many beliefs, but yours suit me better."

"Perhaps it bothers my father, too, that when the time comes, Abril and I will not be here to join with the land of our ancestors."

I tightened my grip on his arm. "Paxton will have to get used to the idea because you're not going to fall here. Not here, not now, not for a long time. I won't allow it. This is still my story."

"You may not be destined to write the ending."

"Try me."

He smiled and touched my cheek. "At times, you are as fierce as a carver."

My pulse raced. "Only when I don't get what I want."

He leaned toward me. The heat from his hand spread from my face through my body. "I'm a soldier, Jess. I lead a rough life with nothing to offer."

"Except your heart." My voice dropped to a whisper. "Whoever says I need more than that is a liar."

The earth seemed to pause to draw a breath. Our lips touched, and I felt that kiss right to my soul. It was an offer and a promise. I didn't need to hear the words. He would stand by my side and love me forever, and I accepted with my entire heart. I slid my hands up his chest to his neck. One thought filled my head. Everything I ever wanted was here. His hands went up my back. He pulled me hard against him, and the burdens I carried slipped away.

Griffin whispered in my ear, "Even as a boy, I sensed something missing from my life. The guard and Abril were enough to ignore the empty space in my heart. Duty and honor were all I required. Then the Rose Stone sent you to me, and the emptiness vanished." Griffin drew back. He cupped his hands around my face and gave me a searching look. "I have no right to your heart."

"Too late. It's already yours." I kissed him again and then laid my head against his chest and smiled. His heart beat as wildly as mine. "I want nothing more out of life than to stay here with you."

"As do I, but you will be called down the other road soon, back to your old life," he whispered softly.

"No!" I swallowed a knot in my throat. "Don't say that. I'll fight to stay, use every ounce of strength—"

"You can't." Griffin's eyes held wistful yearning. "Even drummers such as Danya with all their power can't cure your illness. The only hope is with your people. You must go back."

Tears stung my eyes. "That world has nothing to offer me."

"It has life, which no one here can give you." The naked desire in Griffin's face stole my breath. No man had ever looked at me that way. "I never would have believed a few hours with a woman who found me in a dream could fill my heart. Jessica Rose Stone, know that in either world my love is always with you."

"And mine with you."

I clung to him. Was this what my future held—the love of a man who can never be mine?

Thump-THUMP-tap-tap, thump-THUMP-tap-tap.

The bag at my side twitched. I startled and looked around.

"What is it?" asked Griffin.

"Danya's drum."

He gave me a puzzled look. "I hear nothing."

"It's not a sound, but a feeling. The Rose Stone senses it, too." The tug became more insistent, and I pointed into the woods. "She wants to go that way."

The Rose Stone led me through the trees and past a thicket to a small sunlit glade. As we approached, drumbeats became audible. Bram and Abril stood by a tree watching Danya. Her eyes were open, but they had a faraway look as she rapped lightly with palm then fingers, palm then fingers. Unconsciously, I swayed to the rhythm. No words or messages shot into my head, but I got an impression of Danya standing at the edge of a shoreline. She cast a wide net, first one way, then the other, a mystical fisherman hunting an elusive catch.

Bump-BUMP-bump-bump.   Bump-BUMP-bump-bump.

The Rose Stone throbbed against my hip, pulsing in time to the beat. I took her from the sack and stood next to Danya. The stone's light brightened and dimmed, the cadence echoing the drum's rhythm, as if they sang in chorus. The Rose Stone shifted in my grip, and now the tug went toward the hills.

Danya's shoulder's sagged, and then she straightened and drew a deep breath. "I'm sorry. I can't find the path."

"That's okay," I said with excitement. "The Rose Stone can."

Chapter Thirteen

Griffin's eyes widened. "She spoke to you?"

My breath quickened in excitement. "Not in words. But the message came across loud and clear. The Rose Stone knows what we're searching for and will lead us in the right direction."

Griffin peered at the sky. "Little daylight remains and it's too dangerous to explore the hills in the dark. We'll leave at first light." He ordered Bram and Abril to go with him to prepare.

They hurried away, but I lagged behind to walk with Danya. "It's fortunate for us you returned," she said. "The Rose Stone speaks to you more clearly than anyone."

"Actually, I think she spoke to your drum. I got the impression they're old friends."

Danya chuckled. "You may be right. Drummers forged a special connection to the Rose Stone from the beginning. She selected the first drummers and taught us healing and how to walk the mystic trails. Through them, she sounded the alarms and warned of breaches. You are bound with her, though, on an entirely different level." She narrowed her eyes at me. "I sense a change."

"The Rose Stone drew me into the facets again," I said. "The poison knot shrunk. I hope that's good news but can't be sure. It may be wishful thinking."

She patted my arm. "Wishful thinking is my favorite kind."

When we arrived at the farmhouse, Danya excused herself, explaining she also needed to prepare for travel and check her supply of medicinal herbs. Griffin, Abril, and Bram were busy, and I didn't wish to disturb them. Everyone had a purpose except me, so I took my sketchbook and went outside. I sat on a fence rail and surveyed the surroundings.

Soft wind tousled my hair, and a smile played on my lips. My early drawing of the farm had been made with a childish hand and was woefully incomplete. I didn't have the interesting details then.

I turned to a clean sheet of paper determined to start from scratch and capture the rustic beauty. I put the house, the yard, a barn, and the fields in the background. I positioned Griffin in the foreground on Cirrus. I was next to him on Alta. Behind us were Abril and Bram, and the warbirds soared overhead. The pencil practically flew over the page. Wrapped in the joy of capturing the peaceful tranquility, I had no pain or shaking and forgot about the tumor, the treatments, and even the threat of the darkling. Through grit and hard work, Griffin's ancestors had created a special place. I understood how the call to the guard tore Griffin and Abril away but also understood how Paxton would never be content anywhere else.

At the thought of Paxton, I smiled and drew him between rows of vegetables, leaning on a rake, surveying his own little kingdom with pride. He didn't appear the least bit threatening.

"You have a deft hand."

I nearly dropped the sketchbook. Paxton had come

up silently behind me and peered with interest over my shoulder.

"Sorry," he said gruffly. "Didn't mean to startle you."

"That's okay. I'm glad you approve."

"It's fine work. You are an artist?"

"Back in my world—yes."

"Your world?"

"Didn't Griffin tell you how I came here?"

"We don't speak much," he grunted, and his gaze went to the sketchbook again. "You put me in a picture."

"Well, you're part of this story now." I slid off the fence. "Do you want to hear mine?"

He nodded. "I would."

I laughed. "You're not much of a talker, Paxton."

I caught the hint of a smile, and he shrugged. "When I have something to say, I say it and be done." He wiped his brow. "A warm day. We can sit in the shade with a cool drink."

"That sounds lovely." His eyes widened as I slipped my arm around his, pleased he didn't pull away.

We strolled to the front porch. I settled in a rocker, and Paxton went into the house and returned with two mugs and an earthenware jug from which he poured a reddish liquid. "Cider from fruit in the orchards. It's the first press," he added. "That's the finest."

I took a sip. The cider was tangy and refreshing, with a mixture of apple, pear, and cranberry flavors. "Delicious. I could drink this every day."

"Would do you good. It's known to strengthen the blood, and you're a mite peaked."

I chuckled. "Ah, not a man to hold back his words.

I appreciate your honesty, Paxton, but I looked worse not too long ago." I took another sip and told my story. He leaned forward in his chair, the mug of cider forgotten in his hands, hanging on every word. "So, here I am," I said at the end. "On your doorstep, drinking the best cider I have ever had in my life, and enjoying the beauty of this place."

He frowned. "A journey to the hills is a hard ride over rough country, especially for someone ill. The trails aren't safe. Griffin shouldn't allow you to go."

"Griffin has no choice, as I won't be left behind. Besides, I'm the one linked to the Rose Stone. I'll have you know you're not the most stubborn person here," I said with a grin. "I have a reputation for thick-headedness as well. I made a promise to help the Commonwealth, and I'm going to keep it." I placed my hand on his. "I have every faith in your son to help me."

Paxton gazed at the fields. "He has always gone his own way, too, no matter what I say."

"Isn't that for the best? Do you really want him here when Chancellor Emlyn, the Commonwealth, and the Rose Stone need him more?"

Paxton gave me a searching look. "Do you need him, too?"

A flush crawled up my neck. "Well, yes. That is to say, we're in this together…" I broke off as the door opened.

Griffin glanced at our hands resting together, and a faint smile twitched his lips. "The foreman wants to speak with you, Father. He's in the barn." Paxton nodded at me and then hurried away.

Griffin's eyes sparkled in amusement. "You charmed him."

"Like father, like son."

"Charming the son was easy," he said. "But if you've made such a mark on Paxton, perhaps it is merely the hallucination asserting itself and you need another dose of Danya's healing tea."

I chuckled. "I'll take my chances."

Griffin helped me to my feet. "In the morning, Abril, Bram, and I will ride ahead and scout the area. If it's safe, I'll send for you."

"No, I'm coming, too. The medicine is working, but once it quits, I won't be much good to anyone."

"You are to me." We kissed again, and his touch lit an ember inside me. My breath quickened, and the ember burst into a flame. Such delightfully pleasant heat. We held each other tight. With Griffin in my arms, I'd never be cold again.

"I can't promise safety," he said softly. "I fear for this world, but most of all, I fear for you."

"No one can promise safety. If I were at home, I could walk across the street and get hit by a bus."

"A bus?"

"Never mind." I laughed softly. "I'm happy here and now. That's what matters most."

From around the back of the house came a shout from Bram for Griffin. "Duty calls," said Griffin with a sigh. He kissed me again and left, but the warm glow in my heart remained.

I spent the rest of the day adding more sketches to the tablet—the mad race from the wind surge, High Point Garrison, Danya's garden, the ruins in the hills, the Rose Stone's tower, the barge journey upriver. Racer and Sojourn returned at dusk to report on the trail and advised we should be able to ride the lyrs far into the hills before having to dismount. After dinner, Paxton offered to show us old land surveys from his father's time. The others pored over them, discussing possible routes while I stood back and watched. Was it my imagination or were the exchanges between Paxton and his son less frosty? I hoped so.

****

Abril's rap on the door woke me before dawn. I threw on my clothes, slinging the Rose Stone's sack across my shoulders. The heat radiating against me was warmer than usual. It seemed she was eager to get underway, too.

I hurried downstairs, the drawing tablet under my arm. The others had finished eating and went to saddle the lyrs, so I sat at the table alone. By the time I went outside, they were tightening the last cinches. Racer and Sojourn perched on a nearby fence rail. With eyes on the horizon, they stretched out their wings, as if testing the strength of the breeze.

Paxton stood on the porch, silently watching. "Thank you for your hospitality," I said.

"You are always welcome here." He stepped into the yard and hugged Abril goodbye. "Be careful."

She kissed his cheek. "I will, Grandfather."

I slipped the sketchbook into the saddlebag and then grabbed Alta's pommel. Griffin, who had been making adjustments to Cirrus' pack, moved to assist me, but Paxton rushed forward and cupped his hands as a boost. "You be careful, too," he said gruffly.

I smiled at him. "I promise. See you soon."

Griffin swung onto Cirrus, shoulders stiff as if anticipating a parting argument. Paxton shot him a glance. "Safe journey," he muttered, so low I barely made out the words.

The tenseness drained from Griffin. "Thank you, Father."

Abril urged her lyr forward and winked at me as she trotted away. The first rays of the sun peeked over the horizon as the four of us headed down the lane. The warbirds launched into the air. I looked over my shoulder. Paxton stood on the porch, watching us, and I waved goodbye. He raised his hand and then we turned a corner, and he was hidden by rows of grain.

Racer and Sojourn circled high overhead, two black dots against the rising sun. Once past the fields, we came to a narrow path toward the hills that forced us to ride single file. The woods closed in on both sides. Leafy branches blocked the sky, and I lost sight of the warbirds. The ground was so thick with brush it hardly qualified as a path, but the steady thrum from the Rose Stone prodded me ahead.

Although the narrowness of the route slowed the lyrs to a trot, they continued to press forward with surefooted confidence. We reached the base of the hills, and the route took a sharp incline. Jumbled piles of boulders and loose soil dotted the ground, and occasionally, we had to circumvent jagged cracks. Something had once violently torn this land apart. I warily eyed the broken slabs looming overhead, and a nervous knot formed in my stomach. Massive explosions had blasted chunks from the hillsides, canting them toward us at unnatural angles. Periodically, a shower of gravel and pebbles skittered down the slope, and the knot tightened. The rocks above seemed so delicately balanced the slightest breeze would send them tumbling.

The path split. *East*, the Rose Stone commanded, and we pressed on. As the sun rose high in the sky, the warbirds warned of more landslide debris ahead. A winding turn brought us to a towering ridge that blocked the route, but a narrow rift in the center tunneled into the rockface. It was barely wide enough for one lyr and rider to pass. No wonder the warbirds had a tough time spotting passage from the air.

The clop, clop, clop of the lyrs' hooves eerily echoed down the tunnel. When we reached the end, Griffin whistled. Seconds later, Racer and Sojourn descended, pulling up at the last second for graceful landings on the pommels.

Racer stretched his wings. *High walls of sliding rock. The track is gone.*

The Rose Stone thrummed against me. "We keep going," I said. "But to where?"

The warbirds took to the air again to circle overhead. There was no obvious passage, merely boulders mixed with piles of sand and pebbles that shifted with the slightest touch. We dismounted, and I took the Rose Stone from the bag. She made a subtle movement toward a cleft blocked by scrubby brush.

Griffin pulled his sword and hacked at the greenery to reveal an opening in the rock. "It's too narrow for lyrs, but wide enough for us to pass single file. I'll go first." He squeezed through, and I went next with Bram, Danya, and Abril right behind me. My shoulders had barely a few inches clearance on either side, and it was a snug fit for Griffin ahead of me. Our bodies blocked much of the sunlight, and I fought a wave of claustrophobia. The rocks here were gray, but strangely smooth, and I suddenly realized we were between slabs of concrete. Twisted bits of rusted metal rebar stuck out above our heads. This wasn't a recess in the cliff, but the remains of a wall.

Griffin edged his way out the other side and gave me his hand. I stumbled into an area shielded by another ridge. It had a weird shape, high and very narrow, with parts made up of more broken concrete slabs. He shaded his eyes and peered overhead. "There's the boundary. We can't go farther." I followed his gaze and caught the barest hint of a glimmer peeking from behind the tops of the crests.

Racer circled overhead with a jubilant screech. *The rose!*

I caught his meaning and gave a gleeful cry. "He's right. The shape of this area caused the same pinched contour lines in my picture. The location of the rose on the map must be nearby."

Griffin looked around. "There is nothing here of interest, simply more of the same."

The Rose Stone's persistent tug continued, but sheer walls penned us in. "She wants to keep going, but I don't see a way." My words echoed with a hollow reverberation that bounced between the rocks and faded away.

"We can try to climb over the top," said Griffin. "Perhaps a better passage exists on the other side." He touched the rockface, and his face lit with excitement. "Fresh air is blowing through the cracks. Move the debris."

As I bent over to lift a rock, a stab of pain sliced through my head, and I staggered. Griffin's hand shot out to steady me. "Jess?"

"I'm fine."

"You are not," he said gently. "We should rest."

"You mean, I should rest." I shook my head, regretting the maneuver instantly, as another piercing stab burrowed behind my eyes. "The medication is wearing off, but I'm okay. It's only a headache, no muscle weakness yet."

"Jess—"

"Don't. I need to keep going as long as I can."

Griffin pressed his lips together and continued to dig with Bram and Abril. The sandy dirt shifted easily. Soon, they unearthed an old, battered door on rusty hinges and the breeze strengthened.

Danya placed her hand on the surface. "This goes into one of the old places destroyed in the Great War."

Sunlight glinted off a shiny object on the ground. I picked up a smooth gray globule, a chunk of glass shattered and warped by high heat. Touching it gave me a funny sinking feeling. I dropped it immediately and rubbed my fingers against my jacket.

The door had several huge cracks running from top to bottom. Griffin put a shoulder against it, and with one good shove, the door split apart. He peered inside and wrinkled his nose. "The air is musty, but breathable. I can't see far, but the opening appears to lead straight into the hillside."

A beam of light shot through the top of the bag. I removed the Rose Stone and held her in front to illuminate the entrance. "Better than a flashlight," I said and took a step forward. Griffin held me back.

"Wait. I'll call the warbirds." He closed his eyes. A few seconds later, they dove from above. Racer perched on his shoulder, and Sojourn alit on Bram.

Griffin stayed at my side. The others followed

close behind. Instead of a rocky path, smooth concrete lay beneath our feet. Soft footfalls stirred years of dust. No one had been here for a very long time.

Danya began to drum a slow, measured rhythm that collided with the walls and then ricocheted along the passageway ahead of us. "The drum speaks but nothing answers," she said.

"Other dangers?" asked Griffin.

"None the drum can sense."

Racer gave a soft chirrup. *No life remains.*

"Stay alert." Griffin pulled his sword. Bram and Abril did the same.

The path took a twisty turn, and the light from the opening vanished. The single illumination was the soft glow of the Rose Stone, a steady beacon to guide our way. The corridor reached another and branched. Bram and Abril used their daggers to scratch symbols on the walls to mark the route. Guided by the unwavering Rose Stone, we passed a multitude of passageways. This place was a maze. It didn't take long for me to be hopelessly lost, but the Rose Stone led without hesitation.

Cracks and pockmarks marred the floors. Slabs of concrete ripped from the walls lay in crumbled piles, scorch marks burned into the surfaces. The destruction wasn't the result of structural weaknesses caused by the passage of time, but something more sinister.

"Soldiers fought a battle here," whispered Bram. "Hand to hand, close quarters."

Abril shuddered. "A place like this would not be their choice, too difficult to defend. The enemy must have swarmed and pushed them back."

"No bodies," muttered Griffin. "What happened?

Where did they go?"

I feared we'd find out. We did.

The corridor ended at an opening, and Danya's drumming quickened. "Death touched here," she said in a hushed tone. "Not recently, but the memory lingers."

I stopped and held the Rose Stone in front of me. Her light flared, spilling into a cavern—no, not a cavern, but a massive bay. The warbirds launched to scout ahead. Tangles of metal bits littered the ground and something more. Ahead of us, an airplane wingtip jutted from a jumbled pile of sticks and rocks, and everywhere the ground was discolored with sooty scorch marks. We moved forward, and I froze in horror. Those weren't sticks and rocks, but human bones. Hundreds of them, thousands of them, everywhere I looked. A shudder ran through me at the thought of how many perished here.

"Their last stand," said Griffin, his tone as dark as the great bay. "They must have known the battle was hopeless, yet here they stayed and fell, perhaps to give their comrades a chance of escape."

The Rose Stone shifted ahead. "Oh, you've got to be kidding," I moaned and eyed Griffin in despair. "She wants us to enter."

"Then we shall," said Griffin. "The dead have no power over the living."

Trust a soldier to state the obvious. I pulled myself together and took a cautious step forward, grimacing as my boot came down on something crunchy. I didn't look and kept my focus straight ahead. We slowly advanced across the bay. Griffin stayed at my side, his presence easing fears of monsters prowling in the half-light.

No one spoke. The only sounds that broke the silence were the *tap-tap-tap* from Danya's drum, the crunching of the occasional "something" underfoot, and the unnerving creaks and groans from shifting metal supports overhead. My heart skipped a beat each time, and I shot jittery glances at the ceiling. The ancient rafters supported tons of weight, an entire hilltop over our heads. If they collapsed now, we'd end up with the rest of the dead in the bay, lost and forgotten, our bones mixed with theirs.

The lack of light made it impossible to see the other side, but the unfaltering Rose Stone continued to gently nudge me in the same direction. The warbirds returned, so did a dull cramp in my legs. I stepped on an uneven surface, and my foot slipped.

Griffin grabbed my arm. "Are you hurt?"

"No, I'm fine." My legs shook, and I sagged against him.

"Jess—"

"There's no point in telling me to stop and rest." I straightened. "I refuse to sit on a pile of bones, and we have to keep going."

At last, we reached the other side and found a staircase. The Rose Stone shifted in my hand, exerting slight pressure toward the ground. "You would," I said with a sigh and warily eyed the entrance. "She wants to descend."

Griffin paused and turned back to survey the wreckage. "Come, then, and let us leave them in peace." He saluted the dead with his sword, paying homage to the fallen comrades' bravery. Bram and Abril did the same.

The staircase wasn't any darker than the bay, but

the psychological impact of descending under the bowels of the burial chamber made my heart thump hard against my ribs.

Racer craned his neck. *Fresh air.*

"Father, I feel air coming from below," said Abril.

"So do I," said Bram, excitement rising in his voice. "There must be another exit."

At the bottom of the steps were the remains of a huge metal door. It lay in shattered pieces, raked by long claw marks. Fear fired a round of adrenaline through my veins. The door had been ripped apart by carvers.

Beyond the opening was a room littered with smashed electrical equipment. Charring from multiple fires and explosions stained the walls. Etched into the floor were two burn marks the shape of human bodies. My heart skipped another beat as I gingerly stepped around them.

In the center of the room, three steps led up to a circular platform holding a large silver rectangle made from two upright metal posts about nine feet high and a horizontal bar spanning the approximate six feet between them. There were no seams, as if it had been forged in a single piece. Age weighed heavily on the mounds of wreckage in the room, but the silver rectangle was glossy and without a scratch. Not even a speck of dust marred the perfectly smooth surface.

"Strange," I murmured, moving closer for a better look. "It's so shiny I should be able to see a reflected image of the room, but I don't."

"What is this place?" asked Griffin. "I've never seen the like."

"It's a laboratory, but I have no idea what they did

here. Not much is left intact, and nothing looks familiar." My headache pounded, and I rubbed my brow, willing the pain to go away. It didn't.

Griffin motioned toward a far wall where a smaller door hung lopsided off a broken hinge. "The breeze comes from there."

Bram and Abril sheathed their swords and forced it open. "There's another stairway, and I see sunlight," said Abril.

The Rose Stone shifted in the opposite direction. "Hang on," I said. "She doesn't want to leave yet." The movement of the Rose Stone led to the platform with the strange rectangle. I put my foot on the first step and her color brightened. "She wants me on top."

"To what end?" asked Griffin.

"I've no idea."

"Curious," murmured Danya. "The outline reminds me of a breach. They are of similar size and shape."

I climbed up to the rectangle and then turned to survey the room from the new vantage point. A pattern emerged. "The machines below are clustered together and facing the same direction. They must have been workstations, but I don't get it. This thing is perfectly smooth, no dials or readouts, nothing that hints it's more than a hunk of metal. Were they watching something up here or the rectangle itself?"

"That's the one undamaged object in the room," said Bram. "The metal must be very strong."

"Weird," I murmured. "There's no reflection of me, either." I placed my hand on the surface and then jerked back in surprise. "It's warm. That makes no sense. This place is dead."

The others hurried to climb the steps. Griffin

touched the rectangle and gave a puzzled look. "I feel no heat."

"Nor do I," said Abril, placing her hand next to his.

"The true meaning may be meant for the bearer of the Rose Stone," said Danya. She closed her eyes, tapping lightly on the surface of the rectangle. "The Rose Stone and metal whisper to each other, but not in a language I understand. Perhaps, Jess, together we can determine the truth."

"I'm game," I said. "What do we do?"

"I will drum, and the Rose Stone will guide." Danya's fingers lightly brushed the drumhead and began a steady *tap-tap-tap*. First slow and then the beat increased.

I surrendered to the hypnotic rhythm, body swaying in response. The heat from the Rose Stone filtered up my arm. I held her to my eyes and peered inside. "I'm here. Show me." My hands shook so hard I nearly dropped her.

As if in response, the gentle warmth from the Rose Stone flooded my body and eased the tremor. A pulsing thrum issued from the rectangle, matched perfectly to the drum's tempo, and I shivered as goosebumps danced up my arm. Energy lapped at my skin with the same mysterious ebb and flow as when I traveled between worlds.

"Do you feel anything, Jess?" asked Griffin.

"Yes, but I'm not sure how to describe it. A change, shifting movement, almost like a river..." The underlying reality hit me in a flash. "This isn't simply a piece of metal. It's a doorway."

"Where does it lead?" asked Griffin.

Danya stopped drumming and peered at the

rectangle. "The old tales of the ancestors mentioned seekers of knowledge who opened portals to other worlds. They quested far and wide, perhaps too far."

Abril gasped. "They found the world of the darkling."

"No," I said with a frown. "I sense the connection between the Rose Stone and the darkling is deeper than that." I touched the rectangle again, and this time it was cold instead of warm. A frigid shard raced to my chest and threatened to freeze the breath in my lungs. Flashes of indecipherable numbers and symbols winked in and out. They made a pattern, birthed a purpose. Not life as we defined it, but something else…the full horror of the truth struck me. I gasped and stumbled back into Griffin's arms. "I understand why the Rose Stone brought us here. The darkling is an AI, artificial intelligence."

"What's that?" asked Griffin.

I struggled to explain. "It's a kind of machine that thinks and acts on its own—a spark of mechanical life. These people didn't find the darkling on another world, they created it here."

"The darkling came from our ancestors?" His voice was a shocked whisper. "How can that be?"

I sighed. "They didn't understand what they set loose. Mistakes happen to the smartest, even in my world. People blunder ahead without considering the consequences of their actions."

"All this death…" Abril's voice shook. "They nearly destroyed us and for what?"

"I don't know, but they didn't plan for this to happen and probably started with good intentions."

"They must have found a way to force the darkling

through the portal," murmured Danya. She touched the rectangle and then jerked back her hand. "Even from here, its hate comes through. The darkling is watching from the other side, testing our defenses, searching for a way to bring us to our knees and take this world again."

"The darkling and the Rose Stone are connected," I said. "The flow of poison decreased, but the link between them remains. The way to sever it must be in the darkling's world. That's why the Rose Stone led me here."

Bram cast a woeful glance at the shattered workstations. "But how? If this is a portal, the machines to open it require a spark. Even with such, the skill to repair them no longer exists."

A thought occurred to me, and I peered at the Rose Stone. *Can we do this?* The facets gleamed with inner light, imbuing me with confidence. "I shut a breach with her help. Maybe I can open a portal."

Griffin gave a terse nod. "We are with you."

I drew a deep breath. The Rose Stone glowed, bathing the surface of the metal with light. I held her in front of my eyes and cleared my mind. "Open," I whispered.

My fingertips tingled, not with muscle weakness but a concentration of energy. It beat against the rectangle trying to get inside, but the flow struck a barrier as if a door had been shut tight. If so, I was certain I held the key. I shifted the Rose Stone to one hand and laid the other flat against the surface. The tingle swelled to a fiery surge as power cascaded into me from the Rose Stone, building in intensity with no way out unless it found an escape. I wasn't frightened. I knew exactly where it should go.

"Open." This time it was a command and not a request.

Blinding light coursed from my hand, flowing into the metal until three were one—the stone, the portal, and me. Images of numbers, letters, and symbols flooded my mind. I didn't understand the code's meaning, but it didn't matter. I sensed the proper path, and all it needed to open was a tiny thrust of force here and a bit more power there. Mist formed in the center of the rectangle. The surface shimmered and became transparent. Dim light spilled from the other side through sickly yellow murk. There was no green expanse, no blue sky, merely obscuring haze. The energy pouring from my hands halted.

"We won't be able to mark a trail through that," said Bram. "I can't see more than a few feet ahead."

Danya tapped on her drum, the vibrations continued to channel through the Rose Stone. "My drum speaks to the stone and she to Jess. Together, they will guide you home."

I shot her a nervous glance. "We're not exactly at the boundary and this isn't exactly a breach, but what if it causes a wind surge?"

"The Rose Stone will protect us." She spoke with utter confidence, but I wasn't so sure.

"Racer, Sojourn, fly through that other door to the surface," said Griffin. "Find a path for the lyrs to reach the top of the stairway. Guide them there so we needn't travel through this compound again." The warbirds launched, and he turned to us. "We must move quickly before the darkling discovers an opening exists to our world. Stay close."

I held the Rose Stone in front of me, and one by

one, we crossed to the other side.

Chapter Fourteen

I inhaled and coughed. The haze in the air left a nasty, bitter taste in my mouth.

Abril gasped. "Danya is gone."

I turned around and for a horrible moment saw nothing but swirling clouds. Then they drifted apart, and I spotted Danya on the other side of the rectangle. Her hand moved, striking the drum, but no sound other than a low drone came through the portal. I reached my hand toward her and bumped into a slick surface with the feel of oily glass. The portal had closed. Panic welled up until I detected the subtle vibrations from the Rose Stone throbbing against me and breathed a sigh of relief. "It's okay. The Rose Stone and Danya's drum are still connected."

"Where to now?" asked Griffin.

"Good question." I looked at the Rose Stone. "Lead the way."

Her glow became a beacon, and the gentle nudge left no doubt as to our direction—straight ahead. The haze lifted in front of us. The bay in the compound had been enormous, but a mere matchbox in size compared to this. Banks of machinery lined the walls. No—they formed the walls and loomed overhead, rising until they disappeared from view. It was impossible to tell whether we were inside a massive building, or a structure set deep within the bowels of a planet. Some of the machinery hummed with power and had peculiar gauges emitting glints of light. Others were quiescent, whether dead or merely shut down, I had no clue.

Here is the darkling's home.

I stared at the Rose Stone. "I hear you clearly now."

Our connection strengthens.

"Does the darkling know we're here?"

Our energy gave the portal life for only a brief instant, and my power will keep us shielded from its eyes for a time.

"We're safe, so far," I told Griffin and the others. "The Rose Stone says the darkling can't see us yet."

"Where is here?" asked Griffin.

This is not our world, answered the Rose Stone. *The darkling's creators explored here and released it to delve the secrets. They did not know this place was heir to an ancient power long asleep. It awoke when the darkling spoke and in return gave the darkling power and purpose—to live at the expense of all else. Since then, the energy is nearly spent, and little spark remains. The darkling needs me to awaken more. Then it will be unstoppable.*

"I get it," I said. "The people in the laboratory were explorers and hoped to learn from the alien technology, but something happened. The AI and the machinery's programming merged and changed. Instead of hunting technology, now the AI hunts power and it's never satisfied. The energy here is fading, and it needs the Rose Stone to find more. If the Commonwealth falls, the Rose Stone will come under the darkling's control. Once that happens..." The awful words stuck in my throat.

Griffin's jaw tightened. "Nothing will defeat the darkling. Every world will bow before it."

We reached the end of the corridor. Lights from the active machinery illuminated more of the surroundings and showed a vast expanse. This wasn't a corridor, but a stanchion. It linked to others, forming an interlocking grid, miles in width, that radiated from a massive central core. I couldn't see the end. A mechanical drone reverberated around us, and the ground vibrated under our feet. A macabre image came to mind of a monster awakening ready to feed. I shivered, and not from the chill in the air.

Griffin tensed and pointed across the void. "Carvers," he whispered.

Gooseflesh crawled up my neck. Ahead were rows and rows of transparent tubes, stacked as high as the stanchions. Each contained a single motionless carver.

Carvers belonged to the old ones and did their bidding, said the Rose Stone. *Then the old ones were gone, and they had no purpose. After the darkling came, they had a master once more. They wait to receive the command to wake.*

We left the corridor, and the Rose Stone guided me to a crossbar. There were lights in the floor, but no guardrails. I eased to the edge to have a look and immediately wished I hadn't. Rows of spokes vanished down the unlit abyss, and I hurriedly backed away.

Abril peered at the machines in wonder. "The original purpose of this place was merely to open portals?"

"It doesn't seem probable," I said. "The people in the lab opened a portal with much less, and most of these machines look dead. I can't even guess why this

239

was built, but the darkling tapped into whatever power remained."

Ahead, lights flashed from the central core. Other machines duplicated the pattern, glimmers rippling from one to another as if linked in an electronic wave. Back and forth, up and down and across. The unceasing movement was spellbinding, and I forced my gaze away.

We continued to follow the outer rim. Embedded in the walls were rectangles identical to the one that brought us here, but none gave any impression of activity. I stopped at a rectangle and grimaced. Pain shot through my legs, and the headache had escalated to a constant aching stab. "So many portals," I murmured. "I wonder where they lead?"

See, said the Rose Stone.

It had been a rhetorical question, and I jumped as the center of the rectangle shimmered. The distortion spread to the edges and then disappeared to display the panorama of a world that may once have been lush and beautiful but now lay in smoking ruins.

The darkling came. Fed on the spark. Destroyed what remained.

My heart sank. "These are portals to dead worlds. They had no Rose Stone to protect them. The darkling fed on their spark, but it's never satisfied. This is what will happen if the darkling isn't stopped."

Bram gripped his sword tight. "The end will not come while one Rose Guard lives and breathes. We fight to the end."

Abril scanned the vast expanse and shuddered. "Against this? How?"

"We stopped them before," said Bram.

"With the power of the Rose Stone, but she is ailing."

"Then we find a cure," I said. "It must be here, or she wouldn't have brought us to this place."

"Strange, no guards, not even a single carver on patrol," said Griffin.

I snorted. "The darkling obviously doesn't expect company." A horrific idea struck me, and I gaped at the banks of machinery. "This entire complex is the darkling now."

Bram's eyes widened. "How can we fight an enemy such as this? It has no body. We cannot strike at a heart, nor sever a head."

"Machines are powerful and able to do amazing things," I said. "But they aren't invincible."

"Prepare." The rasping command boomed from the tower.

I stiffened. "I've heard that voice before. It's the darkling."

Griffin motioned for silence. "Listen—footsteps."

In the distance came a shuffling sound, and my heart pounded. The noise grew louder and louder until it overshadowed the ever-present electronic hum. Vibrations echoed through the soles of my boots from the movement of many bodies.

Griffin dropped to his knees and looked over the side. "Cover her light," he whispered.

I dropped the Rose Stone in the sack. The flashes from the great machines rippled in the direction of the approaching sound, and out of the gloom came figures moving in a straight line toward the central core. The entire crossbar filled with rows upon rows of carvers, too many to count. As they passed a tube, the door snapped open, and with tentacles waving, another carver stepped forward to join them. The line seemed endless as they moved with deadly purpose.

Griffin grabbed my arm and pointed below us. "War machines."

On another stanchion, strange devices sailed over the carvers' heads. They had smooth, metallic surfaces and no windows or openings. Around the sides and on top were long tubes bristling like porcupine quills. My mouth dried. Gun barrels.

"I've read old accounts," whispered Griffin. "Those tubes spit fire. A single blast can destroy a village." The carvers and hovercraft filled every spoke until they disappeared into the dark. Then without warning the carvers stopped their march, and the war machines hovered in the air. Griffin tensed. "They're readying a massive breach as in the last great wave before the arrival of the Rose Stone."

Eighteen years ago, the darkling attacked and failed because it could not hold so many breaches at once. It learned to gather power slowly and is determined to succeed.

I felt sick. "Over the years, the darkling stored energy and is almost ready to open every portal to the Commonwealth at once."

Abril gasped. "There will be hundreds of breaches, millions of carvers."

"The wind surge from so many will topple the walls of Stone Keep," said Bram. "If they break through, the Commonwealth is doomed."

The rectangles in front of the rows of immobile carvers and war machines glowed, but haze clouded the centers. As I watched, it cleared enough to make out different landscapes. The views wavered and shifted though, like a TV with a fuzzy cable signal. Then the haze thickened again, and the glow disappeared.

My heart raced. Despite the blur, I had recognized Stone Keep and High Point Garrison among them. In the foregrounds, Rose Guards on lyrs, swords and bows drawn, prepared to do battle. This was the great evil the drummers sensed building. Soon the portals would have enough power to stabilize, and the darkling's army would pour through them. My legs shook, and not because of the tumor.

Time is short. This way.

The Rose Stone thrummed against the side of my leg, and the slight touch ignited a blaze of pain. The ground rumbled from below, and I peered over the edge. A mass of carvers broke away from the main body. Their heads lifted, tentacles waving.

"I don't like this," muttered Griffin. "Do they suspect uninvited guests?"

The carvers stir at our presence, but the darkling does not see, said the Rose Stone.

"Not yet, but let's not hang around here," I said.

The Rose Stone urged me on, and I led with my shambling gait. The pain soared to become fiery shards worming into my muscles, tearing at me with each step. My legs trembled, so did my hands, the weakness in them coming faster than before.

Griffin must have noticed because he took my elbow. "Bear your weight on me."

We arrived at another spoke that led to a second vertical stanchion. It was narrower than the central core and didn't reach to the ceiling but stopped fifty feet overhead. On the top was a tower studded with spikes.

They moved in rhythmic circles, reminiscent of the carvers' waving tentacles.

This device hunts through the recesses of time and space for the spark. The source of the poison lies within, but once inside the darkling will know intruders have entered its realm. I will keep us shielded as long as I can.

"Griffin, the Rose Stone wants me to go inside, but as soon as I do, the darkling will know something's up," I said.

He gave a terse nod. "I am with you. Bram, Abril, stand guard."

The wall of the tower seemed solid, and I opened the sack and looked at the Rose Stone. "How do we get in?"

Touch.

I held her against the wall. An opening appeared into a circular room. Griffin and I stepped inside. I froze, waiting for alarm bells to scream, but only a faint prickle of energy danced against my skin. I gazed around with a sinking feeling. Electronic devices covered the walls. Lights rippled and flowed, not encased in separate machinery, but part of the metal. I couldn't begin to guess their purpose. The tingle on my skin increased, but unlike electricity, it was cold instead of hot.

"Can the darkling see us?" I asked the Rose Stone.

No, but soon.

"What am I looking for?"

The poison lies within.

I made a face. "You're kidding, right? That's truly helpful."

"What is?" asked Griffin.

"Nothing. Apparently, the Rose Stone doesn't understand sarcasm." I was exhausted and fighting the sense of a ticking clock, trying to ignore the painful lashes from spasms in my legs, and failing miserably. The headache burrowed behind my eyes and felt as if it were boring a window through my forehead. My thoughts muddied, concentrating was agony. Even worse, I was certain the Rose Stone didn't lie. The answer was here.

I stared in frustration at the lights. Their ceaseless blinking mocked me. The complex was gigantic, built by beings that weren't human. Even if I studied this one room for a thousand years, I had no way to delve into its secrets. I couldn't even guess where to begin.

Griffin put his arm around my shoulders. "The pain is worse."

I never felt so horrible, both mentally and physically. I leaned against Griffin and drew a shuddering breath. "I brought you this far and don't know what to do next. I'm sorry."

His grip tightened. "You didn't bring us. The Rose Stone did because she has faith in you. So do I. You will find the answer. Of that, I'm certain."

Not a bit of doubt colored his words. I drew a deep breath and closed my eyes. I'd never understand the forces that opened a bridge to my world and allowed me to cross over, yet with the help of the Rose Stone, I found the way.

No. Not really—I sensed the way. Maybe I needed to tap into the same method here. Not knowledge, but perception. I held the Rose Stone out in front and slowly turned in place. What struck me most? The air was cool and dry, but there was also an effect from the machinery, waves of sharp prickly static electricity brushing against my bare skin. It came from everywhere.

Or did it? I stopped turning. One array of lights definitely emitted more than others. Their flashes blinked an enigmatic message. I couldn't read it, but the meaning came through loud and clear. What I sought was here.

My hand shook badly, and the Rose Stone nearly slipped from my grasp. Without a word, Griffin took my other hand, his warmth wrapped my fingers. The tremor eased. I smiled at him and let my mind go. Beneath the icy bite in the air lurked another sensation, dark and evil. I fought an upwelling of fear as every instinct screamed at me to run.

Every instinct be damned. "Follow the trail," I murmured and held the Rose Stone up to my eyes. "Take me in."

Mental restraints evaporated, and I willingly allowed my mind to fall into the depths of the machine. The power was incredible but offered none of the comforting peace of the Rose Stone. Instead, energy waves beat against me as fetid, oily slime. This was the poison, and I needed to find the source.

Down, down, down…there!

Ahead was a black knot with pulsating tendrils. The outline was familiar. I'd seen an MRI with the same shape not long ago. Surrounding this one was a barrier of pure crimson light.

You and I are connected, and the darkling attacks both of us, said the Rose Stone. *The medicine from your people made the evil smaller, but it is still powerful.*

Energy rippled through the knot. A tendril broke

from the surface, and a bead of black oil oozed from the end to form a glistening arrow tip. It shot out and lodged in a facet. The luminous radiance faded for an instant and then flared bright white. The tendril erupted in flames, but the dart stayed embedded in the barrier— and it wasn't alone. Dozens of little black darts marred the perfection of the light.

"The light is you, isn't it?" I asked. "The darkling attacks with the poison darts."

Yes. The link to the darkling was forged at my creation, and the darkling's assault is unending. To destroy the link or the poison and maintain the boundary around the Commonwealth is beyond my ability.

The crimson light shimmered, and I sensed the Rose Stone's pain. No—I felt it. It was worse than mine and she battled on, defending the world that bore her name and symbol.

Another tendril formed. It twitched, and more slimy oil dribbled from the tip. My temper boiled over. This evil was trying to destroy something precious in front of my eyes. I ignored my aching limbs and pounding head and without hesitation commanded, "Hold it right there."

The tendril twisted toward me. "You are here?" The voice of the darkling registered a mixture of astonishment and rage. "This cannot be."

"Well, it is," I said. "Suck it." I snatched the tendril. Pain ripped through my hand, as if I had punched a solid block of ice. The tendril jerked from my grasp. I had to find a weapon.

Use our power, said the Rose Stone.

Energy coursed through me, clean and shining. The

Rose Stone and I had our own bridge, and it was stronger than the one maintained by the darkling. "A weapon," I said, and a palette knife winked into existence. Well, why not? I was no soldier, but it destroyed a tendril on a carver once before. That palette knife broke apart because it wasn't strong enough. This one needed more. As if in response, the metal blade became flame. I reached for it and the handle fitted to my grasp as if forged for this purpose alone. It felt good. It felt right. It felt kick ass. I smiled.

The tendril was on the move again toward the light. I tightened my grip on the handle, ignoring the ache in my fingers. "I said, stop." The tendril froze and turned to me, quivering. "Yeah, you heard me. Not another inch."

"You have no power here," snarled the darkling.

"Then you have nothing to worry about."

I swung hard, and the palette knife connected with the tendril. The blow sent a shock wave through my arm. With an ear-piercing metallic shriek, the tendril vaporized into wispy trails of fetid gray smoke.

I laughed through the pain. "Nice."

Another tendril shot toward me. I destroyed it, and another one appeared. Again and again, I lashed out until the atmosphere was hazy with vapor trails. Finally, the attack ceased. No more tendrils erupted. I had weakened the poison knot considerably, but it wasn't over yet. Every trace of the knot had to be obliterated. I closed in, palette knife in hand, determined to end the horror once and for all and free the Rose Stone from its poison. One more strike at the heart and the battle was finished.

"Jess," said Melanie. "You're finished."

"No!" The palette knife and the knot vanished as I was dragged backward. "Griffin!" I yelled.

"Here!"

I hurled myself toward his voice. A crimson blur clouded my vision and then Griffin's face appeared. Around me the lights in the walls flashed a frantic beat as the color changed from white to blood red.

I see you, thundered the darkling.

My pulse raced. "We're not a secret anymore."

Abril and Bram burst through the door. "Carvers headed this way," said Bram. "We have to move."

I dropped the Rose Stone in the sack and took a staggering step. Stabbing pain exploded through every nerve ending. I would have fallen to my knees if Griffin hadn't grabbed me. "Help Jess," he said to Abril.

"Come on, Jess," said Melanie, in a wheedling tone. "The treatment is done. Open your eyes."

I gritted my teeth as pink haze crept into my peripheral vision. "Griffin, we have to hurry. I'm being pulled back."

Griffin and Bram led the way from the tower. Abril slipped my arm over her shoulders and with a firm grip around my waist we followed.

"Find them. Find them. Find them…" The darkling's strident command surrounded us, rebounding against the banks of machinery.

From a walkway beneath us came a snarling roar. Carvers had the scent. In a seething mass, bodies piled on top of each other as they scrambled to reach our level. Without regard for safety, they shouldered the slowest aside. Dozens tumbled into the abyss below, but nothing distracted them from their advance.

We reached the first cross span, and I cursed my

shambling gait for slowing our pace. Sweat poured into my eyes and every breath was tearing agony. I stumbled back as a carver's arm shot above the span and claws slammed into the walkway. They took hold and then another arm reached overhead, frantically scrabbling at the air. Griffin charged and swung his sword, cleaving both at the wrists. Sparks crackled from the stumps, and the carver fell back with a howl, the eerie screech fading away as it tumbled into the dark. Ten yards ahead, a dozen arms rose at once from below, all flailing for a grip.

"The path is blocked," shouted Bram.

The sack pulled away from me. *The drum calls. This way.*

"The Rose Stone hears Danya's drum," I cried. "Hurry." Following the tug from the Rose Stone, I led them to another dim corridor and across a span. Behind us, guttural shrieks soon came from every direction.

"The hunting party has spread out," said Griffin. "We're penned in the middle of the horde."

We raced around a corner, and I stumbled to a sudden halt. The passageway was a dead end. "Oh, no," I moaned. "Where's Danya?" At the end, haze clouded the wall and then it cleared to show a wavy image of Danya beating her drum. I touched the surface. "It's getting warmer," I shouted in excitement. "She and the Rose Stone are forming the portal. Any second now."

A carver lumbered into the passageway, tendrils fluttering. Another one appeared behind it and then a third. They opened their mouths and howled. From every direction came wailing responses. The horde was coming for us.

"Jess?"

"Danya?" I said. Her voice sounded funny.

"Who's Danya?" said Melanie.

Blind panic rose in a wave. "I can't go yet," I yelled. "I have to open the portal."

"What portal?" Melanie said, her voice anxious. "Jess, you're not making sense. Wake up."

Rosy mist blurred my vision. I banged on the portal and then in desperation snatched the Rose Stone from the bag and touched her to the wall. "Please, open the door, now."

Nothing happened, and I locked eyes with Griffin. "I love you," I said.

"I love you, too." He turned to face the carvers, Bram and Abril at his side. The mist thickened, and they disappeared.

I was falling, falling, falling. Nothing existed but frigid emptiness. A tiny wire sparked in the distance and the grating voice of the darkling filled my head. *No one escapes the dark.*

****

Melanie peered down at me, Dr. Turner at her side. Behind them a nurse watched the medical monitors. "Hey, I was getting worried," Melanie said. "You were harder to wake this time. Heck of a dream, huh?"

"Yeah." I swallowed hard, fighting to keep from sinking into despair. I was back in the hospital. Griffin and the others were gone. I left them facing an army of carvers. What could three people with swords do against that?

Nothing. They're dead.

"This treatment packs more of a wallop with you than my other patients," said Dr. Turner. "You look drained. How are you feeling?"

Feeling? Griffin was dead. I fought back tears, shifted my weight, and winced at the roaring pain in my head and limbs. It almost overshadowed the agony in my heart. Almost. "I-I hurt."

Dr. Turner nodded to the nurse. "She needs more pain medication. Give her another dose."

"So soon?" said Melanie with a worried frown. "It's wearing off faster."

"We'll take another MRI tomorrow and then see what the treatment accomplished."

"Or if it did anything, you mean," I said. What did it matter now? What did anything matter?

Dr. Turner squeezed my shoulder. "I'm not giving up on you," he said gently. "Don't you dare, either. It's bad for my reputation."

I forced a smile. "Not me." Who cared about a stupid tumor when my heart had shattered in a million pieces?

The nurse injected the medication. Warmth seeped into my aching limbs and my headache disappeared. "Better?" said Dr. Turner.

I stretched out my legs. "Much. Thanks."

"You're still pale," said Melanie. "Can I get you some water?"

"I'm good. I want to go home." To mourn, to cry, to hide away from these kindly faces who'd never understand why I was breathing, yet dead inside. I barely held it together.

The nurse unhooked the IV, and I climbed off the bed. Melanie peered over my shoulder with a puzzled expression. "What's that?"

I followed her gaze. The drawing tablet lay on the sheet where I left it, but a shiny object peeked from beneath the cover. I flipped it open, and my heart dropped.

The Rose Stone was inside.

Chapter Fifteen

I snatched the Rose Stone, and every coherent thought flew from my head.

"Pretty paperweight," said Melanie. "Where'd you get it?"

I drew a steadying breath. "I-I found it rooting through stuff at home and decided to bring it along for a good luck charm."

"Hey, it's the same as the gem in the painting. Did you use it for inspiration?"

"Sure. Right. She's inspiration." I stared at the Rose Stone, beaming a flurry of questions, but no gentle voice answered in my head.

Melanie regarded me with a quizzical expression. "Did you say she?"

"I meant to say it. Can we get going? This place gives me agita." I dropped the tablet in my purse and hopped from bed with renewed vigor, the Rose Stone clutched tight in my fist. Lucky for me, the nurse had already detached the monitors because my heart beat a wild tattoo. How did this happen? Was it a good omen or bad? Either way, I needed answers.

Thanks to Dr. Turner, the pain in my limbs was gone. I walked with a steady gait and didn't lean on the cane. Melanie chatted on the way home, and I grunted clipped responses, my attention fixed on the Rose Stone. I rubbed a thumb across the surface, willing answers to come but felt no corresponding warmth, other than the friction and heat from my hand. This Rose Stone was a dead ringer to the one in the Commonwealth, the same shape and weight. The Rose Stone in every way, but frustratingly quiet with no internal light.

I jumped in the seat as Melanie jabbed me in the ribs. "I said, do you want to stop for dinner?"

"What? Oh, no, I have food at home and I'm not hungry."

I turned the Rose Stone over and over in my fingers. Melanie stopped trying to strike up a conversation, but now and then, shot me a curious look. To add to my frustration, she insisted on escorting me to the loft, but I only wanted to be alone with the Rose Stone.

"What's the fascination with that thing?" she said as I unlocked the door. "You haven't taken your eyes off it since the hospital."

"Like I said, inspiration."

Melanie pursed her lips together. "Those are my words. You only agreed. Now that I think about it, you seemed surprised to find it in the bed. Maybe you should put it away for a while." She stepped toward me as if to take the Rose Stone from my hand.

"No!" I jumped back. Melanie's eyes widened, and I blurted, "It feels good to hold her."

"Her?"

"I mean *it*. I'm using it like those—what do you call them—worry beads. People fiddle with them and let worry slip through their fingers. This is mine."

"Jess…" She didn't look convinced.

I rubbed my brow. "It's been a long day, Mel, and

I'm beat. I've got the appointment with Dr. Turner tomorrow and I'm nervous. After all, my entire future is on the line, and it may be a very short one." I clutched the Rose Stone tight to my chest. "I'll take any little bit of comfort from wherever I can get it." That, at least, was no lie.

The lines of concern around her eyes softened and she hugged me goodbye. "I understand. It'll be okay. Owen is optimistic, I can tell."

"Oh?" I teased. "Got a handle on his personal vibes so soon?"

Melanie made a face. "Shut up and go to bed. I'll see you in the morning."

I locked the door behind her and then sank into the couch. "We're alone," I whispered to the Rose Stone. "Please, talk to me. Are Griffin and the others okay?" I gazed deep into the facets, struggling to hear a response, but none came. An icy knot of fear settled in my stomach. The Rose Stone protected the Commonwealth, and somehow, I'd stolen her away. The darkling simply needed her to weaken enough for the boundary to fall and then multiple breaches would open. Had I done the dirty work for it and allowed everyone there to become prey for the carvers?

Images of the horror to befall the Commonwealth flashed in front of my eyes. In a millennium, would another portal open and explorers from a distant world arrive to find nothing but oddly shaped hills covering bones and debris?

So mired in grief, the slight tingle was imperceptible at first and then gentle pressure touched my hand. I jerked straight up. The traffic sounds outside my window muted, as I focused every ounce of attention on the Rose Stone.

"I'm here," I whispered. "Speak to me." From deep inside a facet came a tiny flicker of light. "You're alive," I choked out, swallowing a lump in my throat.

I am here.

"How did I bring you with me?"

Instead of an answer, the Rose Stone said, *The knot of poison remains.*

"I know. I didn't have enough time to destroy it. I'm sorry."

Illness saps your strength, and the cure cannot be found in the Commonwealth. When the time is right, my power is yours.

Understanding dawned on me. "I didn't bring you; you chose to come with me. You think you can help me heal. Forget about the tumor; you can't do anything. It's more important to keep the Commonwealth safe. Does the boundary hold from here?"

For now. Her voice faded. The flicker disappeared.

"Wait! Are Griffin and the others alive? How do I get back? I have to find Griffin."

My hand shook, and not from the tumor. "You shouldn't have left. You should have stayed to protect them."

No comfort came, but instead the weight of the day pressed on my shoulders. I experienced a sense of being poised on the brink, waiting for events to unfold. The next step was unclear, and I sagged with fatigue. Maybe sleep would bring me to Griffin. I staggered to bed, threw my clothes on the floor, and climbed under the covers. Still clutching the Rose Stone, I entered a dreamless sleep.

****

I woke the next morning, refreshed in body, but not in spirit. I hadn't returned to the Commonwealth, no call came from Danya's drum, not even a glimpse of Griffin's face. An image rose of his body lying bloody on a field of carnage, carvers howling in triumph. Enraged, I brushed it aside. Until I had proof, Griffin was alive and waiting for me to return.

The Rose Stone lay on the pillow next to me, and I held her tight. "Griffin loves me. Those were the last words he said before I disappeared, but you know that. I love him, too. The kind of love I've always wanted but never believed possible. The true happily-ever-after kind, but I suppose you know that, too."

I had gladly surrendered my heart to Griffin. My old life was fast becoming the dream, less real by the minute, and I filled with resolute purpose. No matter the cost, I'd find the way to the Commonwealth again and say the words to Griffin in person. Even if the strain on my body made it the last thing I did.

I gazed out the window. It was early, barely dawn. Melanie wasn't due for a few hours yet. I jumped out of bed and quickly showered and dressed in a clean T-shirt and jeans. I kept the Rose Stone in my pocket with a strong need to feel her nearby. The hot water had done nothing to soothe my restless spirit, and I paced like a caged animal. The sketchbook caught my eye. I had tossed it on the couch the night before and now skimmed the pages. The new pictures I'd drawn at Paxton's farm were there. The others remained the same…no, not quite. The shadowy form in the center of the Rose Stone was smaller and without a single tendril.

My spirits soared. I went to the easel, dismayed to see the ugly blot had returned to the painting. The amount of color I used hadn't been enough, and it bled through, making a grotesque scar on the canvas. I grabbed a brush and palette knife and with savage swipes obliterated the stain on my creation. I added color, vibrant green leaves and masses of violet, crimson, and yellow. I stepped back and nodded in satisfaction. The blot was gone, and a garden with a flowered border took its place.

"Never to return," I said with iron determination.

My hand moved of its own accord. Details filled the canvas without conscious thought. I added fields of grain, waving in a gentle breeze. Paxton grasped a hoe, surrounded by those beautiful blue and white blossoms, sunshine beamed from an azure sky. Warbirds soared over Abril and Bram. The Commonwealth flowed with life, and Griffin and I were in the middle of it. With a final swipe of the brush, I stepped back and surveyed my creation with pride. Not a taint of evil lingered. That was the way the Commonwealth was meant to be.

Edginess built inside me like a summer storm. Something was missing. The perimeter of the canvas seemed barren. I filled my brush with crimson and in the upper left corner painted a rose. It still felt lacking, so I added radiant green to make a colored vine that looped and entwined as it ran to the upper right corner. I painted another rose, smaller this time. Then a vine plummeting straight down to the lower right. Another delicate rose on the lower left, and vines linking the four roses together—one large blossom and three small, a single cohesive frame to encircle the painting.

Beads of sweat dotted my forehead, and I slipped off the smock and drew a steadying breath. The vines and roses had drawn color from the brush, but it also felt as if their creation absorbed energy from me. I stepped back to survey the finished picture. I never had the compulsion to put a border on a painting before, and this was oddly unbalanced, with the biggest rose in the upper left corner near Paxton.

The ceiling light flickered. *A mere painting is no barrier to my glory.*

I froze, heart racing, and stared at the light.

The lamp on the end table switched on. So did the TV. "The power brownouts continue," said a newscaster. "A company spokesperson says technicians are working around the clock to resolve issues and expect the plant to return to normal operation soon."

They do not see me. They cannot stop me. The lamp and TV clicked off. With a snap, a spark dislodged from an outlet and danced in the air. *Return the stone. It belongs to me.*

I stumbled back, my hand covered the pocket holding the Rose Stone. "Never."

The spark flared. *My handiwork.*

I glared at it in disbelief. "You made the Rose Stone? Impossible."

Ripples of hate rolled against me, staggering in their intensity. *With the knowledge of the old ones, I built the stone to discover and control sources of new power. It disobeys my commands, but not for much longer.* The tiny flame spit and crackled, and I flinched from the heat.

With a scowl, I brandished the palette knife. "You know what? I don't care where the Rose Stone came from. Just try to take her from me." The spark hung in the air. My heart thumped waiting for the attack. I was alone and except for a pathetically impractical palette knife, had no weapons. Nor did I have the ability to call on hidden energy sources. Without the guidance of the Rose Stone, I didn't know how.

Seconds ticked away. The darkling and I squared off, neither giving an inch, and a suspicion began to take shape. "You can't take her by force. I broke those tendrils, and that weakened you."

My power stretches thin to this place but holds strong in the other. As we speak, breaches form. Soon carvers ravage the land. War machines follow. The world will burn to cinders. I am immortal.

"You are buried in the wires, hiding," I sneered. "But I'll find a way to kill you."

Your power isn't great enough, nor is that of the stone.

The appalling truth hit me like a slap in the face. The darkling was right. I had called upon the Rose Stone in the battle against the tendrils, but that weakened her, too.

The stone cannot protect both worlds. I have traveled the wires here, tasting the spark. The power comes slowly, but it comes, and soon every bit will be at my command. This world has nothing to equal the stone, but it will feed me for a time.

"We'll fight."

And lose. Bring the stone to me and I vow to leave this world forever.

"You lie," I spit out.

I never lie. I have no need.

I believed every vile word. "And the Commonwealth?"

Ties with the stone must be severed, and those who stand against me destroyed. Then there will be no purpose for the stone. I will give it purpose. It will answer to me and hunt the spark forever. This world or that world. One dies and one lives. You choose.

"I-I can't take the Rose Stone to you," I stammered. "I don't know how to get from here back to the Commonwealth."

Find the way or your world ends.

I jumped at a knock on the door. "Jess, are you ready?" called Melanie.

She has importance to you. The dispassionate statement of fact sent warning bells firing off in my head.

"Get out," I ordered the darkling between clenched teeth. "We're done here."

"Jess?" said Melanie, rattling the knob. "Who are you talking to?"

"Shouting at the TV. I hate conservative news shows, nothing but a bunch of fascists." I snatched my purse and yanked open the door. "Let's go."

Melanie startled, her hand on the knob. "Um, okay. I'm early, though. We have time for coffee. I can make a pot."

"We'll stop on the way."

"Okay," she said with a quizzical look, hand still on the doorknob.

The spark oozed through the lock and streaked toward Melanie. There was a loud *snap*. "Ow!" Melanie jumped and shook her fingers. "Wow, that hurt." I gaped in horror, but from Melanie's unfazed expression, she clearly didn't see it hovering in the air, inches from her face.

These creatures are so fragile, crooned the darkling.

"Stop it," I hissed.

"Stop what?" said Melanie.

"Nothing. Let's go."

So sensitive to pain.

The spark dove toward Melanie again. *Snap!* She grimaced. "Geez, that smarts, and I wasn't even touching the knob this time. You've got a real static electricity issue in here. Maybe you should get a humidifier."

Their hearts depend on the spark. So easy to start, so easy to stop.

I shoved Melanie into the hall, slammed the door shut, and locked it. "Let's go."

"Your cane—"

"I'm fine. Don't need it today."

"What's the big rush?" sputtered Melanie, as I half-dragged her down the stairs.

I cast a nervous glance over my shoulder, but the darkling had vanished. "Nothing. I'm eager to get going and hear what Dr. Turner has to say."

Melanie smiled. "You're optimistic, aren't you? So am I. Jess, I believe this treatment is going to work. Have you had any pain medication today?"

"No," I said as I got into the car. "I haven't needed it yet."

"That's a good sign, don't you think?"

"Yeah. Sure." As the car pulled from the curb, I peered up at the loft's windows and suppressed a shiver. "I'm totally optimistic about the future."

We went to the drive-thru at the coffee shop. "Have you heard more about the power outages?" I asked as we waited for our order.

"The news reported a few scattered across the city,

but they ended in seconds. I haven't noticed any. They must have nearly run their course."

My fingers drummed on the armrest. Despite the boast, the darkling didn't have unlimited power. Maybe it was stretched thin, struggling to balance between worlds. *Time, time, time.* The lack of it beat against me as surely as Danya's drum. Even if the darkling's attack was delayed, it would eventually control the grid, feed on the energy, and renew the assault on the Commonwealth.

I tensed at every stoplight, fearing they'd turn green at the same time and cause massive pileups. To my relief, nothing happened. Meanwhile, the darkling bided its time, building power, waiting for me to choose. My chest muscles knotted so tight it was hard to breathe, as the fate of two worlds pressed on my shoulders. I wrapped my hands around the cup, hoping the heat seeping into them would jumpstart inspiration, but no such luck.

I glanced at Melanie. How could I warn her? She turned her head, caught my eye, and gave a puzzled smile. "Why are you looking at me that way?"

"I-I just wanted to say thanks for everything you've done. You've been my best friend since we were kids and have always stood by me. It couldn't have been easy."

"I can say the same of you. Remember those late-night study sessions in med school when I swore I was drowning in text books? I'd call you for moral support and then suddenly you'd be at the door with coffee, junk food, and a sympathetic ear. Once, you even cut out on a date. I ragged on you for that."

"He was no big deal, and frankly, I think he was

relieved." I gave her a sharp look. "Owen Turner is a big deal. Have you asked him out?"

Melanie blushed. "You're awfully pushy about Owen. This isn't the right time to talk about him."

I grabbed her arm. "Promise me, Mel, you'll ask him out soon. Forget about it being the right time. No one knows how much time they have left. He's shy and you can't wait for him to make a move."

"You should have only the treatment on your mind now," she chided. "Why the sudden interest in my love life?"

"Because Owen Turner will make you happy. I'm certain he's the one you've been searching for. When you find a man as perfect as that, you have to hang on tight to him and never let go. You deserve happily ever after."

"So do you," she said gently.

I don't know how to get mine back. I blinked away tears. Not here, not now. "Promise me."

"All right. I promise. As soon as I'm sure you've made a full recovery. Until then, I can't think of anything else."

I relaxed in the seat. I dropped Melanie's hand and rested mine lightly on the pocket with the Rose Stone inside. Melanie never broke a promise to me. She would ask out Dr. Turner and they'd fall headfirst in love. I saw everything clearly; my best friend's future was set.

The smile faded from my lips. A happily ever after would never last with the darkling poised to strike. One thing was certain, I'd never sacrifice one world for another, both were part of me. There had to be a way to save them.

L. A. Kelley

I slipped a hand into my pocket and wrapped my fingers around the Rose Stone, concentrating my thoughts on her. *Take whatever you need from me, and we'll find a solution together.*

Dr. Turner met us at the MRI. His face lit up when I told him I had no pain. I went to the changing room and slipped into hospital scrubs. I tucked the Rose Stone in the waistband and tried not to think where I would have had to hide it if the outfit were a gown instead of scrubs. I tied the drawstring tight. Fortunately, scrubs are hardly form fitting.

I shot a glance around as the technician readied the MRI. There was no sign of the darkling since we left the loft, and anticipation built inside me. The last time I was shoved in one of these contraptions, I woke in the Commonwealth. The technician asked if I wanted medication to relax me.

"Yes, please," I said.

In a half-drowsy state, the sound of Danya's drumbeat would surely carry me along the path to the Commonwealth. The technician returned with a pill and a glass of water. I swallowed it down and then lay on the table, the Rose Stone pressing into my side. The MRI table slid into position, and dopey lethargy clouded my mind as the drug kicked in. I was floating, lighthearted. Any minute now, I'd be back with Griffin. The banging from the machine rattled around in my head. I closed my eyes and pictured his face.

Yup, any minute now.

Time ticked away, but nothing happened. Why was it taking so long? I licked my lips and shifted my hand over the Rose Stone.

"Please remain still," said the technician through

266

the intercom.

I listened hard for Danya's drum, but the only sound was the incessant banging of the MRI. The last image I had of Griffin played over and over in my mind. He faced the carvers. They rushed toward him claws outstretched, ready to rip apart flesh and bone.

The brassy taste of fear flooded my mouth. An awful thought clung to me that the carvers broke past Griffin, Bram, and Abril. They entered the portal. Danya didn't drum because Danya was no more.

The banging stopped. I opened my eyes, and my heart sank. I hadn't budged an inch from the MRI tube.

"That's it," said the technician, as the table retracted. "You're finished." So had my chance to return to the Commonwealth.

Melanie sat in the booth and leaned over the mic. "I'll meet you in Owen's office."

I waved an acknowledgment in her direction and hurried to the dressing room to discard the scrubs. I peered into the Rose Stone with rising dread. "Why are we still here? Please, tell me it isn't too late." Then I asked the question I feared most. "Is Griffin alive?" No answer came, but I caught a glimmer among the facets that gave me a surge of hope. It might only be wishful thinking, Danya's favorite kind, but I held onto it.

I paused at Dr. Turner's door to steady my nerves and then entered. He and Melanie huddled over a computer monitor. She jumped up to greet me with a big smile on her face. "Don't look so glum," she burst out. "I'll let Owen explain the details, but..." She grabbed me in a bear hug. "The treatment is working, Jess. Better than we ever dreamed."

A tumult of emotions crashed in on me. I didn't

know whether to laugh or cry and sank into a chair, unable to speak.

Dr. Turner had the same beaming smile as Melanie. "The scan looks fantastic. The improvement is incredible. I've never had such a positive result. Look." He turned the monitor around. I was too familiar with the sight of my rotten brain with the glowing mass in the center, but the image had definitely changed. The tumor was half the size, every tendril gone, identical in shape to the remainder of the poison knot in the Rose Stone.

"This explains the lack of pain in your limbs," said Melanie. "How's the headache?"

"Nonexistent," I said feeling numb and spent.

"I'm beyond pleased," said Dr. Turner. "The success with other patients was nothing as dramatic as this. The whole process was much slower and took more treatments. It's as if an added ingredient jumpstarted the healing."

I placed my hand on my pocket, the comforting shape of the Rose Stone nestled underneath. Tears welled in my eyes, and I blinked them back. The special ingredient was right here. That's why the Rose Stone was so drained of energy. I swallowed hard. "T-that's good news."

"The best." He shot a glance at Melanie. "So good, in fact, I'm going to schedule your surgery for tomorrow."

I blinked. "So soon?"

"Yes. The medication didn't destroy the tumor but made it accessible. Ordinarily, I'd order additional treatment to shrink it further, but…" Dr. Turner's gaze went to the scan, his expression creased with worry.

My internal alarms screamed. "But what?" I demanded.

"The new scan shows unexpected strain on nearby blood vessels. Since it's possible to operate now, I want to remove the tumor at once. If we wait, it'll start to grow again, and this time affect blood flow to the brain. When that happens…" He shot Melanie another wary look. "I'll be candid. The operation is feasible, but dangerous. I wish we had more time."

"Time hasn't been my friend lately," I said dryly. "But I trust your judgement. I'm ready."

Melanie put her hand on top of mine and gave a little squeeze. "I'll be right there with you every step of the way."

"Go home and pack a bag and then hurry back," Dr. Turner said. "I want you checked into the hospital as soon as possible. I'll schedule the operation for the first thing tomorrow morning."

Melanie and I were quiet on the drive home, both wrapped in our own thoughts. She helped me pack. I tossed my sketchbook on top and patted the Rose Stone in my pocket for good luck. We returned to the hospital, and I went to my room to settle in for the night.

"I'll take your purse home with me," said Melanie. "You won't need it for a while."

"Fine, but I'm counting my money first—even the nickels. You have sticky fingers."

"Wow, so funny. Now, get some rest. They'll prep you before dawn."

I fingered the Rose Stone. "Will you be in the operating room with me?"

"Yes. I already got permission from Owen."

"If this procedure works, how long will I be out of

it?"

"Hard to say, a day or longer. You'll be heavily sedated."

I gazed at the Rose Stone. "May I keep this with me during surgery?"

"I can hold it for you."

"Please, Mel, as a good luck charm. I-I really need to touch it."

Her expression softened. "I'll be back in the morning and make sure it's in your hand. Good night, Jess."

No solid food for the patient allowed, but a nurse came in with flavored gelatin in case I developed an appetite. I politely refused. Stress and worry took a toll on me and left no desire to eat. Besides, I hated the nasty stuff and wouldn't touch it even if I was starving, let alone as a last meal. I crawled into bed and stared at the ceiling, clenching the Rose Stone tight to my chest, hoping for answers. None came, and I was too stressed to sleep. I tossed and turned for hours, dozing off for a few minutes and then jerking awake. A tight ball of anxiety settled in my stomach, and I finally called it quits while still dark outside on what was either the last day of my old sick life or the first day of a new healthy one.

I took out my sketchbook and flipped to the page with Griffin as a youngster riding Cirrus. My finger traced the outline of the drawing as I sought respite for my troubled heart, but none came.

The door opened, and Melanie and Dr. Turner entered. "Hey, you're awake. Sleep well?" Melanie asked.

"Nope," I said, tossing the sketchbook aside. "Let's

get this circus started."

Other medical personnel arrived to insert IVs and attach monitors. My heart pounded, nerves shredded raw. Melanie wiped the Rose Stone with antiseptic and fixed her to my palm with surgical tape. "There, safe and sound. It'll be with you through the whole operation."

I had no fear and took comfort in the touch of the Rose Stone. "Just you and me," I whispered. "We'll fight this together."

The light over the bed flickered, and my mouth dried.

Dr. Turner looked at the ceiling with a frown. "I thought we were done with those brownouts. Despite the backup generator, I'm leery of continuing with the operation if the power quits. We can delay a day."

"It flickered, but it's fine now," said Melanie.

Bring me the stone or she dies. A spark shot from an outlet and landed on Melanie's hand where it rested on the bedframe.

Crack! Melanie jumped back, clutching her shirt. "Wow, that hurt. My heart skipped a beat."

Bring me the stone or she dies before you!

"I told you I don't know how," I shouted. Everyone stared at me as I struggled to get out of bed and attack the spark hovering in the air.

Dr. Turner rushed to my side and pinned back my shoulders. "Don't move. You'll pull out the IVs."

The spark brushed lightly against Melanie's arm, and she flinched.

"Leave her alone," I yelled. "Melanie, the darkling is here. It's after you. Don't touch anything metal."

Bring me the stone!

"It's okay, Jess," soothed Melanie, her voice breaking. "It was static. There's nothing here."

"It's a spark, only I can see it. It's not a hallucination. Just now you felt the darkling touch you."

Melanie shot a desperate look at Dr. Turner. He barked orders to a nurse, and she injected a liquid into the IV. Warm lethargy spread across my body. They didn't believe me. I couldn't protect them.

Bring me the stone!

"I don't know how to get back," I mumbled. My lips went numb, and it was hard to speak. "Don't worry, Mel. I'll stop it or die…"

"Jess, relax," Melanie said in a trembling voice.

"Get her to OR stat," ordered Dr. Turner. There was a flurry of voices, and I felt the bed move.

The spark stabbed at my hand. An arrow of fiery pain rocketed up my arm and into my chest. I couldn't breathe.

You die first and then your world burns.

Unchained energy rushed from the Rose Stone through the surgical tape and into my fingers, my arms, my shoulders. I embraced the power, directing healing waves at my chest, snuffing the pain like a candlewick.

Crimson haze blurred my vision. Voices faded away. "We're losing her," shouted Dr. Turner.

"Griffin," I whispered. "Find me." A light shone through the haze and Griffin called, "I am here."

****

"Be easy, I've sent for him. He's inspecting the front line."

"The front?" I mumbled and opened my eyes to a flood of happiness. Lady Emlyn hovered over me. "I'm back." I sat up, weak with relief. No longer in a crumbling ruin, but on a cot in a tent. "Where are Griffin and the others? I left them fighting carvers—"

"They're alive, massing with the rest of the forces. I've sent word to the captain."

My heart flooded with happiness as the tent flap jerked aside and Griffin entered. I jumped to my feet, and he gathered me in his arms. "I feared I'd lost you."

I clung to him. "But you didn't give up. I felt your heart out there."

"And I felt yours." His lips met mine, and fears for the future vanished. No matter what happened, Griffin loved me.

"Ahem." Lady Emlyn looked at us with a gleam in her eye.

I flushed. "Sorry. I don't suppose this is the right time or place." I glanced down, suddenly aware of the hospital gown. "Or outfit."

Danya entered with an armload of clothing and put them on the cot. "The drum said you returned, and I assumed you needed these. It's good to see you again."

"And you." I hugged her tight. "The last sight I had was through the portal. I was afraid the carvers reached you."

"Not yet." Her solemn tone stirred a chill.

I turned to Griffin. "Abril and Bram?"

"Safe. The portal opened as the carvers rushed the corridor and then shut immediately after we entered. When we reached the other side, you were gone. Since then, breaches have occurred one after another. Dozens of carvers forced their way into the Commonwealth."

"War machines?"

"Not yet, but they will assuredly come. So far, the

Rose Guard has stopped the carvers' advance, but enemy numbers are increasing. We can't hold the line much longer. Now that you've returned with the Rose Stone, we have a chance."

I had forgotten about the Rose Stone and peered at my hand. The surgical tape was loose, a section distended. I ripped it off and saw nothing but my empty palm. In a panic, I patted down my clothing, but the hospital gown didn't have pockets. The horrific truth struck me with the strength of a two-by-four. "The Rose Stone is gone."

Chapter Sixteen

Stunned faces gaped at me. "Gone?" said Griffin.

"T-they were getting ready to operate," I stammered, holding out my hand. "She was right here."

"She stayed in your world then."

"No, I felt her with me when I left, but now…" I stared in numb disbelief at my palm, willing the Rose Stone to appear, but to no avail.

Lady Emlyn steadied herself against a chair. The color drained from her complexion. "If the Rose Stone is lost…"

No one needed to say it. I had doomed the Commonwealth.

A Rose Guard entered the tent. "The drummers have returned."

"I'll speak to them," said Danya and she hurried away.

Lady Emlyn straightened. "Captain, we must inform Commander Tian."

Griffin gently touched my cheek. "Get dressed. I'll see you soon."

He had no condemnation in his eyes, but that did nothing to assuage the despair wrapped tight around me. I threw on clothing, hands shaking. How could I have done this to them? Why didn't the Rose Stone stay with me? Where was she now? Did I surrender her to the mystic recesses between two worlds? I sank onto the cot and gulped back a sob. Why wasn't I strong enough to hold on?

Danya's hands pulled me to my feet. "It's not your fault," she said, holding me tight.

"Then, where is she?"

"I do not know." She gently stroked my hair as I burrowed my face in her shoulder. "The Rose Stone has her own ways. Who are we to question them? Perhaps what happened is as it should be."

"I don't see how."

"Nor do I, but do not cry." She brushed a tear from my cheek. "The answer will come."

"Since when did you become such an optimist?"

"We've fought the darkling for so long I refuse to believe the struggle was in vain. Yes, the barrier is weak, but the Rose Guards continue to drive back the carvers, drummers stopped the wind surges, and none of the killing machines have entered. Griffin described the army waiting in the darkling's lair, but it isn't able to rip apart the boundary yet or the land would have been overrun by now. Do not abandon hope. Come, the others are waiting."

"What's the news from the drummers?" I asked. Danya didn't answer, but looked away, and my heart sank. "It's bad, isn't it?"

She lifted the tent flap. "The future is dark, but we still live and breathe."

Her words held little comfort. I stepped outside and blinked in the bright sunlight. Tents filled the open spaces, blocking the view beyond. Rose Guards mounted on lyrs rode through the encampment while the rallying screeches of warbirds came from overhead. At each tent were poles with crossbars at the top. A warbird swooped down and landed on one.

"Racer," I said. "I'm glad you're okay."

He bowed his head. *Rose Stone.*

The other warbirds circling the sky took up the chant. *Rose Stone, Rose Stone, Rose Stone.*

I swallowed hard. "She's not here."

Racer studied me with his brilliant blue eyes. *When called, the Rose Stone will answer, and warbirds will be ready.* Before I said anything, he stretched his wings and launched from the perch to join the legion.

I looked at Danya. "What did Racer mean by that?"

"I don't know," Danya murmured. "But warbirds have abilities we do not."

I gazed at the sky and intercepted a flurry of excited avian thoughts that rushed by too fast for me to understand. Something obviously had them riled. "Where are we?" I asked. "Lady Emlyn said it's the front."

"A guard encampment, not far from Paxton's farm and the Last Stand River. See?" She waved her hand and above the tent tops was a glimpse of the crooked hills.

"What happened after I disappeared?"

"The four of you entered the portal, but you weren't with them when they reached me on the other side. Griffin tried to return, but the opening vanished as if it had never been. When you didn't appear, we feared the worst, capture by the darkling. I sent word to Stone Keep, but Griffin insisted you were alive and unharmed."

She gave me a knowing look. "You and Griffin have a powerful connection, formed even before each of you knew the other existed. He was the one who said we mustn't leave this place and you would return. He was right."

"I love him, and he loves me," I said.

Danya touched my cheek. "That much is plain. I searched the mystic trails for you and found nothing. My drum did not lead you here, Griffin did, and you are together once more. All is as it should be."

"How can you say that?" I sputtered. "The Rose Stone is lost."

"Yet, the fight isn't over."

Danya ushered me to a tent flying the banner of the Commonwealth. Inside, Griffin was speaking with Lady Emlyn and Commander Tian. He saw me and hurried to my side, but Commander Tian stiffened. "Captain Griffin said the Rose Stone is missing."

It was hard to meet his eyes. "She followed me into the other world. I held onto her as I returned, but she was gone when I woke. I'm sorry. I don't know what happened to her."

"Danya, what did the drummers report?" Lady Emlyn asked.

"They have no message from the Rose Stone but sense the multitude of breaches are applying mounting pressure on the boundary. When it falls, carvers and war machines will break through to every corner of the Commonwealth."

Lady Emlyn clasped her hands. "Such a wind surge will scour the earth clean."

"How long?" asked Griffin.

"Before sunset."

Rising tension built in the air like static electricity. "This is my fault," I said in a choked voice. "The darkling found the portal to my world and gave me a choice. If I surrendered the Rose Stone, it would leave my world and never return, but the Commonwealth was doomed." My shoulders sagged. "Even if I had the Rose Stone, I'd never turn her over, no matter the consequences."

"It seems the decision has been taken from your hands." Commander Tian grunted. "The darkling is coming, and we can't stop it."

"You have no idea where the Rose Stone is?" asked Lady Emlyn.

"None," I said. "The treatment worked, shrinking the tumor. Dr. Turner was ready to begin the operation, and I wanted the Rose Stone near me. My friend taped her securely to my hand so I couldn't let go. The darkling appeared and tried to take her, but I fought back. It was as if, for an instant, the Rose Stone guided me."

"Explain," demanded Danya with surprising fervor.

I rubbed the back of my neck. "Honestly, I don't know how I broke free, but the power had to come from the Rose Stone. When I woke here, the tape was intact, bound to my hand. I was so careful, but she disappeared."

I turned away, unable to face them, but Griffin pulled me close. "You bear no fault and have only tried to help us."

"I wonder," mused Danya. Without warning, she shoved Griffin aside and grabbed both my hands in hers.

"Um, Danya?" I said.

She studied my face, and her eyes widened. "The Rose Stone is here."

I swept my head back and forth, scanning the tent.

"Where?"

"You and she are one." Danya said with wonder. "I understand now. The warbirds sensed it first."

"What does that mean?" demanded Commander Tian.

"It means we have hope," said Griffin.

"Hope for what?" I sputtered, staring at my hands. "Even if what Danya says is true and we've joined together, I have no clue how to access her power."

"You already have," said Griffin with confidence. "The boundary holds."

I saw their hopeful faces and knew what they wanted me to say. I had the power of the Rose Stone, everything would be fine, but I couldn't lie. I didn't feel any different. If something changed, it was news to me. "I need air."

I rushed from the tent and heard a familiar nicker. Alta was saddled and tied to a nearby post. She pawed the ground, straining against the reins to reach me. I patted her neck, taking comfort in the touch of her velvety hide. She butted me gently with her head. "At least, you don't think I've changed."

"Nor do I," said Griffin, who had followed me. "You are the same Jess, stubborn and half mad."

I gave a weak laugh. "I guess some things are eternal." The momentary lightness in my heart faded. "Danya insists the Rose Stone's power is within me, but I don't sense anything. If Danya's right, what's the point if I can't turn it on?"

Griffin said nothing but pulled me toward him. I leaned against his chest, pressing my cheek against the Rose Stone emblem, his arms wrapped tight around me. "The weakness is gone from your hands and legs," he said. "I see no pain in your eyes. The medics from your world healed you."

We're losing her. Dr. Turner's shout came back to me with icy foreboding.

"No, they didn't. The darkling attacked the hospital before they had a chance." I pulled back from Griffin. "I don't think I have much time left in my world."

"What are you saying, Jess?" He gently tilted my face so that his gaze locked on mine. I read his fear and knew he yearned for me to offer hope.

I had none to give him. "I'm dying, Griffin."

"That can't be true."

"It is. I feel it."

He tenderly caressed my cheek, his eyes a well of pain. "Don't say that."

"The Rose Stone came to my world with me because she knew the tumor was a death sentence. She couldn't heal me from the Commonwealth because the power stretched too thin. She tried in my world but had been weakened and only able to do so much. The doctors took over from there, but it doesn't look good."

Griffin's head turned toward the hills and then back to me. "When the call comes to your world, as it surely will, don't fight it. Allow the healers to complete their work."

Pain shot through my heart. "My home is here with you."

"I wish it were so with all my heart, but this world is falling into an abyss, one from which it will never emerge. The Rose Guard will make a final stand to protect the people and I will be with them. I won't have your last sight of the Commonwealth be our annihilation on a hopeless battlefield. Remember us as we were."

My throat tightened. "I want to fight by your side."

"I know, but my love does more harm than good." Griffin pushed me away. "It's more than the Rose Stone that ties you to this place. I do, too."

"Griffin—"

"No, Jess. Much as we wish it, you have no future here with me. Your hope lies in the healers of your world. That is your true place. Go home."

"I can't leave you." Every word was a hot shard in my throat. I barely got them out.

"You can. You must. I believe the Rose Stone is with you now and gave you the ability to find the route home. The next time, I won't try to stop you and will forbid Danya to use her drum to search." Griffin stepped back. "I'll take you to my father's farm. He refused to evacuate with the rest, but perhaps concern for your safety will change his mind." Griffin's voice softened. "I can't have you on the battlefield when there is nothing you can do."

I could barely breathe. "I'm a distraction."

"Yes." A pained look crossed his face. Those words didn't come easily. "My guard and I will hold the front line as long as we can. Find the way home, Jess, and be happy."

"Griffin, don't." He was silent, but his eyes spoke volumes. Nothing would alter his decision. I held my arms out to him, but Griffin turned his back on me and strode away.

I leaned against Alta, chest so tight it was hard to breathe. My heart left with Griffin, and yet for a strange reason continued to beat inside me. The sudden weakness in my legs had nothing to do with the tumor invading my brain.

Alta nuzzled me gently, offering a lyr's version of comfort. I stood with her, mired in misery. Why couldn't I help these people? Griffin was right. I was useless in combat, a distraction he didn't need. Had the Rose Stone brought me back to say a final goodbye? Half-formed thoughts stirred inside me, and I felt as if an answer floated within reach. My mind snatched for it, but the meaning slipped away. If only I had more time. I pressed my lips together, raging at my stupidity. I was here for a reason, something the Rose Stone and I were meant to do together.

Danya exited the tent. "Griffin said he was taking you to the farm. I will go, too, and see you settled. He wished Lady Emlyn to come, but she refused."

"She's not a distraction," I said bitterly. "Aren't you needed here with the other drummers?"

"There is time for me to return and join them."

"Not much."

Danya gazed past the tents. "I told the drummers how we opened the portal in the hills. Before the final attack begins, we have decided to try to open another one as an escape route."

I regarded her in disbelief. "You had the Rose Stone then to help. Can you do that without her? How can the drummers create an opening large enough save a world?"

"Perhaps drumming together, we have a chance, but any formed would be small and not hold long. If fortune favors us, a handful will escape, enough so that the story of the Commonwealth continues."

"That's crazy," I blurted. "You have no way of knowing the other side of a random portal isn't worse.

It might lead to a world already ravaged. Besides, the darkling will eventually come after you. It wants revenge and every remnant of the Commonwealth destroyed."

Danya patted Alta's neck with a wistful smile. "Since the beginning, the drummers' gift from the Rose Stone has not only been to heal and guide but also offer hope in the darkest times. That is what we offer now—hope that the fight against the darkling isn't in vain."

I opened my mouth to protest what was surely a suicide mission and then shut it again. The Commonwealth was reduced to acts of desperation and I had no alternative to offer, not even hope. Anger and frustration ate at me.

"Jess!" I turned at Abril's shout and felt a moment of cheer. She and Bram waved and led their lyrs toward me.

I ran over and hugged them both. "I heard you were alive and well, but I'm so glad to see for myself."

"As are we," said Abril. She gave me a sympathetic look. "Father said you returned, and he will take you to Grandfather."

"Not my choice," I said, biting off the sour words.

"He means to protect you," said Bram. His glance at Abril told me he'd be perfectly content if Griffin ordered her to stay at the farm, too.

As if reading his mind, Abril snapped, "I am Rose Guard and won't be left behind, no matter what he says. Father finally accepts that. So should you."

"He tried to convince you to stay at the farm?" I asked.

"He said I was needed to protect you and Grandfather." Abril drew herself up proudly. "Everyone knows the truth. This is the Last Stand of the Hills, where the Rose Guard will have its finest hour."

And no one will remember because everyone will die. I bit my lip.

Griffin rode up to us on Cirrus. "It's time to go." He didn't look at me, but kept his eyes straight ahead, focused on the horizon. We mounted and left camp. Griffin urged the lyrs to a gallop. Racer and Sojourn soared overhead. We sped past other farms, but the air was eerily still. Crops stood in the fields, but no farmers. Doors were barred and windows shuttered. Everyone had evacuated behind the lines. Perhaps those people would be the lucky few to escape if the drummers managed to open a portal.

My stomach tightened in a knot. No, they wouldn't. Escape was impossible. I didn't need the Rose Stone whispering in my ear to know the drummers' plan was doomed to failure. I felt it. They'd never open a portal without the help of the Rose Stone.

At a full gallop, it didn't take long to arrive at the country lane leading to Paxton's farm. The fields were empty of workers here, too, except one. Paxton hoed the garden, the single piece of normalcy in the deserted landscape. He spotted us and propped the hoe against the fence. His eyes widened at the sight of me, and he flashed a welcoming smile. "You're back," he said. "Griffin told me you vanished when the breach closed. I feared you were dead."

"Not yet," I said, sliding from Alta's back. I couldn't help myself and hugged him. "I'm happy to see you."

To my surprise, he didn't stiffen but returned the hug. "Griffin insisted you'd return, but I had doubts. I was wrong."

"Well, well, Paxton admits he can be wrong," I said with a faint smile. "Perhaps the future isn't bleak after all."

Paxton regarded his son keenly. "Griffin doesn't think so. I read it in his eyes."

"The battle is near," said Griffin. "I brought Jess here for safekeeping. Evacuate now and you can reach a cave in the hills."

Paxton gave me a sharp look. "Will running save us?"

I respected this man and respect demanded an honest answer. "No."

"Then what is the point? I will stay and you are welcome to join me." He turned to Griffin and his voice softened. "As are all of you."

The tenseness Griffin carried in his stance since the encampment melted away. "Thank you, Father, but we must return as soon as the lyrs rest." Neither had to say it. This was their last goodbye.

Everyone dismounted. Bram and Abril took the reins and led the lyrs to the watering trough. I watched, my fingers clenching and unclenching. There was no pain in my limbs anymore, no headache either. The misery eating me had nothing to do with a tumor.

The heaving flanks of the lyrs quickly slowed to a normal rhythm. They bowed their heads and drank deeply. They were powerful animals, and it wouldn't take long for them to recuperate. Then Griffin, Bram, and Abril would ride away from the farm, and I'd never see any of them again. The only thing left was to barricade the door and wait for death to come knocking.

"What happened after you disappeared?" asked

Paxton.

I told him what I learned, and Abril gaped at me in disbelief. "The darkling created the Rose Stone? How can a being so evil be responsible for such beauty?"

"Fortunately for us, the Rose Stone has been a willful child," Paxton said as he looked at Griffin. His expression held pride. "Children have minds of their own and don't always obey. That can even be for the best."

Danya cocked her head. Her hand went to the ever-present drum at her waist and her fingers tapped a subtle beat. She paused, listened again, and then addressed Griffin. "The drummers sent a message. They are coming here with the guard."

My mouth dried. "The darkling must sense the location of the Rose Stone and will force breaches here." Danya said nothing, but the hard lines in her expression painted a clear picture of what was to come.

Griffin turned to Abril and Bram. "We'll secure the house and then rendezvous with them."

Time ticked quickly away. As they shuttered the windows, I paced the yard with pent-up energy. For the first time in many months, I felt alive and strong and, at the same time, absolutely worthless.

With a *whoosh*, Racer descended from the sky and lit on a fence post. *They come.* The faint pounding of hooves now echoed across the plains. In the distance, a dust cloud rose from the movement of thousands of lyrs. Racer gave me a questioning look. He appeared to be waiting for an answer.

"If you know what I'm supposed to do, I wish you'd spit it out," I snapped.

Abril hugged Paxton. "Goodbye, Grandfather. I

must go now."

Goodbye. The word was so final, a death knell. Paxton clung to her, pain etched into his face. "I never did turn you into a farmer."

"I love you, anyway, and I'm sorry to have been a disappointment," she whispered.

"Never," he said, and his voice tightened. "The fault is mine. I tried to mold you to the life I thought best and refused to cherish your gifts." He released her and looked at Griffin and drew a shuddering breath. "I am proud of you both. Can you forgive a stubborn, stupid old man?"

Griffin hugged him. "Stubborn, yes," he said, his voice welling with emotion. "But stupid—never. I am proud to be your son."

Payton blinked hard and wiped his eyes. "You'd best be on your way, then. I will take of care of Jess."

Abril kissed his cheek. "You're sure we can't convince you to leave and make for the river, Grandfather?"

"The darkling is coming," he said gently. "Whether we run or not, there is no escape from this time and place and the final reckoning. If today holds the last sunset, I'd rather see it here."

No escape from this time and place…Paxton's words struck a chord deep inside me.

"He's right," I murmured. Those wispy thoughts that eluded me earlier clicked together like tumblers in a lock falling into place. "There's no safe place here, not with the darkling hunting us. A sword is useless against a spark."

But something else might work. A shape that wove and stretched, winding and twisting, laying trails through time and space. A shape that held enough power to forge a link between two worlds. A very familiar shape.

I turned to Danya. "Even the power of every drummer combined can't open a portal, but you and I can, or rather you, I, and the Rose Stone can." I faced the others. "The Rose Stone sent me a message."

"What kind?" demanded Griffin.

"It was in the painting, but I didn't understand. Maybe I wasn't ready." The words spilled from my lips. "I painted a border, one I was compelled to finish, roses with winding stems. I couldn't figure out the point. It didn't add anything special to the picture and I never did borders around my work. But this one was different. When I was a child, the Rose Stone gave me a map because she wanted me to find the darkling's lair. Now she's given me another. The border is a map."

"To where?" asked Griffin. "A second place in the hills?"

"No. It wasn't a contour map. There were no recognizable landscapes or markings, simply a long twisting line." I gazed into the distance. "I see it in my mind's eye. It's a wonder I couldn't read it before. Each corner of the painting had a tiny rose, but the first was the largest and nearest to the farm. It marks the place for a portal to open. I have to go through and follow the trail." Excitement rose in my voice as certainty filled me. "I have to find and destroy the darkling."

Chapter Seventeen

Griffin rested his hand on the sword haft. "Not alone."

Danya unhooked the drum from her belt and held it under the crook of her arm. Her hand poised over the surface, and she flexed her fingers. "I am ready."

Bram nodded at Abril. "We are, too."

"As am I," said Paxton.

Griffin raised an eyebrow. "Father?"

"This is my farm," he grunted. "If you're going to open a portal, I have as much right to see what's on the other side as anyone."

I nodded at Danya. The slow tap-tap-tap of her drum filled the air. "Show me the way," I whispered. An edgy tingle danced over my skin. Power built inside me, and I made a promise: my heart and soul sworn to the protection of the Commonwealth.

And to me? At last, the gentle tones of the Rose Stone surfaced.

"Yes. Whatever you offer, I willingly accept." The crimson haze rushed into my vision, but I didn't blink it away. I pulled it in, new energy to flood my veins. I wasn't using the Rose Stone, I had become the Rose Stone.

Together we are one.

"Together we are one." I glanced at Danya. "Louder."

She switched from fingers to palm, the tempo increased as she slapped the drumhead. My mind snatched the beats from the air, infusing them with power, bending and shaping the notes to my will. A rectangle formed with a misty center.

Abril pointed at the army in the distance. "Look." The atmosphere shimmered in front of the advancing line of Rose Guards. An excited chorus came from above as the warbirds screeched an alarm. Breaches began to form, dozens upon dozens, larger than before, big enough to allow entry of the war machines. This was the darkling's final stand, too, as it readied to use all its might to open them at once.

A combined roar issued from the guard. "Rose Stone! Rose Stone! Rose Stone!" Swords held high, their lyrs thundered across the plain.

The mist thinned on the rectangles, and the shapes of carvers became visible. Soon, the horde would emerge with only death on their minds. After them, the wind surges and war machines would wipe the Rose Guard and every inhabitant of the Commonwealth from the face of the earth.

I turned away and faced the portal. An ember burned inside me. It flared, an incandescent inferno begging for release. I touched the portal, and the surface glowed white. "Open," I commanded with no hesitation. No world existed on the other side, only the essence of time. A mystic expanse with a vibrant crimson rose hovering in the center, motionless, waiting for me.

Bram eyed the portal with a sinking expression. "That's not a battlefield. Sword and bow are useless in there."

Griffin took my hand. "Then the Rose Stone may call upon my strength instead. Whatever I have is hers to wield. Protect Danya. Guard the portal. Keep it open for us as long as you can." Abril and Bram drew their swords, Racer and Sojourn took to the skies. Danya beat the drum, her face a mask of concentration.

Paxton grabbed the hoe leaning against the fence and hefted it overhead. "For the Rose Stone," he shouted.

"For the Rose Stone," echoed Griffin.

I touched the rose.

To save the present, we must search the past and plant the seeds of the darkling's destruction.

The rose sprouted a vine that shot into the mist. It developed dozens of offshoots, vines upon vines. I couldn't see the end.

Hold tight to the trail of time.

Griffin and I were yanked forward. Hundreds of vines twisted and turned, but I knew the correct route to follow. I had painted it smooth, green, and straight through the offshoots.

We jerked to a halt, and the haze lifted. I had been in this room before when it was a ruin. Now the machinery was shiny and undamaged. A man and a woman in lab coats burst through the entrance and ran past us without a look.

"They don't see us," said Griffin.

The woman slammed her hand down on a panel, and a door slid into place. "The lab is shielded but won't stay secure long." She leaned against a desk as if her legs no longer supported her weight. "The AI is in everything." She moaned. "How did it find the way back?"

"T-those things…" The man trembled. "They're killing everyone." From above came the carvers' howls, human screams, and explosions that rocked the floor.

The large metallic rectangle was on the dais. This time, a crystal floated in the middle, the same size and shape of the Rose Stone, but not the same crimson color. Instead, a muddy gray haze obscured the perfect clarity of the facets. Sparks crackled in the center.

The blood drained from the man's face. "Oh, no. It's working. It wants this back. What have we done?"

The light overhead blinked. An alarm wailed, and the woman cringed. "The shield collapsed. It knows we're here. We have to destroy the crystal."

"No!" The disembodied voice of the darkling thundered from every speaker in the room. "The stone is mine."

The woman touched a panel. A hum emanated from the rectangle and filled the air. "We've got one shot. There's no time to destroy the crystal, but we have enough power left to send it through a portal. The crystal is an unimaginable energy source, controlling time and space. If it falls to the AI, nothing will ever stop it."

"The AI will follow," said the man.

Something heavy pounded on the door. The unearthly bellows of the carvers were right outside.

"It can't," said the woman adjusting the controls. "The coordinates are random. It won't know where it's gone."

The rectangle glowed.

"Mine!" roared the darkling.

Flames burst from the machinery and struck the man and the woman. They screamed as they collapsed and their bodies burst into ashes. Fire sprouted from a dozen different devices and heavy smoke clouded view of the lab.

Awaken me, said the Rose Stone.

Griffin squeezed my hand. "I heard her, too."

We ran to the dais. I released Griffin's hand and grabbed the gray crystal. Intense, stabbing pain sliced through my head. It nearly sent me staggering back, but I held on tight. Angry sparks flitted around the interior of the stone, bouncing off the facets and sending lashes of white-hot agony up my arm.

"No, you don't," I said through gritted teeth.

Power flooded my hands. It cascaded through me and poured into the crystal. The muddy color disappeared, and the Rose Stone smoldered with pure crimson light. "There you are," I whispered. One shadowy bit remained buried deep inside. The black knot.

Fire shot from every monitor; the temperature soared as flames licked the dais. We were trapped in an inferno. The pounding at the door increased. Hinges warped and bent.

Give her purpose. Show her how to protect this world. Take her through the portal.

Mist formed in the center of the rectangle and inside was a rose attached to a vine. Griffin slipped his arm around my waist, and I touched the floating rose. We were yanked off our feet and thrown into a whirlwind, racing at an impossible speed as the vine tunneled a path through time and space.

The vine disappeared. Griffin and I stood next to a pile of smoking rubble, surrounded by a roaring din. We had landed in the middle of a battlefield. Pieces of tanks and armored carriers lay in broken bits. The darkling's great war machines poured through multiple breaches. Their surfaces bristled with long thin tubes moving in circles, like carvers' tendrils homing in on prey. Engine contrails crisscrossed the sky, and I watched in horror as multiple missiles streaked toward earth. We were right in the path of destruction.

Tendrils from a hovering war machine locked on and spewed fire, plucking each missile from the sky with a booming explosion. None reached the darkling's forces, and they continued their unwavering advance. A squadron of aircraft screamed from behind distant hills. Beams from the darkling's war machines sliced through them as if they were tissue paper.

Every weapon of the last great army of the world is now destroyed, said the Rose Stone.

Griffin gazed at the carnage with horrified eyes. "Was this the Commonwealth?"

At its inception, she said. *The battle is nearly lost. The tattered remnants of humanity have banded together, with lyrs and warbirds at their sides, but nothing can stand against the darkling. The carvers will destroy the remaining defenders and the wind surge will kill the rest. The darkling found my design in that alien complex and had those people create me. They did not suspect, once under its control, my power would open tens of thousands of portals for the darkling to feed on the galaxy, to drain the universe.*

"Unless it is stopped," Griffin said. Behind us, riders on lyrs advanced toward the carvers, a final desperate stand as they faced the enemy. A carver spotted us and charged. Without hesitation, Griffin drew his sword and ran to meet it. "For the Rose

Stone," he shouted.

The Rose Stone you hold is nothing but unfulfilled potential. Give her purpose. Show her how to become the protector of this world. Close the portals, stop the wind surges from forming.

I peered into the Rose Stone's depths. "Watch and learn." I opened my heart and mind, and the world bathed in crimson light. The Rose Stone of then and now became one with Jessica Rose Stone, and the three of us stood together. The darkling built the crystal to seek power for its own use but didn't count on one determined human to spoil the plan.

Pathways of energy appeared before me. I snatched power from the earth and the sky and rammed it against a breach. "Close."

The breach disappeared. I absorbed the wind surge, adding the energy to the Rose Stone and focused on the next breach. "Close." The breach vanished in a puff of air as if it were no more than a dust cloud stirred by an errant breeze.

Nothing stands against me! the darkling screeched.

"The Rose Stone does." A shard of hot pain burrowed deep into my brain.

The stone is mine. I will destroy you.

"Maybe but not today," I said between gritted teeth. I launched the force of the Rose Stone in cannon rounds, absorbing the wind shear until only a few breaches remained.

A carver screamed. Griffin backed it against the wreckage of a tank and lunged. One slash of the sword and the carver's head bounced to the ground. Two more bodies lay at his feet. From across the field, three more charged him.

"Say goodbye," I said and released the power of the wind shear, but this time, instead of being expelled from the breach, the force rushed inward.

The carvers emitted ear-shattering wails as the wind surge sucked them across the battlefield. They tumbled unchecked, bodies breaking against the ground, and vanished from sight. I wrapped the savage wind around the darkling's war machines, plucking them from the earth and sky. As the last one disappeared, I slammed the final breach shut. The Rose Stone glistened, and the protective boundary around the Commonwealth snapped into place.

My chest heaved in ragged gasps, and I swayed on my feet. Griffin ran up and put his arm around me. "Jess?" he said.

I sagged against him and forced a weak smile. "I'm fine but don't want to do that twice in one day." I looked at the stone. "You okay in there?"

Yes. Thank you. My purpose is clear.

"Protect this world."

I swear it.

The Rose Stone was back where she belonged.

A soldier rode up on a lyr. She sheathed her sword and slid from the saddle. "How did you do that?"

"I didn't. This did." I tossed her the Rose Stone.

A warbird dropped from the sky and landed on the saddle's pommel. *Rose Stone.*

"What's a Rose Stone?" she asked.

"A protector. Listen hard and the Rose Stone will guide your people and tell them how to protect the Commonwealth from the darkling."

"Commonwealth?"

I felt a mystic tug. A haze lifted from the ground,

and the outline of the soldier blurred. A rose with a twisted vine hovered in the air. I took Griffin's hand. The haze thickened, and she disappeared.

"Wait," called the soldier. "Where are you going?"

"Haven't a clue," I said over my shoulder.

I latched onto the supernatural flow and touched the rose. The sounds and smells of the battlefield vanished. Through the mystic paths of time and space we flew, pulled along on the spiraling vine. The third corner of the painting would be dead ahead. What truths would it reveal?

The vine deposited us in a room. Two little girls lay on the floor, reading a book, heads together. Neither noticed our arrival.

Griffin looked at one of the girls and then to me. "It's you."

My eyes widened in wonder. "Yes, and my friend, Melanie."

"This book is boring," said Melanie, slamming it shut. "You can do better."

"Someday, I'll write one," said my childish self. She took a sketchbook and colored pencils from a backpack. "Wanna draw?"

"Okay." Little Me ripped out a sheet and handed it to her. Melanie got to work while my hand poised over the blank page.

Griffin nudged me. "She needs inspiration."

I crouched beside the girl and laid a hand on top of hers, guiding it this way and that to form a shape. Lips pressed tight together, Little Me concentrated on keeping the lines at their proper angles.

Melanie looked over her shoulder. "Ooh, a jewel. It's so pretty."

"Rose Stone," I whispered in her ear.

"It's called the Rose Stone," said Little Me.

"That's cool," said Melanie.

"The story is going to be an awesome adventure with a hero and everything."

"What's the hero's name?"

"Griffin," I whispered.

"Griffin," Little Me echoed.

"That's a weird name," said Melanie, wrinkling her nose. "Why don't you call him Kyle?"

"I don't like Kyle. You like Kyle."

"Do not."

"Do so."

Melanie giggled. "You should call him Wesley. You think he's cool."

"Not anymore. He's a poop head. I'll draw Griffin for you."

I chuckled. "Don't forget the scar."

"He has a scar, too," added Little Me as she sketched Griffin's face.

Melanie put her drawing aside. "I'm hungry. I'll ask Mom to make us a snack and then we can play my new video game."

"Okay."

Melanie left the room and Little Me finished the sketch of Griffin, and then the farmhouse, and the contour map.

I stood up. "I guess we're done here."

Griffin peered at me with a quizzical expression and then regarded Little Me with a whimsical look on his face. "No, we're not." He knelt and placed a hand on her shoulder. "Across time and distance, we bind together this night. My heart will wait for you. Find me

299

when you're ready."

Little Me's lips formed a dreamy smile. "Okay."

Melanie came in with a bowl of popcorn. "Did you say something?" she asked.

Little Me blinked. "Uh-uh."

Griffin stood and took my hand. I touched the rose. We raced along the vine to the fourth corner. This time I knew exactly where we'd land and what I had to do. The world came into focus. Stark metallic walls of machinery surrounded us. A siren blared.

Griffin looked around in surprise. "We're inside the tower."

"Yes, and we don't have much time. The darkling knows we're here. I have to finish what I started. The essence of the poison is a bridge between the Rose Stone and the darkling. But a bridge can be crossed from two directions, and I intend to use it. The darkling will do whatever it takes to stop me." There was a roar outside the tower, and then loud hammering at the door. The floor shook under the assault.

Griffin kissed me. "None shall pass." He drew his sword and turned to face the enemy.

Power flooded my body, pure and perfect. Behind me came an eerie howl that iced my blood. I glanced back. The door had been hammered ajar. A carver hooked claws around the jamb to yank it open. One slice from Griffin's blade and the hand tumbled to the floor.

"Go!" shouted Griffin.

I turned away knowing I couldn't help him now. "Let's end this," I said to the Rose Stone. "Take me in." Once again, I was drawn into the icy depths of the darkling's heart. Ahead was the knot, surrounded with protective sparks. The power at the darkling's command beat against me, brittle shards stabbing my skin.

You damaged my perfection, but my power will rise again. Where is the stone? roared the darkling.

"You want the Rose Stone," I mocked. "You've got the Rose Stone."

The palette knife reformed in my hand, shining with crimson flame, and the shards of brutal cold parted like a drawn curtain. A spark struck at me. I stabbed it with the blade and a spasm of pain exploded in my head as it vaporized to ashes.

Impossible! You are weak, dying.

"Yet here I am."

The darkling's voice rose to a maddened screech. *Your world will be drained of life, bodies rotting in the sun.*

"Not if I kill you first." Sparks shot toward me. The palette knife flashed, slicing a fiery arc and turning them to vapor. I grimaced at the burning torment but pressed forward. More sparks sprang from the knot, black arrows directed right at my heart. Another swipe sent them into oblivion.

"Is that the best you've got?" I mocked. "I can do this all day."

You cannot stop me. Accepting the power of the stone has a price. My poison festers in you. You will die long before I am defeated, and the stone will be mine once more.

I bit my lip against an exploding assault of pounding throbs in my head. "Do I hear a touch of panic? There should be." The darkling sent a third volley, smaller this time. The protective ring of sparks around the knot shrunk to one third the size. I crowed in triumph, "You're the one who's weakening."

I am strong enough to open the portal to your world first.

"Never!" I embraced a swell of hatred for the black, ugly thing.

Mine! You are mine! The stone is mine! The sparks launched a frenzied assault to bind my power and overwhelm the Rose Stone. My strength ebbed. The hand with the palette knife sagged.

Past, present, and future binds us together, said the Rose Stone. *Now, call on all our power.*

With blistering rage, I summoned every ounce of strength to drive the palette knife into the black knot. The darkling screamed, not in anger, but abject terror. The knot ruptured into a thousand pieces. Beyond that was the beating heart of the darkling itself, not a spark, but a core of pure energy, buried deep within the alien machines that powered the portals.

You cannot hold such power, said the darkling. *I will die, but you will die, too.* The voice soared to a high-pitched scream.

"I don't care," I shouted in triumph. "My world and the Commonwealth will live."

Stop the attack, the darkling quavered. *The link with the stone infected you with my poison, but I will withdraw and give back your life.* Waves of force hammered at me, dismal, unyielding clouds that sought to crush my defenses and leave me broken and lifeless. *I promise to retreat from both worlds and seek the spark elsewhere. Either that or die. Here. Now.*

"And allow you to invade another innocent world, rob it of life? I have a better idea. You will never seek the spark again."

A crimson glow surrounded me. The pain vanished. I no longer had a body to suffer as I became one with the Rose Stone, mistress of her power. I snared the darkling and held on tight.

Noooo!

The pulsing core became a flame, white-hot and mad as hell. Scorching heat beat against my skin, but I ripped into the fire and plummeted into the darkling's heart. Electric currents vibrated around me, crackling waves controlling the machines at its command. Alien machines whose sole purpose had been redirected to find new sources of power to keep the darkling alive. I touched no soul, no conscience, only an endless pit of hunger.

The darkling vibrated with rage and tried to run and hide in a myriad of circuits, a galaxy of sparks, but I detected the heart of evil. Hidden deep inside was the primary program, the original source code, the essence of the darkling. It couldn't run anymore. It couldn't hide. I tasted shock, then felt tremors of the darkling's terror as it surrendered to the inconceivable truth.

It was mine.

One little deletion from the code and power drained away until only a flickering spark remained.

You will die. You will die. You will die. Agony ripped through my head with every word.

A second deletion, and the spark weakened to barely an ember. *No. Please. Help.*

Nothing existed for me but pain—and determination. At hand was the most important line of code. The one that gave the darkling life. "Delete," I commanded.

With the darkling's dying scream echoing through my head, the spark snuffed out.

So did the world.

Chapter Eighteen

The ground rocked beneath my feet, but strong arms kept me upright. "Jess," said Griffin. "Everything is collapsing. We have to go now."

I blinked and my mind cleared. We were still in the tower, but most of the machines were dark. The only lights came from several flickering monitors belching curls of fetid smoke.

"This way." Griffin grabbed my hand, and I stumbled toward the door. It had been ripped off its hinges and the opening partially blocked by the bodies of two carvers minus their heads. Behind them lay dozens of others with no signs of wounds. I shot a look at Griffin. "You were busy."

"These weren't my doing," Griffin said as we climbed over the bodies. "The lights dimmed and then the carvers collapsed." He motioned around us. "The rest of the machines are failing as we speak."

I peered over the gangway. Carver bodies covered the walkways. One by one, lights in the depths winked out. The gloom deepened as total darkness inched toward our level. There was an ear-shattering *boom!* and a section of the tower exploded. Streams of liquid metal erupted, cascading down stanchions, and tumbling into the pit. The rumbling staccato of multiple detonations echoed through the air.

Griffin and I ran; the creaking, grinding roar of

total annihilation dogged our heels. Machines ignited and smoke decreased visibility even more. The darkling's world was disintegrating around us. We sprinted across stanchions, not knowing where we were, racing to keep obliteration at bay.

We turned a corridor and then slid to a halt. A computer bank had toppled over, blocking the route. "Back that way," shouted Griffin. With a tinny crash, the one behind us shattered, boxing us in. My heart hammered, and I drew a ragged breath, coughing from the smoke. The ground shuddered again, and a huge crack zigzagged across the floor. The annihilation of the darkling's lair was imminent, and we were hemmed in with no escape. Without words, Griffin gathered me in his arms. No need to say it. This was as far as we'd go. He kissed me as the world ended. "I have no regrets."

"Neither do I." I clung tightly to him, and fear melted away. If his heartbeat was the last sound I heard, his arms the last touch I received, then so be it. I closed my eyes, content to die.

Thump-thump-thump. The beat thrummed within me. *Thump-thump-thump-thump.* "A drum," I said with growing excitement. "A lot of drums. Danya and the others are trying to open a portal."

I held out my hands and waves of sound struck them, Danya's drum louder than the rest. "The rhythm is strongest over here." I touched the wall and felt a flicker of heat. "We can follow it, just like the vine."

I reached for the power of the Rose Stone, and she answered willingly. I latched on and funneled energy to the wall. Through the clouds of gathering smoke, the hazy outline of Danya and her drum appeared.

With a thunderous *crack*, a rift split under our feet. Griffin grabbed my hand. "Jump!" he yelled. We leapt into the portal as the ground crumbled away.

Falling, falling, falling into a crimson haze…*wham*! A hard jolt brought me to my knees. The haze parted and a cheer rose. The beaming faces of Abril, Bram, Danya, and Paxton surrounded us along with dozens of drummers and other members of the guard. Bodies of several carvers littered the ground. Through the portal came a volley of rapid-fire explosions as Griffin helped me to my feet.

"Jess, shut the portal," called out Danya.

I reeled in the power, and with a shimmer, it vanished. Another cheer sounded and well-wishers rushed us. Paxton dropped his hoe, stained with carver blood. He grabbed his son by the shoulders and drew him into an embrace. To my surprise, he then turned to me and did the same.

I laughed. "I'm glad to see you, too. Are you all right? How many carvers made it through?"

"They poured through breaches like water," said Abril. "The guard dropped the front line, but even Commander Tian's forces couldn't stop the horde and they had to fall back here." Her expression soured. "It didn't look good for the Rose Guard, but then without warning the carvers fell in their tracks."

"I've never seen anything to compare," said Bram with a shake of his head. "They simply collapsed, broken marionettes whose strings had been cut. We thought the wind surge would destroy us, but, instead, the wind reversed, dragging in the carvers and war machines. Then the breaches vanished, and Danya called the other drummers to help find you."

L. A. Kelley

Lady Emlyn pushed her way through the crowd with Commander Tian at her side. At the sight of us, Lady Emlyn's face lit with a smile. "I received word you were both alive and well. The darkling?"

"Destroyed, thanks to Jess," said Griffin.

"Thanks to both of us," I said. "I couldn't have done it alone."

"What of the Rose Stone?" asked Commander Tian.

Unsure, I looked at where the portal had been a moment before. "I-I don't know. She spoke to me plainly. We joined to defeat the darkling, but I don't hear her any longer."

The chancellor nodded with a thoughtful expression. "Perhaps her duty is finished. Our world is finally safe."

A spontaneous shout rose from the crowd. "Rose Stone, Rose Stone, Rose Stone." It swelled to a triumphant roar as word passed to every member of the army that the enemy they had fought for so long would never threaten the Commonwealth again. The chant echoed from the hills and flooded the sky. For all I knew, it rippled through the galaxy.

The rest of the day was a blur. Lady Emlyn and Commander Tian insisted on a full recounting of our adventures. Warbirds arrived from around the Commonwealth. Everyplace within the boundary reported the same result. A massive wave of carvers spewed from the breaches. The Rose Guard fought back and when the battle seemed lost, the carvers collapsed. The breaches stayed open long enough for a reverse wind to scour the land clean and then vanish.

The sun had long set, but people continued to

arrive at the farmhouse to hear our story. A dull throb sprouted behind my eyes, and I rubbed my forehead. Griffin ordered them away, even to my amusement, Commander Tian. He left with a slight grumble and advised he'd see me first thing in the morning.

"You need rest now," said Griffin to me. "Go upstairs. I'll send a servant with a tray to your room. Eat and then sleep. That's an order."

"Are you always so bossy?" I said with a laugh.

"Only when I'm right," he said with a sparkle in his eyes. "And a captain of the Rose Guard is always right. Ask my people."

"No argument from me, Captain," said a grinning Abril who walked toward us. "The chancellor summons you."

"Tell her I'm coming." Abril hurried away and Griffin pulled me close and into a long, deep kiss that I felt to my toes. "I'll see you in the morning," he said softly.

I wrapped my arms around his neck. "It's not necessary to wait that long. You know the way to your old bedroom, and the door will be unlocked."

He nuzzled my neck, sending a delicious flutter of desire cascading through me. "If only my duties were so simple to escape."

"Why not?" I chuckled. "We'll take Cirrus and Alta and head for the hills. They'll never catch us."

With a tender light in his eyes, Griffin took my hands in his. "I am naught but a soldier with little to offer, but everything I have is yours."

My heart beat against my ribs. "Your love is more than enough."

"Then will you honor me by becoming my wife?"

"Yes, oh, yes," I said and kissed him again. "The offer to my bedroom still stands."

Griffin pressed my fingertips to his lips. "I fear duties will keep us apart tonight, but I'll speak with my father and ask if he will host the wedding here. No matter where Commander Tian chooses to send me next, you will be at my side."

I went upstairs, tired to the bone, but heart light as a feather. I'd found my place and a man who loved me with his whole heart. I didn't know what the future held and didn't care, as long as I was here in the Commonwealth with Griffin, never to be parted.

****

Tap-tap-tap.

The noise jerked me awake. Sunlight streamed into the bedroom. I'd slept through the night and nearly half the day and was fully refreshed. I hadn't budged from Griffin's old room, and contentment flooded my heart. Part of me feared I would be yanked to my old life, but I remained firmly anchored in the Commonwealth. I'd never leave again.

Tap-tap-tap.

Racer sat on the sill impatiently pecking at the pane with his beak. I threw open the window. "Good to see you again. The warbirds?"

Unscathed. Victory was ours. The legion triumphed in the kill. He scrutinized me with those crystal blue eyes.

"I know," I said with a tinge of melancholy. "The Rose Stone is gone."

So you say. The world has changed. Some things stay as they were, some do not. He flew off, leaving me with a distinct impression of amusement.

"We're going to have to work on those communication skills," I yelled after him.

I turned from the window. My gaze caught the unrumpled pillow next to mine, and I sighed. Dang it, Griffin was right. Duties had kept us apart last night. A smile teased my lips. But not for long. Soon, our lives would officially join. I was meant to be with him. Every ounce of tension I had carried was gone. The darkling was destroyed. This was my place. I'd never be dragged back to my old life. I was here to stay.

My smile faded, and in rushed wistful sadness. Did Melanie stand at my bedside in the other world? Was I dead or in a coma? She and Owen Turner were meant for each other, but would grief for me overshadow her emotions and they drift apart? The thought of Melanie unleashed bitter sorrow. She'd done so much for me. We shared everything in our lives, but I'd never see her again to explain I found happiness and it was time to find hers. If only there were some way to pay her back.

I dressed and went downstairs. Paxton stood in the kitchen. The gruff shell was gone, and he greeted me with a warm smile. "Sleep well?"

"Yes, thank you."

"Good. Sit. I made tea. Would you care for a cup?"

"I'd love one. Where is everyone?"

"You mean, my son?" Paxton gave a sly grin. "Or, should I say, your future husband?" He set a steaming cup in front of me, leaned over, and kissed my cheek. "I am pleased with the news and honored to host the wedding."

"Thank you, Paxton. I wouldn't want to be married anyplace else."

He sat across the table from me and blew on his

tea. "Maybe we'll have a new addition to the family soon—a farmer, this time," he said with a smile.

I laughed. "Griffin and I will do our best. Speaking of Griffin, where is he? He didn't come to…" I coughed. "I mean, I haven't seen him since yesterday."

"He's with the chancellor and the others. They've been talking through the night." He snorted. "It's a wonder anything ever gets done."

"So why are you in here fixing tea and not out there hassling the servants?" I said with a grin. "Haven't you heard, there's plenty of work on a farm. Not to mention, you offered to host a wedding."

"My people haven't returned from the evacuation yet. With Rose Guards clomping over my fields, there is naught for me to do but tend the livestock. Abril and Bram helped with that."

"I hope the guards didn't destroy your crops."

"Whatever damage done was worth the price." He added with a gleam in his eye, "Besides, Chancellor Emlyn offered a generous settlement from the Commonwealth. It will be enough to cover the loss and make more improvements to the farm."

I laughed. "Good. Tell me about them." As Paxton described his plans, I sipped my tea, unconsciously rubbing my temple.

Paxton's sharp eyes took note. "You are in pain."

"A little headache, a remnant from the excitement of the last few days." I dropped my hand to my lap. The ache buried itself deep inside me, and the rubbing didn't help. It seemed to make it worse. Maybe I needed to eat.

Abril rushed into the kitchen. "Good. I hoped you were here." She hugged me. "Father said you will be married. I'm so happy for both of you."

"Thanks, Abril. That means a lot to me."

"I never thought I'd have a stepmother." She said with an impish grin, "Father was so picky."

"Speaking of your father, where is he?"

"Outside with Chancellor Emlyn. Much has happened since last night. The council met in the headquarters tent. Then Commander Tian summoned Father and other Rose Guard captains. Everyone talked for hours. Father and the chancellor just emerged, and he sent me to see if you were awake."

"So, what's the big news?" I asked. "I can see you're bursting to tell."

"I'll let Father do that. He is waiting by the garden gate."

"Jess has a headache," said Paxton.

"I'll find Danya," said Abril. "She'll make a remedy."

That's what I needed. One of Danya's tonics was the ticket. I hurried outside. Lady Emlyn stood with Griffin. They both looked tired. Lady Emlyn had dark circles under her eyes and Griffin's shoulders sagged, but at the sight of me coming toward him he straightened. His loving smile momentarily dulled the headache, which was now more of a needle than a throb.

Lady Emlyn clasped my hands. "Captain Griffin told me of your upcoming wedding. Congratulations. The Commonwealth owes you a debt that can never be repaid."

"You don't owe me anything." I glanced at Griffin and felt a flush rising up my neck. "I only want to make a life here."

"That is readily granted, but the Council and I have another request."

I raised an eyebrow. "Oh?"

She chuckled. "My, my—such suspicion. Now that the darkling is vanquished, we are no longer constrained by the boundary set for our protection long ago. I received confirmation it fell across the Commonwealth. People are eager for new lands, but the old knowledge of the world is lost and there are but a few stories of what lies beyond the garrisons. We have no wish to repeat the mistakes of the ancestors and stumble blindly into the unknown. Progress must be slow and thoughtful. Rose Guards will lead, but their mission has changed. We need exploration and mapping. Dangers may need to be overcome before lands are ready for settlers. It's possible some carvers survived, hiding in the wilds and must be dealt with. Rose Guards will be the pathfinders and protectors of this world. Leadership will be a heavy burden and not meant for one person to carry."

Lady Emlyn nodded at Griffin. "I have named him Marshall of High Point Garrison and the Northern Realm, and he has accepted. He will return with a force of Rose Guards and begin exploration. Will you also accept the responsibility, Lady Jess, to be the voice of the Rose Stone at his side and help open the new northern province for us?"

"I'm honored, but I haven't heard the Rose Stone's voice," I said. "She doesn't speak to me any longer."

Lady Emlyn gave me a sharp look. "I believe she does, but not in the same way."

Griffin took my hand. "I can't promise an easy life."

I smiled at him. "I don't need one. I gladly accept. It would be an honor to serve the Commonwealth." I flinched at a stab of pain.

"Jess, you have to fight," said Melanie.

I felt the blood drain from my face. "No," I shouted at the sky. "I'm not leaving."

Griffin stared at me. "Jess?"

"I-I hear Melanie." Griffin caught me as my legs gave out. The pain soared, a hot knife slicing into my head.

Danya and Abril ran across the yard. I peered at Danya though a fog of pain, a crimson fog clouding my vision. I felt stretched tight like a rubber band, any more and I'd snap. "I won't go," I moaned. "I have to stay." I screamed at another tearing pain in my head.

Danya laid a cool hand on my brow. "Her body is linked to the other world. Healers are removing the evil inside her. I can do nothing. She must go back there or die in both."

"No," I cried. "I won't leave you, Griffin."

"You must. Let go, Jess, I beg you."

"Jess," said Melanie. "I'm here."

Griffin kissed me. "I will love you forever," he whispered.

My strength failed me. The fight was over. The crimson haze closed in, and I slipped away.

Chapter Nineteen

"She's waking up," said a man, but not Griffin. He wasn't here. I'd never see him again. The voice belonged to Dr. Turner.

"Thank God," said Melanie. "I thought she'd never come back to us." A gentle hand squeezed my fingers. "Come on, sleepy head. You're home."

My eyelids fluttered open. I was in a hospital bed surrounded by faintly beeping monitors and people with concerned faces.

Melanie leaned over me. "Do you know who I am?"

"M-Melanie." My throat was dry, and my voice had a raspy croak. The crimson haze had vanished, and so had the terrible ache in my head.

She heaved a sigh. "It was a rough road for a while. How are you feeling?"

My heart had broken in a thousand pieces, but I managed to say, "O-okay, I guess."

Dr. Turner smiled. "Remember me?"

"Dr. Turner."

He tested the muscle responses in my arms and legs, and I assured him I had no pain. What a lie. He checked my eyes and asked me to squeeze his fingers. "Good grip," he said cheerfully. "Muscle response and reflexes are excellent. Jess, I'm delighted to say the operation was a complete success. Every trace of the tumor is gone. You're going to live a long, happy life."

A tear squeezed from the corner of my eye. "Don't cry," said Melanie. "We almost lost you on the operating table, but everything is all right now."

"H-how long?" I was numb, physically and emotionally.

"You've been unconscious for five days," said Melanie. "It was touch and go for a while."

"She shouldn't try to talk anymore," said Dr. Turner.

Melanie leaned over and kissed my forehead. "I'll come back later. You'll be up and around in no time."

"I'll walk you out," said Dr. Turner to Melanie. "Rest now, Jess. Everything looks perfect."

Nurses fussed over me, checking the medical monitors and IV bags. My mind was a cloudy mess with one anguished thought tearing my heart. I was alive, but Griffin was gone forever.

****

I remained in the hospital for three more days. As each one passed, my body strengthened. Dr. Turner, or Owen, as I now called him, said he'd never seen anything akin to my recovery. Recovery? The tumor was gone, but so was my heart, lost at the other end of a mystic trail. I didn't allow Melanie or Owen to see my suffering. I couldn't explain it to them in any logical way and had no wish to go from the ICU to the psych ward.

After I was discharged from the hospital, Melanie drove me to the loft. She pressed me to stay at her place for a while, but I refused. This was where I first heard the call of the Rose Stone. This was where I had to be. The trip up three flights of stairs took longer than usual, but I leaned on her and made it home.

Home…such a hollow, empty word now.

After she left, I went to the painting and strained to hear Griffin's voice, yearning for the tug to take me back to him. But try as I might, the Commonwealth was out of reach as if a barrier had been erected. No thoughts or sounds came from the end of the mystic trail. I stood at the easel until my legs ached, and then I sat on the couch and cried until no tears remained.

It's funny how I managed to go through the motions of living when I was hollow inside. Each morning, I went to the painting waiting for a call that didn't come. My heart was in the Commonwealth, but my body anchored here. Melanie stopped by every day after work to fuss over me until I convinced her I managed perfectly well on my own.

"You were at the hospital with me when I passed my two-week checkup with flying colors. Owen even said I can drive again."

"You're not painting yet," she said. "You haven't once picked up a brush."

I couldn't have Melanie wasting any more of her life focused on me, so I grasped for a convenient lie. "I've decided to do something different—that book I always meant to write. I didn't want to tell you about it until it was finished."

"That's wonderful." Melanie hugged me. "I'll buy the first copy."

"Thanks. Now skedaddle, so I can work. You don't need to concentrate on me any longer. It's time for you to think about your own life. Ask Owen out to dinner."

She blushed. "I almost did today but chickened out."

"Call him now. Take him to a nice, romantic restaurant and talk about anything except me and disgusting medical procedures."

Melanie laughed and dug her phone from her purse. A few minutes later, the date was set. After she left, I sat at the desk and stared at the computer. The urge to write my story was irresistible, a way to keep Griffin's memory alive. Words spilled from me to the page; I couldn't type them fast enough. Now and then, I stopped for inspiration and looked at the painting. Maybe it was the light, but the colors seemed brighter than ever.

With every visit, Melanie had new things to tell me about Owen. I heard the change in her voice as she fell headfirst into love. Their relationship progressed swiftly, and they often came to visit together. Their subtle tender touches and loving glances eased the constant ache in my heart. I lost my happily ever after, but Melanie had discovered hers.

Meanwhile, page by page, chapter by chapter, the story of the Rose Stone took shape. I returned to my old sketchbook and filled the remaining blank pages with drawings of Abril and Bram, Danya and the drummers, the warbirds and lyrs, the darkling's fortress and others. Every morning, I went out and purchased a fresh rose from the flower stand on the corner and kept it in a vase at my desk.

At last, I reached the present. No more pictures, no more adventure. I tried to write a different ending. Griffin and I married and then traveled to High Point Garrison and began our new lives, but the words rang empty, so I deleted them. This was a journal, not a novel. Only the painful truth sufficed.

My cellphone rang. Melanie bubbled with excitement. "Owen and I want to stop by. We have news to share."

"You're engaged!" I said.

She laughed. "At least pretend to be surprised."

"I promise to act shocked when you tell me again."

"We'll be there in an hour. You know it's funny, Owen and I would never have met if it hadn't been for your tumor. Who could have predicted something that caused so much pain, would be responsible for so much joy? Without you, I'd never have found my happily-ever-after."

"I'm so thrilled for you both."

"You'll find your happily-ever-after soon, too. I'm certain of it."

"Sure. Absolutely. See you in a bit."

"See you."

I went to the painting and lovingly touched Griffin's face. "Melanie will be happy now."

Then your task is done.

I gasped. Was that real? "The Rose Stone? You're here?"

I have always been with you. We are bound.

The wall around my heart crumbled and light flooded the dark spaces. "I hear you now. Why didn't I weeks ago?"

The love for your friend prevented it. You owed her a debt and wanted her to find happiness before claiming your own. The debt is now settled.

"And Griffin?"

He is also tied to you in a bond neither time nor space can shatter.

The power of the Rose Stone flooded through me,

and I saw the mystic road stretch ahead. Griffin waited at the other end with arms wide. "Come to me, my love."

Joy filled every empty chamber in my heart. "I will." The power was at my command and Griffin's call would lead me home whenever I was ready. I looked at the computer. "But first, I have one last thing to do."

Epilogue

Owen parked the car in front of Jess' building. The window opened, and Jess leaned over the sill. "Hey, you two, it's about time you got here. You drive like an old lady, Owen."

Melanie laughed and waved. "We'll be right up. Don't forget to act surprised when we tell you the big news." She took Owen's hand. They went inside and climbed the three flights. Melanie tried the knob, but the door was locked. She knocked. "Jess, it's us. Open up."

"I love you both," called Jess from inside. "Have a happy life."

Owen chuckled. "That sounds final."

"Jess?" Melanie knocked again, but no one answered. A bright crimson light flared under the door and then vanished.

"What was that?" asked Owen.

"I-I don't know." A niggle of worry poked Melanie and she fished Jess' spare key from her purse. "Jess, we're coming in."

She unlocked the door, but it jammed. Owen peered through the crack. "The chain is on."

Fear welled inside her. "Something's wrong. Break it down."

Owen shoved his shoulder against the door, and the chain snapped. They rushed inside, but the loft was empty. "That's impossible," murmured Owen, running a hand through his hair. "We saw Jess at the window, heard her voice. The chain was on the door. No one passed us on the stairs."

Melanie spotted a stack of papers on the coffee table with a rose on top. "The Rose Stone," she said, scanning the title page. "Jess finished her story."

Next to the manuscript was an open sketchbook, and Owen handed it to her. "There's a letter on the last page addressed to you."

Melanie read aloud, "Dear Mel. Don't be sad and don't look for me. I'm not here and won't return. You'll understand when you read the manuscript and see the pictures in the sketchbook. I'm going home to Griffin. I love you." Next to Jess' signature was the tiny figure of a rose.

Out of the corner of her eye, Melanie caught a flash of crimson light from the easel. The old painting was gone, and a new one in its place, Jess and the man with the scar. They were in the country with fields and green hills in the background. Jess had a garland of blue and white flowers in her hair. Both wore wedding rings and their faces glowed with joy.

Melanie gasped, hit by a flood of happiness as she gazed at a painting that now seemed to breathe life. Jess' voice whispered in her ear, "I am home."

"What does the letter mean?" said Owen. "Should we call the police?"

"No. Jess is okay, but she's not coming back." Melanie clutched the tablet to her heart and swallowed a lump in her throat. "She found her happily-ever-after."

A word about the author...

I write fantasy and science fiction adventures with humor, and a little romance because life is dull without them. I don't write either sexy naughty bits or gore, so your mama would approve, but do add a touch of cheeky sass so maybe she wouldn't. The South is home, a place where the heat and humidity have driven everyone slightly mad. In my spare time I call in Bigfoot sightings to the Department of Fish and Wildlife. They are heartily sick of hearing from me.

For information on any of my books, check out my website at https://lakelley.com